# NIGHT
# MARKET

## DANIEL PEMBREY

**NO EXIT PRESS**

First published in 2017 by No Exit Press,
an imprint of Oldcastle Books Ltd,
PO Box 394,
Harpenden, Herts,
AL5 1XJ

noexit.co.uk

ISBN
9781843448815 (print)
9781843449461 (epub)
9781843449478 (mobi)
9781843449485 (pdf)

2 4 6 8 10 9 7 5 3 1

Typeset in 11.5pt Garamond MT
by Avocet Typeset, Somerton, Somerset TA11 6RT
Printed in Great Britain by Clays Ltd, St Ives plc

For more about Crime Fiction go to www.crimetime.co.uk / @crimetimeuk

# CONTENTS

WE FIRST MEET HENK VAN DER POL
IN *THE HARBOUR MASTER* WHICH CONTAINS
PART I, II, AND III.

# Part IV:

## Night Market

# 1

# IF YOU GAZE INTO THE ABYSS...

'Don't go in there.'

I was standing outside a set of double doors on the nineteenth floor of the Ministry for Security and Justice. The brown-carpeted anteroom was dim; much of it was in shadow. I'd been summoned for an after-hours meeting.

'Not yet,' the man added.

He was the assistant to the justice minister.

'What's this about, anyway?' I asked.

'I'm unable to advise,' he replied, his dark features dimly lit by his computer screen. The soft clacking of his keyboard resumed.

I eyed my watch again. My wife was waiting back at our hotel to have dinner. Apparently, global-security considerations no longer respected office hours.

I paced over to the tall windows. It was dark outside and The Hague's skyline winked, orange and white. The westward panorama took in the twin white towers of the International Criminal Court and, far ahead, I could make out the inky darkness of the North Sea... landmarks in the case of Rem Lottman, a kidnapped politician who'd been working for the energy minister, Muriel Crutzen. The case had brought me into contact with her, and she'd encouraged me to consider a job here in The Hague. I still didn't know exactly what it involved, but perhaps I was about to find out.

I turned back to the assistant, about to say something, when the double doors to the ministerial office flew open and there he stood.

'Henk,' he said, appraising me. 'Is it OK to call you Henk?'

'Is it OK to call you Willem?'

He smiled and stepped forward, shaking my hand firmly.

Willem van der Steen was of medium height and a stocky build, with wiry grey hair. His white shirt was open at the neck; his sleeves were rolled up. He looked like he'd be a tough bastard in a fight.

He was a vote winner, *'strong on law and order in uncertain times'*. *'We Dutch remain liberal – within limits'* was another of his election slogans. He was known to be a copper's friend. He'd started off in the force and gone on to run Southern Regions. In some ways he'd remained an old-fashioned bruiser – but now he was one with formidable powers.

He released my hand and led me into his office. There was a pattern to the appearance of these ministers' rooms, I was discovering: modern, workmanlike, unpretentious. In van der Steen's case, I glimpsed an oil painting in the shadows: a marine vista, choppy seas. A ship sat in the centre, listing, valiantly holding its course.

There was a circular glass table strewn with papers. A phone sat in the middle.

'A conference call ran long. The Americans like to keep us late.'

It begged questions that I couldn't ask.

'Drink?' he asked, closing the door behind us.

The offer surprised me.

'Still or sparkling?' he added, correcting my misapprehension.

'Still.'

He poured a glass for me, emptying a small bottle of water.

'Please, take a seat.'

I sat on the opposite side of the table.

'You come highly recommended,' he said, emptying another bottle – sparkling – into his own glass.

'Indeed?'

He sat down. 'The energy minister.'

No surprises then... or none yet.

I waited for him to go on, struck by a tightening sensation in my chest – a wariness of what might be coming.

'You're over from Amsterdam?' he asked. It was as if he were softening me up with small talk. He knew where I was from, surely.

'Just for a few days.'

He studied his fingernails, which were slightly dirty. It looked like he might have been doing some gardening, and not quite managed to scrub away the soil.

'What I'm about to tell you, I'm sharing in confidence. Is that understood?'

'Of course.'

I wondered how much was in my file. Did it mention that my wife was a former features writer for *Het Parool*, the Amsterdam daily newspaper?

'We've got a situation over in Driebergen.'

Driebergen, near Utrecht, was the headquarters of the old Korps Landelijke Politiediensten (KLPD) – the National Police Services Agency. The KLPD was now a unit within a single, newly merged Dutch police force. Not everyone had been happy with the unification. Office politics.

'What kind of situation?'

'There's a specialist team over there which is investigating child exploitation. You may be aware of them?'

I stayed silent, but I knew about the team... more or less. They always seemed to be in flux, given changing police priorities and public perceptions.

'It's a six-person team,' van der Steen went on. 'It needs to grow, but before we grow it, we need to clean house.'

'Oh?' I took a sip of water.

'We had a series of busts lined up. Mid-level members of what we'd managed to identify as a major paedophile network. The busts went bad.'

I noted how the minister used 'we' for what was being described as a tactical operation. The justice ministry oversaw the police of course, but van der Steen's words implied an unusual level of involvement.

'We now believe we've identified a kingpin in the same network,' he went on. 'In your neck of the woods, it turns out, Henk. We can't risk an operational failure this time.'

'You say the bust went bad... How?'

'All the addresses had been hastily abandoned by the time the arrest teams arrived. Cleared of any computer material, cleaned almost forensically. Every single one.'

'Addresses in Holland?'

'Three of them, yes. The other addresses were in Belgium, Luxembourg and southern England.'

I gave a low whistle.

'All recently vacated.' His words reinforced the point.

'A tip-off?'

'Almost certainly, but by who... that's the question.'

'An insider – a plant?'

'That's one theory. A theory that needs proving or disproving, and fast.'

'And you want me to look into it?'

His grey eyes held mine. They shone in the low light, like steel.

'Why me?' I asked, shifting in my seat.

'Four reasons,' he said, holding up the stubby fingers of one hand. 'Evidently you're a man with experience of life.'

I was fifty-six. 'Thanks for reminding me.'

He smiled, briefly. 'You've got an outsider's perspective. At least, that's what I'm told. Don't underestimate the value of being able to sit outside the tribe and see what's going on, in ways that others can't.'

Funny – the energy minister had told me they needed me 'inside the tent' after the discoveries resulting from the Rem Lottman case. Now they wanted me back outside again – but under their supervision. Things evolve.

'And as I said, you come highly recommended. We wouldn't be having this conversation if you weren't.'

I nodded impatiently. 'That's three reasons. You mentioned four.'

He locked eyes with me. 'There's no one else willing and able to do this, Henk.'

In my thirty-plus years as a policeman in Amsterdam, I'd seen a lot. But child abuse cases were known to be different. The images that the investigating teams had to look at each day, the victims' stories they encountered… you can't leave that stuff at the office, can't go home and forget about it. It gets into your mind, your dreams.

'If you take this assignment, it will change you,' van der Steen warned.

'Does that point to an alternate explanation?' I said, stepping back from the precipice of the decision he'd asked me to make. 'That someone on the team turned? Went native?'

Turned into a paedophile, in other words.

He shrugged. 'That's another possibility. These operatives have to stare at a lot of images. Perhaps, yes, it could… *release* certain things in certain men.'

He was looking at me searchingly.

'I don't pretend to understand what motivates older men to become interested in young children,' he went on. 'And let's be clear about this. We're talking about the sick stuff here, Henk. There's a lot of it going on all of a sudden. As many as one in five of us may have leanings that way, one police psychologist in Leiden is now loudly proclaiming.'

I took a sip of water, wondering what response that hypothesis had got from the psychologist's colleagues on the force.

'There's another point to consider – and I'm sure I don't need to spell this out for you as a seasoned policeman. Investigating the investigators: it's not for everyone.'

It contradicted the bond of loyalty among police personnel. I'd been in the army, which had the same ethos – though it was for reasons of survival there.

'A plant, looking for a plant,' I said meditatively.

He gave me a tight smile.

'How would that work?' I asked.

'We'd get you a regular job on the team in Driebergen. You'd be one of the guys. But we'd also pair you with someone from the security services.'

'A handler?'

'You could put it that way, yes. We'd work on your cover – give you an alternative identity of sorts.'

'My existing one's not unblemished.'

'I'd be suspicious if it was. You're a human being.'

There was a crushing silence.

Sexual exploitation, trafficking, drugs, corruption, aggravated assault, homicide cases even – I'd worked them all, but the one area of policing I'd stayed away from was child abuse. Every cop felt in their heart the Friedrich Nietzsche quote: *'Battle not with monsters, lest ye become a monster, and if you gaze into the abyss, the abyss gazes also into you…'*

'I also read about your altercation with the Amsterdam police commissioner.'

My old friend Joost. In abeyance since the Lottman case, but still there… still ready to cause problems in all areas of my professional and personal life.

'Take this assignment, and that problem goes away.'

I didn't doubt the justice minister's ability to make it so.

'And if I say no?'

He paused, choosing his next words carefully.

'Then, like the others I've offered this assignment to, you'll walk out of here. You'll forget this conversation ever happened and, as agreed, you won't mention it to anyone. In your case, Muriel will no doubt send you off to some other ministry. Somewhere easier. Environmental protection, maybe...'

I grimaced. 'Just how important is this to the justice ministry?'

He leaned forward, pressing his palms onto the table. 'I'd say it was vital... but that would be understating it.' He paused for effect. 'You can judge the decency of a society by how it treats its women and its children. If we're not protecting our children, then what the hell *are* we doing?'

He was good, van der Steen. He knew what drove us. The real coppers that is, not the Joosts of the world.

'It's an unusual case,' he continued. 'Outwardly, it's all supranational networks, technology, and collaboration with counterparts from other countries. In another sense, it's a classic little locked-room mystery.'

'How so?'

'At least one of the six men – yes, they're all men – in Driebergen is rotten. Your job, if you think you're up to it, is to determine which, and to ensure that the rot stops there.'

I tried to visualise the airless environment I'd be entering, the smell of it – but couldn't quite get there.

'How do you know the insider is on that team?'

'If you decide to proceed, you'll see the file.' He paused, and then asked with finality: 'Is the mission clear?'

I found myself nodding slowly, and added a more emphatic nod.

'Think about it,' he concluded, sitting back again but still scrutinising me with those steely eyes. 'Talk to your wife – *in general terms* – about a possible posting in Driebergen. You're married?' he asked, as if he might have misheard or misread something.

'Yes.'

I eyed the painting over his shoulder. The ship, attempting to hold its course in the gathering storm, listing badly.

'With a daughter,' I added.

'Then think it over.' His lips twitched. 'But not for too long.'

# 2

## THE FILE

'*DRIEBERGEN?*' MY WIFE ASKED, mouth agape.

'Keep your voice down.'

'Don't tell me to be quiet, Henk. It's not The Hague, nor Delft – like we agreed!'

'No.'

'What do you mean, *no*?'

'No – you're right.'

We were sitting in the bar of our hotel. The lighting was low; the room was full of flat, grey shapes and figures. I was tired of negotiating everything with everyone. Wasn't life supposed to become easier as you neared retirement and cast off children and responsibilities? My life seemed to be going in the opposite direction.

I signalled to the barman for more drinks.

Petra clamped her hand over her cocktail glass, narrowly avoiding the candle flame as she did so. It guttered.

'OK, *one* more drink.' I corrected my order, raising my empty, sudsy glass.

'But why Driebergen?' Petra demanded.

'Because it's the headquarters of the old KLPD.'

'I know that. I was a features writer once, remember?'

*How could I forget?* I felt like saying.

'You were talking about a role with one of the ministries here,' she said. 'Why go there?'

'Because the minister asked me to.'

A fresh Dubbel Bok arrived. *Thank God.*

Petra's face was screwed up with incomprehension in the flickering light. As soon as the barman left she said, 'Which minister?'

My voice was low. 'The justice minister. It's a confidential assignment. They've got a problem with one of the teams there, and that's about all I can share.'

My wife had been a journalist for as long as I'd been a policeman. In putting up a 'Do Not Enter' sign, I might as well have confessed everything on the spot. It was just a matter of time.

But I was taking van der Steen's warning seriously.

'Well,' Petra said, crossing her arms, 'I'm not leaving Amsterdam without good reason.'

'Last week you said that you couldn't wait to get off the houseboat and be nearer Cecilia in Delft.' Cecilia was her favourite cousin.

'Oh, I'll be getting off the houseboat all right,' she said. 'And finding dry land. In Amsterdam, close to our daughter.'

Our daughter Nadia wouldn't be leaving the nation's capital any time soon. Her social set could only countenance living in one Dutch population centre, and it certainly wasn't Driebergen.

'Should we get something to eat?' I suggested. 'It's late.'

'*Too* late.' Petra sniffed. 'I'm no longer hungry.'

I sighed exasperatedly, craning my neck. 'Can I see a menu?' I asked the barman.

'We only do snacks. The restaurant, over there, serves food.'

'Of course.'

We sat in silence.

Finally I said, 'OK. I'll tell you the mission I've been asked to undertake, but you mustn't share it with anyone.'

'As though I would!'

18

'*Anyone*, Petra. Not Nadia... *no one*.'

'Why would I share it with Nadia?'

'You won't.' I paused. 'And you must promise me that.'

'Fine,' she said.

'Van der Steen wants me to look at the team investigating child abuse.'

Her eyes narrowed.

'One of them is suspected of passing on police information to suspected paedophiles.'

Her head dropped.

'They need to plug the leak.'

'Why?' she said, looking up again, her face screwed up in a silent wail. 'Why this, of all the roles you could have taken?'

'Because someone needs to do it.'

'But why you?'

'Would you rather I crossed the road?'

'Oh, don't do your lone-knight thing with me, Henk.' Petra had her head in her hands.

She was right about most things, but not everything.

No one is.

'Child abuse.' She was mumbling. 'There's a reason child offenders live in mortal danger in prison and the rest of society –'

'Well, maybe if there were more women on the team in Driebergen, things would be different.' I was thinking about Liesbeth, a team member of mine who had a knack of winning trust and gaining insight into cases. She was the one who'd helped me break open the Lottman kidnapping case, with an early interview she'd done...

'So it's women to blame now, is it?'

'That's not what I'm saying. I'm just speculating that it's not healthy to have an all-male team –'

'Therefore, some unfortunate woman – or group of women – must now bear a further cost for these men's depravities?'

Jesus, was this not difficult enough without turning it into a full-on gender war?

'Looking at those images changes the neural pathways,' she cried. 'It rewires the brain!'

'Please keep your voice down.'

She shook her head. 'If it's true of legal porn, it must be doubly so with this.'

I was about to challenge her on the pornography point but her words rang true. I thought again of those six men in the office in Driebergen...

'I don't want you looking at that stuff.'

'All right.'

'I'm serious, Henk. I don't want that stuff in your head, and in our house, and in our bed!'

'All right, dammit! Then I'll make that the condition with van der Steen – I'm there to watch the watchers, but not to watch. Now, can we please get something to eat, before the restaurant shuts down and I shut down, too?'

\*

At the justice ministry the following morning, van der Steen's assistant led me into a small meeting room. A beige paper file marked *Confidential* sat on the polished wooden table.

'You can't take it away,' he said.

It felt like an unnecessary piece of theatre – I had my smartphone with me, able to photograph anything inside the file.

'In a few moments, someone from the AIVD will drop by to introduce himself.' The Algemene Inlichtingen en Veiligheidsdienst is the Dutch secret service, charged with 'identifying threats and risks to national security which are not immediately apparent'. It carries out operations at home and abroad, working with more than a hundred different organisations and employing over a thousand people – all of whom are sworn to secrecy about their work.

'My handler?' I clarified.

The assistant didn't answer my question.

'I'll leave you to it,' he said.

The door clicked shut behind him and I opened the file. There appeared to be two parts: a review of the operation van der Steen had mentioned (the bust that had been lined up and failed), and then an overview of the team in Driebergen, SVU X-19.

The nomenclature was familiar. 'SVU' stood for 'Special Victims Unit', the 'X' denoted that it didn't appear as a matter of public record, and the '19' distinguished it from other teams operating in that same capacity.

Conscious that I had little time before my handler arrived, I turned back to the beginning, scanning each page in turn. There are different ways to digest files but I like to avoid reading ahead, instead reliving the experience of the investigation – what was known at which point.

As I discovered, Operation Guardian Angel had grown out of a routine police check in Liège, Belgium. A Belgian police team had paid a house call to Jan Stamms, a convicted sex offender, to ensure that he was abiding by the terms of his early prison parole. They took a cursory look around Stamms's suburban, semi-detached house, including his basement – where they heard a distant cry. The lead officer assumed that the cry had come from the neighbouring property.

Luck (or its absence) can come in many forms in police work, and in this case it was a throwaway remark by the lead officer's partner, Veronique Deschamps, to the neighbour, who happened to be out in her front garden: 'That's quite a pair of lungs someone in your household has,' Deschamps reported commenting.

'But I live alone,' the neighbour replied, perplexed.

Veronique Deschamps then insisted on a more thorough search of Stamms's property. The first team still missed the sealed-up door in the basement, so good had Stamms's handiwork been, but his clear nervousness prompted them to persist and bring in search dogs, which quickly found the location of a passage down to a second basement.

In the concealed chamber were two four-year-old boys, a basic latrine, cameras and lighting equipment… plus a computer with editing software and thousands of hours of video footage. The room also contained a set of workmen's tools.

The twin boys required immediate medical attention. The video footage was too distressing for the local police team to review. However, by interviewing Stamms over a thirty-six-hour period, they elicited a confession to the existence of a video-sharing venue on the Dark Web called 'Night Market'.

I found myself nodding admiringly as I read the report. The Liège team had covered an impressive amount of ground before handing over the case to the Belgian Federal Police, who in turn discovered that Stamms had tried to resolve a payment problem with a bank in Amsterdam. The Federal Police speculated that the payment he'd expected to receive there was in exchange for his supply of video footage. A growing belief that the network was centred in Holland caused overall control to pass to Driebergen.

The door opened and the assistant asked, 'Do you want a drink, by the way?'

I blinked in consternation. 'No. How much longer do I have?'

'A few minutes.'

'Who is my handler, anyway?'

'His name's Rijnsburger. You'll meet him soon enough.'

The name didn't mean anything to me. I waited in silence for the assistant to leave again, returning immediately to the file. There was a lengthy section on the build-up to the arrest teams going into the various different locations to apprehend the mid-level suspects already mentioned by van der Steen…

I wanted to take in all the details. But more than that, I needed to get to the section on SVU X-19 itself. Van der Steen had suspected that the leak (resulting in the failure of the arrests) had come from SVU X-19 – only why?

*If you decide to proceed, you'll see the file…*

I flicked forward, thinking that there must be an elaborate Joint Investigation Team, with investigators from the various countries involved. Any one of them or their immediate colleagues could have had access to information about Operation Guardian Angel, and leaked it…

Aware that Rijnsburger might walk in at any moment, I skipped to the final section. Dumbstruck, I took in each of the SVU X-19 team members' short bios and photos in turn.

Manfred Boomkamp was a twenty-year KLPD veteran.

Jacques Rahm was from Luxembourg's Police Grand-Ducale.

Tommy Franks, formerly with the London Metropolitan Police's Flying Squad, was on secondment from the UK's national Child Exploitation and Online Protection agency.

Ivo Vermeulen represented the Belgian Federal Police.

And there was a fifth nationality involved: Gunther Engelhart was from Germany's Bundeskriminalamt.

SVU X-19 *was* the Joint Investigation Team. They'd built a mini states-of-Europe in Driebergen.

I sat back, and exhaled hard. Was it some kind of experiment? Did they believe that it would be more efficient to centralise the joint investigative work? Had the rationale been to avoid precisely the kind of intelligence failure that had then occurred?

And what of my ability to take on these men?

I leaned forward again, reaching into my inside pocket for my phone, when there came a rap at the door. It swung open to reveal a tall, white-haired man in a tailored navy suit. He was rheumy-eyed.

'Henk van der Pol?'

I didn't deny it.

'My name's Wim Rijnsburger, I believe the minister has mentioned me. We'll be joined by a psychologist shortly. Please, come this way.'

# 3

## THREE DAYS LATER

IT WAS AN OVERCAST morning as I approached the main entrance to the low building situated beside the busy A12. Only when I pulled into the car park did I appreciate how much Driebergen was otherwise surrounded by forest – the kind of dense forest that you no longer expect to find in central Holland. At some level, the location symbolised separation from the newly combined national police force headquartered in The Hague.

I still had a few minutes to spare before I was due to meet with Manfred Boomkamp, the commander of SVU X-19, so I locked up the car and reached for my cigarettes and lighter. My phone reception had dropped to a single bar of coverage.

I got a Marlboro Red going, reflecting on the last few days: the surprisingly small change to my identity required for me to assume the role here; the questions from the police psychologist that I never wanted to hear again..

A man to my right was trying to get his cigarette lit with matches. I recognised him as Tommy Franks, the English member of SVU X-19. His brown eyes were lively, fox-like. He had fine, sandy-coloured hair and a curiously old-fashioned, thick moustache.

I offered him a light.

'Haven't seen you before,' he said, exhaling his first draw.

It felt prudent to reveal nothing about my posting at this point. 'I'm here for a short while. Henk, by the way. And you?'

'Tommy. The same – here for a spell.'

We stood in that spirit of temporary camaraderie afforded by smoking areas.

With his free hand, Franks stroked the tips of his moustache like a pet. I looked away from him, surveying the car park. 'There are some nice cars here.'

'There are,' he agreed.

I was eyeing a midnight-blue BMW 3-Series convertible in particular. The plates were German, temporary.

'It's mine,' he said.

Perhaps he was awaiting a reaction. He didn't get one.

'Damn sight cheaper over here than in the UK,' he added, maybe reading my thoughts. He had the veneer of a well-spoken Englishman, but I could detect a regional British accent beneath. I couldn't tell which.

'Better get back to it,' he said, discarding his half-finished cigarette.

'Nice to meet you.'

'See you around.'

\*

I picked up my security pass at the front desk, and a receptionist escorted me to Manfred Boomkamp's office. The open workspaces I saw on the way were like any others in the police realm: functional, sparsely furnished, and adhering to a 'clean desk' policy – no personal items left out.

Boomkamp had his own office, which had permitted him to hang a framed photo showing two grinning girls on pushbikes. The girls looked to be in their early teens. Boomkamp himself was clean-cut and angular-faced. He had silvery-blond hair and disconcertingly blue eyes. As I approached his desk, he uncoiled himself from behind it. He was one of the taller Dutchmen I'd met, and that was saying something.

'Welcome, Henk. Sit down.' A file was on the desk in front of him. Mine, almost certainly. 'How are you settling into the area?'

'Fine, thanks. I'm staying for a few days at the motel until I find something more permanent.'

I didn't need to name the motel – there was only one in Driebergen.

'Has your wife joined you yet?'

'Not yet.'

'Let me know if we can help. I'm sure my own better half, Mariella, could show' – he paused, glancing at my file – 'Petra around. Driebergen's not everyone's cup of tea, but it grows on you. The forest here can be quite lovely in spring.'

'I'm sure.'

I didn't know whether Boomkamp had been informed of my real mission here. The AIVD had told me to reveal only that I was an internal transfer, further to my job disappearing in Amsterdam. Effectively it was true – things with my former boss, Joost, had ended in a debilitating stalemate. And yet the guilt of my deceit was already starting to grow.

'We need to get you operational as soon as possible.' Boomkamp eyed his watch. 'Helpfully, we have our weekly team meeting at eleven hundred hours. I'm going to have you shadow one of the other men.'

'Which one?'

'Ivo Vermeulen. He's a specialist in technical analysis, which – with child exploitation – usually constitutes the heart of the investigation.'

I digested this information. Vermeulen was from the Belgian Federal Police, so would have been closest to the events in Liège that had launched the ailing Operation Guardian Angel.

'Ivo's a good man,' Boomkamp added, 'but he's busy. We all are. We're behind with our targets.' He gave a tight smile. There were lots of tight smiles going around all of a sudden. 'We don't have enough men, even with your arrival.' Then, almost as an afterthought: 'It didn't need to be this way.'

Perhaps he was referring to the merger between the KLPD and the national police force.

'But,' he conceded, 'we all have marching orders.'

There was a pause in the conversation.

The experience of coming to this remote location in the forest, and of being among such a group of men – even the terminology used by Boomkamp: it was like rejoining the army.

I asked, 'Were you by any chance in the forces?'

'Do I give off that impression?' He laughed. 'In fact, three of the men here were. I'll let you find out which.'

'D'you mind telling me who does what?'

'What do you mean?'

'Roles.' The way army teams are put together, each man has a different, complementary area of expertise.

Boomkamp swivelled his chair from side to side. 'Like I said, Ivo handles technical analysis. Gunther Engelhart specialises in technical surveillance, which is similar but different. Tommy Franks is more versed in traditional forms of surveillance. Similar, but different again. Whereas Jacques Rahm is into suspect psychology. The psychology of suspects, I should clarify.'

'Similar but different?'

'Definitely different. Rahm's work I don't pretend to understand so well. But apparently we need it.'

'Marching orders?'

'Marching orders.'

There was no mention of leaks, or of suspects being tipped off.

He held me with his stare. Just like the justice minister had.

Then I remembered something else from my meeting with the justice minister.

'I thought this was a six-person team?' I'd counted five, including Boomkamp.

'It's six now. Question being what *your* role here turns out to be.'

'Can I ask,' I said, deflecting his remark, 'whose idea it was to staff the team from different countries?'

But before he had a chance to answer, there was a sharp rap at the door.

'Enter,' he said.

A fleshy face appeared round the doorjamb.

'What is it, Engelhart?'

The German's small, dark pupils flicked my way. 'We're all ready in the meeting room.'

'I'll be there in a minute.' The door closed and Boomkamp sighed, then said, 'Put the other men at ease, would you, Henk? Go out for a drink with them or something. They're curious about you, and there's only so much I can tell them. You came here *highly recommended.*'

It was a police euphemism; he was conceding that he'd been instructed to take me. Or was he maintaining a clever cover of his own?

*

The weekly meeting took place in a typical briefing room, brightly lit and smelling of institutional cleaning products. Seated around the long table were the two men I'd already met – Engelhart and Franks, the latter man's eyes widening as he recognised me from the smoking area – plus two others.

Ivo Vermeulen was sitting on the near side of the table, and he turned to shake my hand. He had severe features and wore polished, ankle-high boots. Like Boomkamp, he had the air of a former military man.

Jacques Rahm was slight and olive-skinned. He wore a black

polo neck, and a pancake holster that emphasised his stooped shoulders.

Boomkamp looped his jacket over a chair at the head of the table and gestured for me to sit. 'Let's get started,' he began in English. 'Joining us is Henk van der Pol, on secondment from the Amsterdam police force. Henk's a thirty-year police veteran who's seen the full range of action. Make him welcome.'

There was a smattering of hellos.

'What will your role here be?' Franks asked me directly.

'Good to meet you again –'

Boomkamp answered. 'He's a general bandwidth-extender, if I can call him that.'

'Around here,' Rahm said with a sardonic smile, 'it's more dial-up than broadband, let me warn you.'

No one laughed.

'Henk will help out with a bit of everything,' Boomkamp explained tersely, 'which will also allow him to get up to speed. Ivo, show him the ropes.'

Vermeulen shifted his stare from Boomkamp to me. I could only wonder what horrific images his grey irises had taken in.

There were some housekeeping points about schedules and holidays, then Boomkamp got down to business.

'So where are we with the Karremans case?'

A silence pressed down on the room.

Finally, Franks spoke. 'Why don't we get the new boy's perspective?'

Boomkamp looked from him to me. 'OK, why not? Ivo?'

Vermeulen thwacked a couple of keys on his laptop – a sturdy model favoured by the old KLPD – then spun it round. 'Tell us what you make of this.'

The screen was split crosswise, showing four images. I winced at what was going on in the foregrounds of each.

'What am I looking for?'

'The identifiers.' It was Engelhart, the German, who spoke.

My eyes searched the four photos, trying desperately to block out what was being done to the child.

Trying to channel my three decades of investigative experience, my mind went to the case of Robert M, dubbed 'The Monster of Riga' by the media. Robert M was a Latvian man who had worked as a babysitter and day-care helper in Amsterdam. He'd abused at least eighty babies, filming or photographing his acts. The exact number was unknown because many parents refused to become involved in the investigation, preferring privacy for their children instead.

Robert M's oversight had been to leave a toy with one baby. The toy was a Miffy, originally made in Holland. This narrowed the international search triggered by the discovery of the images online. A modified version of the Miffy photo was shown on the Dutch TV show *Opsporing verzocht* (*Detection Requested*), inviting members of the public to call in if one of them recognised the baby. An elderly man called, identifying the child as his grandson. The grandfather could easily have taken the matter up quietly with the father instead, or stayed silent – or indeed never have watched the show in the first place, in which case Robert Mikelsons might still be at it.

The case shocked Holland for many reasons, not least the revelation that Mikelsons – by now a Dutch citizen – had previously been banned from working in German day-care centres.

That information had never been disseminated.

'The pattern...' Gunther Engelhart prompted me.

Paedophiles operating at any level are by necessity expert dissemblers, but there will always be habits, blind spots... things so familiar that they might go unnoticed – become part of the furniture, even.

'The window fenestration,' I said. It was a metal design that mixed an industrial aesthetic with a faintly art deco style. 'It's distinctive, and it's the same. It's the same built environment – where the suspect feels comfortable.'

Vermeulen nodded approvingly. 'He's a natural.'

'Wait,' I said, stunned. 'Which Karremans are we talking about?'

'*That* Karremans,' Boomkamp confirmed.

Van der Steen had mentioned a kingpin in my 'neck of the woods', only... '*Heinrich* Karremans – the *Rijksbouwmeester*? I find that hard to believe,' I uttered.

'Welcome to the big leagues,' one of the men said.

There's no exact translation for the Dutch title *Rijksbouwmeester*, the closest thing being 'State Architect'. Heinrich Karremans happened to have played a key role in redeveloping the Amsterdam docklands, which I'd lived in since the 80s. His designs had created the physical backdrop to my adult life.

'Why do you find it hard to believe?' Vermeulen challenged.

'I'm just testing your assumptions here,' I said, still rocked by this turn of events. 'Granted, several of Karremans's buildings appear in these photos... but could it be somebody else using them?'

If true, why hadn't the justice minister or Rijnsburger briefed me about this?

Jacques Rahm answered my question. 'There is a *psychologique* concept called confirmation theory, in which subjects seek to integrate the abnormal events of their lives into a coherent narrative, by making troubling events *feel* normal...'

'Meaning?' I said sharply.

'Abused people are predisposed to go on and abuse others. They wish to perceive the behaviour as ordinary – *quotidien*. And if the activity takes place in a familiar environment... *tant mieux*.'

'Apologist,' Gunther Engelhart mumbled under his breath.

Rahm looked genuinely shocked by the accusation.

'Do you even know that Karremans himself was abused?' I asked.

'It's a theory,' Rahm replied.

'Forget the theory,' snapped Ivo Vermeulen. 'The metadata of the images links them to Karremans's IP address.'

I couldn't ask whether the link was via the Night Market site – I hadn't been told by the team about that yet – but it seemed a reasonable assumption. Only, something was missing.

'Looking at this stuff and creating it are two different things,' I said, gesturing at the laptop screen.

'One begets the other, and we don't need psychological theory to tell us *that*,' Boomkamp said. 'Ivo, fill Henk in on the technical analysis later. Now, let's consider the operational plan.'

Tommy Franks spoke up. 'Do you want in-person surveillance? In Amsterdam?'

'No,' Boomkamp ruled. 'The fewer people involved this time, the better.'

'But–' Franks began.

Boomkamp spoke over him. 'Ivo, Gunther – come up with a technical-surveillance recommendation, yes? I don't want a hundred people to coordinate on this one, further to the reorg.'

*Further to the police reorg,* I wondered, *or the leak of information?*

Boomkamp continued: 'Have a recommendation on my desk by day's end.'

The Belgian and the German nodded.

Tommy Franks flicked away a paper clip and sat back in his chair.

Jacques Rahm stared into space.

This was one unhappy family. I needed to find out the particular way in which it was unhappy, and fast.

# 4

## THE REINDEER

I PLUGGED IN MY police laptop at one of the empty workstations. The point of a clean desk policy is that it allows for hot-desking – anyone can sit anywhere. This was one of the gripes related to the police reorg. It made the rank and file feel that bit more interchangeable, and hence dispensable.

I was still replaying the staff meeting in my head: the different team members' words, and where they stood in the political pecking order. Tommy Franks and Jacques Rahm were clearly more on the outside. Was that relevant? Did it give one of them motivation to sabotage operations?

There was an email in my inbox from Petra, asking me to call her. Also one from my former team member Liesbeth, enquiring how I was getting on. She too had been lured to The Hague, where her husband – a fast-rising prosecutor – had taken on a bigger role.

Nothing from the justice ministry, however.

I put my laptop to sleep and went looking for Ivo Vermeulen, my designated mentor. There was no sign of him in the open work area.

I saw Tommy Franks, hunched over his own computer.

'Tommy, have you seen Ivo?'

'Probably in the clean room.'

'What's that?'

'I'll show you.' He got up – possibly grateful for an opportunity to do something – and suddenly looked thoughtful. 'How about a drink later on?'

'Er… sure.'

'The Reindeer?'

'Is there a choice?'

'Not without a drive,' he said. 'Five o'clock?'

It sounded early, but I kept that thought to myself. 'Thanks for offering.'

I made a mental note to make more use of the designated smoking areas.

Franks led me down a long corridor. 'Here,' he said, stopping beside a glass door. 'This is where our Belgian and German compatriots can usually be found.'

'Thank you,' I said to his retreating back.

The door was smoked but I could make out two seated figures. I tapped on the glass.

One of the figures became larger, and the door opened.

'Yes?' Vermeulen said.

'When do you want to get together?'

'About what?'

'Didn't Boomkamp suggest that you showed me the ropes?'

'Oh,' he said. 'Now's not a good time. Didn't you hear him in the meeting? He wants a recommendation on his desk by day's end.'

'Of course.' I looked over Vermeulen's shoulder. Gunther Engelhart was tapping away at a computer.

'What happens in here?' I asked.

'Technical work.'

'What kind?'

'The productive kind.'

Who monitored these monitors? Perhaps Rijnsburger, my handler, might know.

'Listen, Henk.' Vermeulen closed the door behind him and led me down the corridor, away from the open office area. 'I wouldn't be so quick to second-guess what's going on around here, if I were you.'

'What are you talking about?'

'At the meeting earlier – questioning whether we have the right man in Karremans. There's a chain of command.'

'Of course.' I nodded understandingly. 'I was just trying to clarify –'

'Trust the process,' he said over me. 'Things will go smoother for you that way. A lot of thought's gone into the way things work here. Now, if you'll excuse me.'

He walked back to the clean room, and vanished behind the glass door.

\*

There was little to do until Vermeulen or Boomkamp had more time for me, so I set off for the motel in order to make a couple of personal calls. I lit a cigarette as I walked. The air was autumnal.

Driebergen was a small ribbon-town strung out along the old Hoofdstraat road. One road, one motel, one bar… and one reason for me to be there: to find out who was betraying the Dutch police to an international paedophile network. I reminded myself that staying here would allow me to get to know the men of SVU X-19 better. Otherwise, I might as well have stayed in Amsterdam and commuted by train. That would have made things easier with my wife, certainly. I tried to call her as I walked, but there was no reply.

My motel room was musty. It was situated at the back of the dated building, facing out onto the damp forest.

My two bags remained unpacked.

Rijnsburger had asked me to use the cover of a relocation company called ARS Nationwide in order to communicate. A contact there would put us in touch.

I thought about calling, to test the communication method and to talk about Heinrich Karremans. But it felt premature. Perhaps I'd have more to report once I'd been for a drink with Tommy Franks.

I tried Petra again; this time she picked up.

'It's good to hear your voice,' I said.

'How's your first day?' she asked.

'Not over yet. I just came back to the motel to sort out a few things. How's your own day?'

'Quiet.'

There was an unfamiliar, awkward pause.

'It's a curious bunch – the team here,' I said.

'Are you even allowed to discuss it with me?'

'To a point.' I laughed, trying to ease the tension. 'Run by a guy called Boomkamp. He suggested that his wife showed you round here sometime.'

'While the husbands look at child porn?'

'Petra –'

'Will they?'

'Will they what?'

'Will they make you look at that stuff?'

I thought about the four images on Vermeulen's computer that I'd been shown.

'No.'

I'd blocked out what was going on in the foreground of those pictures… hadn't I?

'Did you make it clear to this Boomkamp that you wouldn't be doing that?'

'We haven't had a chance to meet properly… Look, is this the way it's going to be?'

'You tell me.'

'Why don't you come down here, take a look at the place? It's not unpleasant. The forest –'

'One step at a time, Henk. Settle in first, then we'll see.'

'OK,' I said, banking the progress before she had a chance to change her mind. 'Talk later. Give my love to Nadia.'

'Give it yourself.'

The line went dead.

*

Tommy Franks ordered a Dubbel Bok for me and a double Famous Grouse for himself. His brown eyes glinted in the lights of De Rendier – or Reindeer, as he referred to it – where we were leaning against the dark bar top. There was something reassuringly old school about Tommy, and I couldn't help but be drawn to him.

He was explaining how he hailed from Gravesend, near the mouth of the Thames Estuary. 'Just across the water from Middelburg,' he said with a wry smile, referring to one of the islands off the coast of Holland. 'We're old allies, Henk.'

'We might be, if you didn't steal our best football players.'

'Van Persie? Pah.'

'He's scored some nice goals for the national squad.' I winked at him good-naturedly.

'England couldn't hit a cow's arse with a banjo,' Tommy conceded. 'No, I lost interest in van Persie after he left Arsenal.'

His vocal polish had dulled; his regional accent was coming through more.

'Is that your team?' I asked. 'Arsenal?'

'Now and again. What about you? As an Amsterdam man, has to be Ajax.'

'Now and again.'

'So how did you end up *here*?'

It was a friendly enough question, but I sensed he was looking for information.

'My job went away. Someone suggested I looked here – said they needed the men – and the rest, as they say, is history.'

'Who suggested it?'

'Someone in Amsterdam,' I replied. 'You wouldn't know him. You should come up in that new car of yours by the way… see a match. I could show you around.'

'Leave the BMW among a load of Ajax fans? You've got to be fucking joking.' He knocked back his whisky. 'Here, let's get another round in.'

He did so. I'd barely started on my first beer when the second arrived. Tommy had switched to German Pilsner.

'Anyway,' he went on, draining a third of his pint and sighing, 'the ball and chain wouldn't like it.'

'You're married?'

'Was,' he replied. 'No, I'm talking about my girlfriend. She's Dutch, by the way. Maybe that's why I like you.'

'Well, at least you got that one right – unlike your taste in football.'

'Doctoral student in Utrecht, I'll have you know.' He clinked my glass.

It made me see Tommy differently. Dutch women are nothing if not fastidious in their choice of menfolk.

'We've made some nice trips over the border,' he went on. His eyes were dancing in the light behind the bar.

'Which border?'

'All of them.'

'Hmm.' I took a sip of beer. 'Do you get back to London much?'

'Not so often. I like it over here. I like the lifestyle.'

'You like the team?'

'The team?' He looked perplexed. 'Is there a football team *here*?'

'No – SVU X-19.'

'Oh.' He laughed, then smoothed the ends of his moustache. 'Each of 'em has his quirks. But don't we all? You ready for another one?'

'Christ, no. Anyway, it's my round.'

I ordered another Pilsner for him and a jenever for myself, setting the clear spirit alongside my two other drinks.

'Keep up, Henk.'

'Don't worry, my ancestors were sailors.'

'That may be, but I was in the SRR.' He gulped down more of his beer.

'Special Reconnaissance Regiment?'

'Before CEOP and the Flying Squad, yep.' He stifled a belch.

'Now you have my respect.'

The SRR was the surveillance counterpart to Britain's elite SAS. So that accounted for one of the three military men that Boomkamp had mentioned. Boomkamp and Vermeulen must be the other two, surely.

'Tell me something' – I leaned in – 'how do you all keep up? The work, I mean. There must be thousands of images discovered online every day.'

He seemed surprised. Had I overreached?

I added, 'I just don't know if I'm ready for that level of stress.'

'You'll be all right. We don't even try to keep up, is the thing. Each region has its own team.'

I knew that. 'But SVU X-19 –'

'We're not interested in the people who are just looking. We're interested in the ones creating the content in the first place.'

'Even so… each image has been created by *someone*, right? That's still a lot of suspects to have to track down.'

'Many images are created by a few.'

It reminded me of a saying on the Amsterdam police force – that six hundred people account for sixty per cent of the crime in the nation's capital.

I dropped my voice lower. 'Look, I heard about the Night Market operation – Guardian Angel.'

His eyes darkened.

'Sometimes stuff leaks out – to the regions, especially

Amsterdam,' I explained. I was betting that the alcohol had loosened Tommy up just enough. 'Word was, a couple of suspects got to know about it. I'm just trying to make sense of that. I mean, guys like you, Tommy – ex-SRR and all…' I left the last part of the sentence unsaid. *The best.*

He snorted. 'They were small fry. We let them go. We let the bigger fish feel a bit safer, see? We're here to hook the biggest fish – the ones swimming in international waters.'

My voice lower still: 'Heinrich Karremans?'

Tommy drank his beer. 'Enough shop talk. We're in the pub.'

But no sooner had Tommy said that than I spied a familiar face through the now-crowded bar.

'Isn't that Rahm?' I nodded in the direction of the dining area.

Jacques Rahm was sitting at a table for two, alone, eating a bowl of soup and reading a newspaper.

'Jesus, yes. Don't call him over.'

'What's up with him?' I asked conspiratorially.

'I dunno,' Tommy replied. 'He was another one sent our way. God knows why in his case. The psychological shit he spews…'

'Was there any explanation given for his appointment here?'

'What I *heard* was that he was mixed up in that bomber case in Luxembourg, and had to get away for a while.'

'Which bomber case?'

'Is there a news blackout where you come from? You really didn't hear?'

'Hear what?'

He paused. 'A couple of cops in Luxembourg were found to have planted bombs.'

'Bombs that killed people?' I asked, stunned.

'Almost, but they made sure to place them beside electricity pylons, unstaffed police stations and the like.'

'But why?'

'Who knows? One theory is that the Police Grand-Ducale

was resisting budget cuts, and certain members took it upon themselves to make the case for the status quo in their own way.'

'Jesus.'

It gave me an odd sensation in my gut, mirroring as it did the plea made by some in the KLPD against merging with the national police force.

'The cover-up went high – some reckon it went all the way up to the Ducal family.' Tommy nodded in Rahm's direction. 'Our friend over there was involved in the fallout somehow, anyway. But, like I said, enough shop talk.'

He drained the rest of his second Pilsner. 'I want to learn some Dutch sailor-slang so that I can impress Famke,' he said, changing the subject. 'She can be a dirty bitch when she wants to be, and I'm all for encouraging that.' He eyed the drink in my hand. 'One more?'

'Why not?' I said, before draining my own drink. I was catching up with Tommy Franks, and fast.

# 5

## HIDE AND SEEK

'STEP IN HERE, HENK,' Boomkamp ushered me.

My head was still throbbing from the night before. In the bright meeting room sat Ivo Vermeulen and Gunther Engelhart.

It was just the four of us.

The smell of cleaning products was stronger than yesterday. Whatever it was designed to clean up couldn't have smelled worse. I was about to vomit.

'You OK?' Boomkamp asked.

'Something I ate last night,' I said, wondering how and when I became so comfortable with casual lying. Probably right around the time I sat down with van der Steen and Rijnsburger in The Hague. Which reminded me that I needed to make contact with them. I already had things to talk through.

'Time is short,' Boomkamp was saying. 'It felt easier to invite you along, Henk. Ivo can fill you in on the backstory later. Give us a quick overview would you, Gunther?'

I sat next to the German. He looked up from his laptop screen, which I could see easily enough. It showed a chat room conversation.

'I've assumed an alias online: Wonderboy,' Engelhart explained. 'My profile picture has an eight-year-old dressed in a fairy costume.'

No one laughed.

'Deep cover.' Boomkamp broke the silence for my benefit.

'I've got Karremans engaged in a game called hide and seek,' Engelhart continued.

'We're close,' Boomkamp said.

I knew the thrill of the hunt, the belief that an arrest was within reach.

'*Beau soleil*,' Vermeulen said.

My eyes narrowed, not comprehending.

'Squad-room saying,' the Belgian explained. Perhaps it was irony, given the unremitting darkness of the work here.

I hazarded another glance at Engelhart's screen, where there was a message. From Karremans? *You show me yours, I'll show you mine.*

Engelhart typed the response:

*Has to be yours.*

He waited, tapping his teeth. A bottom left one was missing.

An image flashed up on the screen and I looked away. Petra's warning rang loud in my ears.

'But this is entrapment,' I said to the other two.

Vermeulen shot me a censuring look.

'This is war,' Boomkamp corrected me. 'You were in the army once, weren't you?'

'Once,' I echoed, feeling distinctly sick now. I could feel it at the back of my throat. 'As was Tommy Franks. Where is he, by the way? Shouldn't he be in this meeting, too?'

'What?' Boomkamp asked.

He glanced at the others, as though he might have missed something. Vermeulen met his gaze and something passed between them.

Boomkamp then stood up, towering over me. 'Step outside, Henk.'

The team leader left the room and I followed. He walked with astonishingly long strides towards his office.

Once the door closed he turned on me, and only then did I register the depth of his anger.

'What the fuck was that?' he spat. 'Questioning my authority in front of the others? I don't know who sent you, but I've been making enquiries, and I don't see anything in your record that warrants VIP treatment here, van der Pol. Do you understand?'

'Sure.'

'Do. Not. Undermine. Me.'

'My apologies,' I said. 'That wasn't my intent.'

'Was it that bastard Joost at police HQ who put you up for this role?'

Sensing my opportunity, I charged through the open door. 'Actually, that couldn't be further from the truth. I don't know how deep your enquiries went, but I came here to *escape* that bastard Joost.'

Spurned by the ministers in The Hague, my erstwhile boss and nemesis had worked his way deeper into Police head office, resurfacing near the top – near the justice minister.

The anger had softened in Boomkamp's blue eyes but it was still there, burning deeply. 'So who *did* put you up for this?'

'I can't tell you,' I said. 'You'll find that I'm discreet like that. When I work with someone, closely, I always respect the confidence in which anything is shared. Always.'

He looked down at his polished shoes.

I added, 'Surely you'd be worried if I did otherwise, given the sensitivity of the work here?'

For a moment he looked lost.

'Very well, Henk. Maybe I underestimated you. But have regard for my authority here, would you? It's the only way.'

'Of course…' The contradictory impulses of getting closer to Boomkamp and getting away – fast – fought each other. 'Look, something's come up, Man –' I paused. 'Is it OK to call you Manfred?'

He nodded. 'In private, yes. What's come up?'

'My wife doesn't want me here. She doesn't understand the work, she has reservations about it all…' I spoke hesitantly, like I was embarrassed – the henpecked husband.

Boomkamp put a firm hand on my shoulder. 'Why didn't you say that? It took Mariella a while to come to terms…' But the sentence drifted off. Instead, he said, 'You and your wife should come over to the house. This evening, yes?'

'Petra's still in Amsterdam…'

'Well *you* should come over then.'

'OK.'

'Say, seven?'

'Okey dokey.'

\*

Back at my workstation, my first call was to Petra.

No answer.

I called a different number altogether.

'ARS Nationwide,' a male voice answered.

'Could I speak with Mrs Rosen?'

'Who is calling?'

'Henk van der Pol. Your company is delivering some possessions of mine to Driebergen.'

I looked around. There was only Tommy Franks, several workstations away.

A female voice came on the line. 'Mr van der Pol?'

'Yes.'

'I'm just going to ask you a question, to confirm that we're talking about the right account.' The challenge question. 'What possessions are you expecting?'

'Two chairs, a sofa and a mountain bike.'

This was the response to give if I needed a meeting.

'We don't seem to have those items in storage.'

'Can I speak with your manager then?'

'He's busy, but I'm sure we could arrange something.'

'Is tomorrow too soon?' I made sure to sound suitably

indignant, in case Tommy was listening in.

'There's an ALLSAFE storage facility in Leiderdorp,' the agent said. 'The address is Rietschans 68. My manager could meet you outside it, but I'm not sure what time yet.'

There was an ALLSAFE facility in Utrecht, too, I felt like saying – just ten minutes away instead of an hour in bloody traffic. Of course, Leiderdorp was close to The Hague, and Rijnsburger.

'Fine, Leiderdorp ALLSAFE it is.'

'Call back first thing tomorrow and I can confirm the time of the meeting.'

'Will do.'

I set the phone down, wondering how I'd manage to get away for a few hours without suspicion. Suddenly Franks was at my shoulder, surprising me.

'Everything OK?' he asked.

'Yeah, just a mix-up with some possessions.'

'Happens. Here, come look at this.'

He led me back to his workstation.

'How's the head by the way?' he asked.

'Better,' I replied. 'Just.'

We arrived at his computer screen. 'Now, what d'you make of this?'

The girl on the screen looked voluptuous, young and yet grown-up. Was it a trick question? It looked like Tommy was showing me standard soft porn.

'Sixteen-and-a-half years old,' he said.

'Doesn't sound like our remit.'

'That's because it's not. I've been dragged into a cross-regional working group. They're trying to agree the number of underage images a person should be allowed on their computer before an investigation starts.'

'How about one?'

'But look at her again.'

It was hard not to.

47

'Whenever you go to a standard porn website these days, there are invariably under-eighteen images. Ghost copies of the images end up on users' hard drives. So there's a debate about whether it should be ten, fifty, or even a hundred images – otherwise, we'd be impounding the hard drives of most of the male population.'

I remembered him saying something in the pub, though. *We're not interested in the people who are just looking, we're interested in the people creating the content…*

I played his words back to him. 'I thought we were here to hook the biggest fish – the ones operating across borders?'

Something flashed in his brown eyes like a flare of lightning from a dark cloud. 'These are Boomkamp's orders, received just this morning. He wants me to be a "point of contact" for the police regions.'

Was our team leader managing Tommy out of SVU X-19?

I looked back at the screen. 'In America, a sexual act with her would be statutory rape.'

'Land of the free,' he said acidly.

The disconnect between Tommy's credentials – the SRR, CEOP – and his general conduct was becoming impossible to ignore. And something else was wrong.

'Shouldn't you be doing this in the clean room?'

'Shouldn't we all,' he said ruefully. 'You should see the shit Rahm has on his work laptop.'

He was joking… surely?

*

Boomkamp's house was a substantial detached dwelling, built in brick some way into the forest. His wife Mariella greeted me at the doorway in what looked to be gold pyjamas, only they couldn't have been.

'Your wife wasn't able to join you?' she asked with disappointment as she led me inside.

I wiped my feet on the *welkom* mat. 'Not this evening,' I said. 'Hopefully next time.'

The interior was white, pristine; the forced-air heating made it feel arid compared to the damp outdoors. Mariella led me through to a sunroom. Only dark forest and gloomy evening sky were visible through the glass ceiling and walls. I couldn't see any evidence of kids. The personal items dotted about looked curated – like the house had been swept for anything too revealing, or even staged as if for sale. Framed, crocheted designs sat above the fireplace and adorned the walls. Evidently Mariella was an old hand with the needle and thread.

'Henk,' Manfred said. He was sitting on a La-Z-Boy recliner, his long legs elevated on the footrest. He had what looked to be a Scotch in his hand.

'Don't get up,' I said.

'But you need a drink. Mariella, perhaps you could do the honours? And take the man's coat.'

She did. 'What would you like?' she asked brightly, folding my bomber jacket over her arm.

'Do you have jenever?'

'We do, chilled. I was just drinking some, in fact.'

Sure enough, a liqueur glass with lipstick round the rim sat on a low table between Boomkamp's chair and another chair on the far side. He reached over and patted the armrest of the other chair. 'Please.'

I sat.

'So,' he said, setting his glass aside and steepling his fingers. 'Here we are.'

'Yes.'

'What are your first impressions?'

'Of the town?'

'The town, the team...'

Mariella arrived with the jenever, giving me time to think. I thanked her.

'I'm going to leave you boys to talk,' she said, carrying out her own glass.

'Please,' I offered, getting up, 'I didn't mean to –'

'No,' she said, smiling. 'That's fine. I have things to do.'

'Relax, Henk,' Boomkamp said. 'We're off the record here. Cheers, by the way.' He reached for his glass again and clinked mine.

'Cheers,' I reciprocated. I met his eyes and drank.

'First impressions,' I repeated, conscious that he was awaiting an answer. 'It's early days, but –'

'What do you make of the men?' he asked directly. 'Tommy, for example. How does he come across to you?'

Was it a trap? A test of loyalty? I recalled the more peripheral role that he'd assigned to Franks that morning, which clearly hadn't sat well with the Englishman.

'Matter of fact, I was out for a drink with him last night.'

'And?'

'Haven't formed any distinct impressions yet,' I lied.

Boomkamp was silent.

Eventually he said, 'Sometimes I wonder about him… and Rahm.'

'It's difficult work. It's not for everyone, that's for sure.'

'*Beau soleil*.'

'What *is* that?' It was the second time I'd heard it.

'Just an expression from the squad room.' He sighed deeply. 'One day, this will all be over. We'll all be retired, on the beach someplace.'

His blue eyes looked bottomless as he stared out into the gloom. It struck me that the last thing a man like him needed, after a role like this, was time on his hands. There would be far too much to reflect upon, to ruminate over.

'Listen, Manfred,' I said, turning to him. I'd come here with one plan in mind, but decided to change course. 'I need to return to Amsterdam for a long weekend, if that's OK. Things aren't going at all well with my wife – I need to sort them out.'

He took a sip of his Scotch.

'It feels like the right time to go back,' I continued, 'before the workload really hits. Are you OK with that?'

For a second I wondered if he'd even heard me.

'Whatever you need to do, Henk.' He stared out into the forest. 'You don't want to finish up a single man here.'

Mariella walked back in. 'Anyone for a refill?' she asked with a beaming smile.

'No, thank you. I should be going, in fact.' I stood up. 'It really was just a quick call.'

'I'll say,' she remarked, surprised.

'I'll come back with my wife,' I promised. 'I hope,' I added for Boomkamp.

'I'll hold you to that,' he said, raising his near-empty glass.

'Is everything all right?' Mariella asked as she showed me to the door.

'Yes, I just need to be back in Amsterdam for a couple of days.'

She handed me my jacket and I paused on the threshold. 'What about the children?' I said, remembering the framed photo in Boomkamp's office. 'How are they?'

'What children?'

'I thought I saw a photo of two children on pushbikes...' Had I imagined it? 'At the office,' I added.

'What photo?' She looked confused. 'Which children? We don't have any photos of our younger selves. Not ones that we set out, anyway. Manfred hates to dwell on the past.'

Were they distant relatives? Was he trying to create some erroneous impression around the office of a happy family life? I recalled my own family troubles, and forced a smile.

Mariella returned the smile, but as the door closed the smile vanished, her mouth becoming hard-set.

# 6

## ALLSAFE

I WAS GLAD TO escape the claustrophobic, hothouse feeling of Driebergen. The storage facility in Leiderdorp was surrounded by nondescript, light-industrial premises. Along the front of the ALLSAFE building ran a bay of customer parking spots. I pulled into one and waited for Rijnsburger to arrive.

It was just before 2 p.m. on Friday afternoon and there was that sense of things winding down for the weekend. I stared at the garish yellow-and-blue building ahead. ALLSAFE. More and more Dutch households were turning to remote storage arrangements like this for their possessions, space always being at a premium in Holland. I was willing to bet that once most of these possessions were put away, the only trace of their existence would be a recurring monthly bank charge.

I was thinking, too, about the Boomkamps' pristine house, and their domestic arrangements, when I glanced at my watch and noted that Rijnsburger was late.

I wanted to get out of my car and smoke, but the instructions had been clear: *Wait in your vehicle until he arrives.* Was this how it would be now – everything on The Hague's terms? With annoyance, I saw a small tear near the zip of my bomber jacket.

I called Stefan de Windt, another former team member of mine in Amsterdam.

'*Hoi*,' he replied cheerily. A dog barked in the background. A good sign: he was away from the police station…

'Thought I'd see how you're doing.'

'I *was* doing fine,' he joked. 'You?'

'Hey, less of the cheek,' I said. 'I just started in Driebergen.' I'd already told him about my new role – in general terms.

'It's our loss,' Stefan said. 'This place isn't the same without you.'

His words sounded genuine enough, but I noted a more relaxed tone in his voice than when he'd been working for me. He was still in station operations – surveillance – and I needed to tread carefully, given that he had a new boss.

'I'll be back in Amsterdam over the weekend. I wondered if you're free for a drink?'

'*This* weekend?'

'Why not?'

'What's going on?'

'It would be good to catch up.'

'Is there something I can help with?'

He knew me too well. 'I'm no longer your boss, Stefan. That said, I could use a little help…' Just then I saw a large black panel van swing into the parking bay, two spaces over. 'I'm going into a meeting right now, but perhaps we could grab a coffee at De Druif tomorrow or Sunday?'

De Druif was my local bar in Amsterdam.

'I'm free either morning, just text me.'

'Will do. Good to talk.'

As I ended the call, another one was incoming. Mrs Rosen, at ARS Nationwide.

'My manager is available to meet with you right now, Mr van der Pol.'

*

The van's cabin was upholstered in dark leather. Rijnsburger sat in the middle front seat. Rheumy-eyed as before, he greeted me with a stare. A motionless driver sat to his left. I wondered who, or what, was in the back.

'This is too soon to be coming in,' Rijnsburger reproved me. 'What's going on?'

I began my update with the rumours about Jacques Rahm – the bomber scandal in Luxembourg. 'Yes, we're aware of all that,' Rijnsburger interrupted. 'Why set up a crash meeting? What else have you got?'

So this was how it would be? No discussion, just me feeding them information?

I cleared my throat. 'Tommy Franks: there's evidence of unusual personal wealth – expensive car, a girlfriend who sounds considerably younger. It might be worth looking at where the extra money is coming from.'

'You should.'

'Franks and Rahm are definitely on the outside of the power structure within SVU X-19.'

'Loose cannons?' Rijnsburger asked, showing a bit more interest.

'I wouldn't go that far. But something's clearly dysfunctional in the way the team is set up.' I hated reporting on people like this, like some glorified informant. 'It's surprising, in the case of Tommy Franks at least.'

'Why?'

'Because of his background: CEOP in the UK. The Flying Squad, the Special Reconnaissance Regiment...'

Rijnsburger pulled out a little leather-bound notepad, detaching a propelling pencil from its interior. He wrote something down in a way that the words evaded my view.

'Look, could we have some two-way traffic here?'

'Say again?'

'Could you give something back, or at least respond to what I'm saying? Wouldn't our arrangement work better that way?'

His bloodshot eyes found the middle distance. A stray cat

was pacing along the strip of concrete between the parking bay and the ALLSAFE building.

'OK,' he agreed. 'Tommy Franks was never in the Special Reconnaissance Regiment. That much I know for a fact. Is that helpful?'

It was. If Tommy had lied about that, what else had he lied about?

'What about the others?' Rijnsburger demanded.

How to summarise my first impressions of Boomkamp, Vermeulen and Engelhart? 'From what I've seen so far, they're almost exclusively focused on one suspect.'

'Who?'

'Heinrich Karremans.'

'*The* Heinrich –?'

'Yes.'

I had his full attention now.

But did Rijnsburger really not know that? I'd come here ready to complain about him not mentioning Karremans...

'What evidence do they have?' There was an urgency in his voice.

'Images, which they've apparently linked to Karremans's IP address. The images they showed me also appear to have been taken inside buildings that Karremans designed.'

Rijnsburger wrote down several more words, then said, 'What are they planning? How are they moving the operation forward?'

'They're using an online alias to engage Karremans and draw him into a compromising situation.'

Rijnsburger's eyes narrowed. He didn't like what he was hearing. 'How do they know they've got the real Heinrich Karremans? Are they not planning physical surveillance?'

Wouldn't this kind of information be expected, even demanded, by the justice ministry – and passed on to the secret service in relevant cases such as this?

'They haven't planned any physical operations, yet. Or should I say, not ones that they've told me about. They're focused on technical surveillance.'

Rijnsburger contemplated the situation for a few seconds. He said, 'What do *you* make of it?'

The generality of his question caught me off guard.

'Of Karremans potentially being in a paedophile ring, or of how SVU X-19 is progressing the case?'

'Both.'

I wasn't sure, was the problem. 'I find the idea of Karremans's involvement particularly shocking, given how admired he and his buildings are.' I puffed out my cheeks and expelled the air. 'There are two scenarios. One is that Karremans is a legitimate suspect – and that Boomkamp is trying to manage the risk of tip-offs, after the previous leaks. The team does appear to have split, with Vermeulen and Engelhart carrying out the lion's share of the surveillance work. Franks and Rahm are effectively sidelined.'

Rijnsburger looked up from the notes he was writing. 'You mentioned two scenarios.'

'If Karremans is not guilty, evidence is being misinterpreted, or worse.'

'Worse?' he prompted me.

'The team is clearly feeling the pressure to get a result, to maintain its independence… the more so after the merger with the national police force.'

Rijnsburger was nodding.

'That's what I inferred from Boomkamp's off-the-record remarks, anyway,' I said.

'Have you spent much time with him?'

'Enough to have formed a reasonably solid first impression. I went to his house last night.'

'You did?'

'Yes. Look, shouldn't we be trying to get out in front of this?

What do you think about initiating alternate surveillance of Karremans?'

'By who?'

'Whoever you think makes sense.'

I was fishing for what Rijnsburger might be planning. I needed to know, before asking my favour of Stefan in Amsterdam.

'We're going to need a few days to work through the implications of this,' Rijnsburger said.

'OK.' If true, that might buy me just enough time. Quickly, I changed subject. 'Here's another suggestion: what about bringing in someone who could do a psychological assessment of the different team members?'

'Who? Why?'

'Someone in an ongoing training-slash-counselling role. Something required by Police HQ.'

'Do you not think that might stir up a hornet's nest? Why would we take that risk?' Rijnsburger was clearly considering it, though.

'They're doing a lot of things on the computers there at Driebergen.' I was thinking of Tommy's comment about the content on Jacques Rahm's laptop. 'The question is, who's monitoring the monitors?'

'Boomkamp, in the first instance. He's the commander.'

'So who's monitoring *him*?'

'You are, on the ground.'

'I have no idea what they're doing on those computers, and I doubt I'll be allowed to find out anytime soon.'

'It's not hard to remote-access the computers at Driebergen,' Rijnsburger said, thinking aloud.

I liked the way he was opening up now, like a reluctant liqueur, past ideal drinking age but worth persevering with.

'That's good, but all it will show us is that a lot of illicit material is being viewed,' I challenged him. 'It doesn't tell us anything about their states of mind, their intentions…'

What had the justice minister said in our very first meeting? *These operatives have to stare at a lot of images. Perhaps, yes, it could...* release *certain things in certain men...*

It had been Petra's warning and objection, too.

'Ongoing training,' Rijnsburger repeated, meditatively. 'There's a police psychologist near here – in Leiden – who might be interesting for that role.'

'Not the one claiming that as many as one in five of us have paedophilic leanings?' I shook my head. 'That would be too much indeed. That might put them *too* much on the defensive. We want them to *act*, not pull back.'

Rijnsburger's bloodshot eyes stared again into the middle distance. 'Let's keep it as an option.'

'OK,' I agreed, eager to preserve the newfound spirit of cooperation.

He appeared to be thinking again. 'We should wrap things up here. What else do you have?'

There was something I'd observed in Driebergen that was nagging at me, which I couldn't quite put my finger on. It's really true, what they say about short-term memory going as you get older. Things that had happened ten or twenty years ago I could recall with absolute clarity; events that had occurred more recently seemed lost in some memory soup.

Conscious of the seconds ticking by, I said, 'I can't think of anything else right now.'

'Nothing about the leaks relating to Night Market and Operation Guardian Angel?'

There was Tommy Franks's remark about the leaked suspects being small fry... *We let them go. We let the bigger fish feel a bit safer, see? We're here to hook the biggest fish...* But could Franks be trusted now that he'd been caught in a lie?

'I'm afraid not,' I replied.

'Well, keep going,' Rijnsburger urged. 'We should speak again next week.'

I agreed and we shook hands.

As soon as I got out of the van, its engine started. It disappeared into the grey afternoon, leaving me alone once more.

*

Driving up to Amsterdam, I put my headset on and tried Petra again. She still wasn't picking up, and I was becoming concerned.

I tried my daughter Nadia instead.

'Can I come over?' she asked.

I glanced at the phone to make sure I'd dialled the right number. 'Nadia?'

'Oh, Dad. I thought you were –'

'The boyfriend?'

'He has a name,' she said.

I'd heard the rebuke before. 'And how is Sergei?'

'He's just bought a place here, and I'm due over –'

'Bought a place where?'

'Amsterdam,' she said. 'Where else?'

'Are you moving in together?'

I'd almost forgotten why I was calling now.

'I don't have time for this,' she said.

'Neither do I. Is everything OK with your mum?

'Why don't you ask Petra yourself?'

My wife had started encouraging Nadia to call her by her first name; their relationship had grown up. They were as much friends as mother and daughter now.

'She's not picking up,' I said.

'Well, maybe if you didn't spend your days looking at child porn, she might!'

Jesus, Petra had told her that? We'd specifically agreed she wouldn't.

A car swerved in front of me and I broke hard; the juddering anti-lock braking system cut in. I shoved my palm hard against the centre of the steering wheel and kept it there, the horn blaring.

'What the hell's going on?' Nadia said.

'I need to concentrate on my driving.'

I was about to end the call when a very unwelcome thought intruded. 'Have you mentioned any of this to Sergei?

'What, about your job? Please,' she said with a faintly disgusted tone. 'The last thing I'd want to own up to is –'

'Then that's all,' I said, hanging up.

# 7

## SEPARATION

THE DOOR WAS UNLOCKED when I arrived back at our houseboat on Entrepotdok in Amsterdam's docklands.

I could hear the shower running. The air was warm, humid and sour-smelling. Unwashed dishes sat in the sink.

I hung my jacket over a dining chair. On the table sat orange plastic cylinders. Pharmacy medication. I picked one up: *Bioglan Fluoxetine.*

Antidepressants were not prescribed lightly by family clinicians in the Netherlands.

A shriek split the air. 'What are you doing creeping around?' Petra cried.

'Excuse me?' I set down the antidepressants. 'Do I not live here anymore?'

'You startled me!' she said, grabbing a towel.

She padded across to me, leaving wet footprints on the wooden deck, and gathered up the objects from the kitchen table. 'Leave these alone.'

'You didn't return my calls. I'd no idea what was going on.'

She put away the medication in a wooden cabinet above the sink. I remembered fitting it... Happier times. Or, at least, *easier* times. Dark tendrils of hair curled down Petra's back as she reached up into the cabinet. The towel unravelled and she hastily gathered it back up to chest height. I was torn between the anger I still felt over Nadia's revelation and the need to

61

make up with my wife. I sat down, waiting for that tug of war to resolve.

Petra leaned over the sink, facing away from me.

'Henk,' she said in a tone of voice that filled me with sudden dread. 'I didn't want to speak with you until I'd arrived at a decision, but I think we should consider a separation.'

'Oh?' I tried to hide my surprise but felt my face flush red. Shock – and anger, too. 'All because of this new role I've taken?'

She turned to face me. Her eyes looked dulled.

My phone rang: Stefan. I pressed ignore.

She sighed angrily. 'It feels like the life has gone out of our relationship. I don't know why it left, or where it went... or how to get it back. I should be excited to see you again on occasions such as this, to be around you. I'm not.'

I was silent.

'But,' she conceded, '*everything* has turned into a struggle, a daily battle of late...'

'This is sudden,' I managed.

'It's not, really.'

Lost, I waited for her to go on.

'Ever since I left my job at the newspaper...' The sentence trailed off. Her eyes were moist.

'Maybe we can talk about it over dinner.'

She shook her head. 'I'm not hungry.'

'OK then,' I said. 'Skip dinner. But one thing we need to be absolutely clear about is what we agreed: not to share my new role with anyone, including Nadia.'

'Nadia found out that I was depressed, so we talked.'

I felt banished from my own family.

She continued: 'And you promised that you wouldn't look at images – that you were there only to "watch the watchers". Tell me that you haven't!'

Not good enough. 'Would you have revealed one of your

journalist sources so easily, just because you and Nadia *talked*?'

'Oh, you and your fucking job!'

'Just stop right there!' I said loudly, standing up. 'I'll stay elsewhere tonight. Let's speak again in the morning, when we've had a chance to calm down.'

'Where will you stay?'

Things were really starting to unravel.

'Johan's.' I could always rely on my old army friend, though I had no idea whether he was free, or even in town.

In the bedroom I found a gym bag and began filling it with some of the items I'd meant to pick up for Driebergen: a favourite bottle of jenever from the galley, a book I'd been meaning to read – a Herman Koch novel called *The Dinner*... My outreached hand hovered in front of the bookcase, settling on a coffee-table hardback about Heinrich Karremans.

'*Why* did you have to take that job?'

The inside flap was loose and there was a small portrait of him, his too-close-together eyes staring at me through round glasses.

'Because I was asked to. Duty.'

Petra grabbed my arm. 'Tell me again,' she said, 'to my face.'

Her beseeching look ate the heart out of whatever defences I had left.

'Why did you take that job when I was so against it?'

'I don't entirely know, Petra.' I had to acknowledge that there was something else. 'It's not just about catching the bad guys, or the supposed good ones who are helping the bad guys...' There was some deeper curiosity, as well. 'I need to know why so much child abuse is going on. And...'

'What?'

'There's something I need to understand about myself, too.'

The arousing image that Tommy had showed me, now flashing up in my mind?

'*What?*' she repeated, her jaw quivering.

Could *I* have ended up with that image on my laptop – an image of a teenager, officially classified as child porn?

'I'll have my phone switched on,' I said, holding the device up as if it contained our salvation.

Then I swung the gym bag over my shoulder and left.

\*

Once outside I didn't call Johan, rather Stefan.

'Boss,' he replied.

'Not anymore.'

'True,' he conceded.

I walked past my car, which I'd parked on Entrepotdok. 'How is the new boss, by the way?'

'Not the same as the old one,' he grumbled. 'Does the job. Did you want to meet?'

'We could. I'm heading to De Druif right now.'

'I'm stuck at the police station.'

'In which case, would you mind looking something up?'

'How did I guess…'

'Heinrich Karremans – you know who he is?'

'The name's familiar.'

'He's the *Rijksbouwmeester*. Could you check the station transcripts, quietly, to see whether he has a record?'

'Erm…'

'Not necessarily convictions. Official complaints he might have made, too – or a role as a witness, even. The complete picture.'

'Does he have a connection to the precinct?'

'Look at the buildings around you, Stefan. He's designed enough of them.'

'Hold on.'

I heard the rattle of his fingertips at his keyboard.

'His address is on IJburg.'

It was a new town reclaimed from the water, a few kilometres to the east of us.

'Could you give it to me?'

Stefan did. 'Looks like this is his office, too. Karremans Architectuur. So, not our precinct.' He paused. 'I could go into the national police database for his full record...'

The query would leave a trail, with Stefan as requester. Could that be traced back to me, given that we were on the same team until recently? I took the risk. 'Do it. Go back a few years.'

'I would have done that anyway.' He was typing. 'Oh, there's a second address listed for him.'

'Where?'

'Norway. Looks like he's got a cabin up there, near Trondheim.'

'Why Norway?'

'Why not? Nice place, lots of space up there.'

I liked how Stefan's confidence had grown.

'I wonder where he is,' I said. 'Here, there?'

De Druif was invitingly lit. I walked inside and Gert, the owner, nodded. I hung back from the bar to finish the call in private – hard to do in a bar as small as this one.

'Establishing his whereabouts – passport use and the like – we'd need to go through the proper channels,' Stefan was saying.

'Fair enough. Then let's stick to his police record for now. Please let me know as soon as you've got something.'

*

I'd never needed a Dubbel Bok more in my life. I ordered a jenever chaser, downed both, and sat at a table by the window with a second beer. Why on earth had I brought my gym bag with me? I'd meant to leave it in the car.

There was nothing to do about Petra until the morning. But memories of my last drink at this same table – with Johan – made me hesitant about calling my old army buddy. He'd done enough for me already, and one thing in particular that had caused him no end of trouble. Maybe I'd be staying at the local Ibis hotel instead.

As I sipped my beer I thought about my next move, hypnotised by the burble of after-work conversation in the bar. I looked down. The gym bag had become oblong-shaped, owing to the Karremans book. I pulled it out, set it before me and began flipping the glossy pages.

There it was: the distinctive art deco, industrial fenestration, in this case featuring in a double-page colour spread devoted to the twelve-storey Sea Berg building, which stood a mere kilometre or so from where I was sitting. The experimental structure had established Karremans's reputation.

Gert was clearing away empty glasses, including two of mine. 'What do you think of this?' I asked him.

He stooped and stared at the building, which was iceberg-like – stacked slabs of translucent glass sliced down one side, topped off with a matte-black splotch...

'Looks like a toe gone bad,' Gert said. The light was low by the window; he peered closer at the photo. 'What was that movie – the one with Paul Newman and Steve McQueen?'

'*The Towering Inferno*? I think that's the only one they were in together.'

'Yeah, that's the one. McQueen was the fireman, right? The one who questioned why we insist on building so high when the fire department can't reach a fire above seven floors. Do you remember? I think you could apply that to living, too. Why do we keep building places that people don't want to live in? What was wrong with the traditional way, when buildings in this city were no taller than four storeys? People seemed a lot happier.'

He shrugged, and carried on collecting glasses.

I looked out of the window at the traditional merchants' houses across the canal and supped my beer. It felt as though I was missing something. Only – what? I couldn't think, or rather couldn't recall, and shook my head ruefully. Advancing age, no doubt.

The Karremans book went on to feature other buildings designed by him over his long and distinguished career, the *Rijksbouwmeester* being in his seventies now. Buildings in Rotterdam, Ghent and Antwerp. Oslo, China...

*Oslo.*

My military training had been in Norway, and an old acquaintance from the army, Olaf Magnusson, had spent his subsequent career in the Oslo Police District. He had only recently retired.

I dialled his number.

'Is that Henk again?'

I'd called him a few months prior, about a separate matter.

'Guilty as charged.'

'To what do I owe the honour this time?'

'A man named Heinrich Karremans.'

'Name's vaguely familiar.'

'Do elaborate,' I encouraged.

'No, I insist. You first.'

'He's an architect, well known here in Holland, with a cabin near Trondheim. He's also designed buildings in Oslo, so he must have spent time in Norway professionally.'

'Throwing out more lobster pots, are we?'

The last time I'd contacted Magnusson, I'd been fishing in the wrong place.

'Is it lobster season up there already?'

Magnusson gave a short laugh. He had good contacts in Kripos, the Norwegian National Criminal Investigation Service, which handled serious crimes – including organised child abuse. I was betting that any enquiries up there wouldn't be linked back to me.

'Could you have someone run his background?'

'In aid of what? What would we be looking for this time?'

I thought of mentioning the child abuse, then checked myself. That was how rumours started.

'Justice,' I said.

He sighed. 'I'll have someone confirm whether or not he has a record, but that's all I can do. What's the address of his cabin?'

'I'll try to find out.'

'You do that.'

He hung up.

It was one of the less abrupt ways in which the old bruiser had ended a conversation over the years.

I put my mobile phone down on the table. My eyes settled on a section of the book discussing *liquid forms* and *fluid identities*. The latter was a term coined by a Polish sociologist, but Karremans had made it his own. It caused me to think of the game of hide and seek that he'd allegedly been drawn into, online, by SVU X-19. *Architects are friendly intruders*, Karremans was quoted as saying in the book, *articulating what the mainstream doesn't always express or even know that it wants...*

My phone was vibrating on the table.

Petra?

No – Stefan.

'*Hoi*,' I answered.

'I found three records.'

'That was fast.'

'Just the summaries.'

'Good.' Something briefer – sooner – was invariably better for investigative momentum. 'Well, go on,' I prompted.

'The first was the reported theft of Karremans's electric car last year. It turns out that some drunk students pushed it into the IJmeer.'

'Did it float?'

'It doesn't say –'

'A joke, Stefan. Keep going.'

'Seven years ago he was called as a witness in a dispute

between the developers of a residence on IJburg and the consulting engineers. The cantilevered section of a house had started to list –'

'Never mind that, either. Is he married, by the way? With a family?'

'Karremans?'

'Yep.'

There was a pause as Stefan checked something. 'I don't think so.'

'Keep going. What was the third record?'

'This is going back some way…'

'What is?'

'There's a statement from 1985. Karremans propositioned a boy at a foster home in Ghent.'

My heart rate quickened. 'In Belgium?'

'Yes.'

'Which boy?'

'A ten-year-old called Paul Ruiter.'

Thoughts of Liège, Night Market and Operation Guardian Angel flooded in, only… 'Was he Dutch? The alleged victim?'

'Yep, that's why it's still on the system.'

'What happened?'

'Nothing. No action taken.'

I was thinking fast, trying to work out what questions to ask. 'What year was this?'

'85, like I said.'

'And what was the name of the foster home–' But another call was incoming. 'Hold on, Stefan.' Still not Petra, dammit. It was Magnusson.

'Olaf…'

'You know, it is indeed lobster season up here…'

'I'm sorry?'

'Would you like to come up over the weekend? Quick fishing trip?'

I thought about Petra, and Johan, and instinctively said yes without giving it too much thought. Then: 'I'm just on another call. I'll ring you straight back, OK?'

I returned to Stefan.

'You still there?'

'Boss. I mean Henk… Do I call you Henk now?'

'Whatever floats your boat. Could you look into that foster home complaint?'

'Not easily, unless we coordinate with the Belgians.'

'There's no need for that.' I racked my brain – there had to be something else. 'Look at the complainant, would you? The Dutch boy.'

'Ruiter? He'd be in his forties by now.'

'True.'

'Is Monday OK?'

I couldn't argue. 'Monday is good.'

'Till then.'

'Oh – and Stefan?'

'Yes?'

'What's the address of Karremans's cabin?'

# 8

# THE FISHING EXPEDITION

THE SKY WAS CLEAR and jelly-pink as my plane touched down at Torp Sandefjord, the smaller of the two airports serving the Oslo region. Torp also served the peninsula to the south of Norway's capital. Retired police captain Magnusson kept a holiday home in Stavern, a fishing village near the peninsula's southernmost tip.

Petra had gone to stay with her cousin in Delft. I'd learned this by calling her from the Ibis hotel the previous night. She'd sounded serious about the separation, but I was trying not to think about it.

I'd managed to catch a direct flight that morning: one hour and forty minutes. The airport terminal was blessedly small, the air crystalline as I got outside. I was soon in my Budget rental car, driving out onto the E18 motorway, comforted by the sense of space and openness that I'd come to love up here.

Holland had traded with Norway for centuries. At one point, a fifth of the Dutch navy was made up of Norwegian sailors. Over the years, many Dutch had bought property here. Heinrich Karremans hadn't exactly settled in Norway, but it sounded like he'd spent enough time in the country that my enquiries might yield something.

A veil of mist lay draped over the coastal hills. It called to mind my army training, and first meeting Olaf Magnusson as a young man. Norway shared a border with Russia in the

High North and, under NATO guidance, had moved its army's headquarters from Oslo to the remote town of Bardufoss, where Magnusson and I had been stationed together.

When I'd first arrived, Norway felt like a basic, primitive place. I recalled the training in winter forests, the northern lights and midnight sun. Norway can afford many things now, not least Heinrich Karremans's architectural wonders in Oslo, but in the early 1980s oil production was only just beginning to ramp up.

I pulled into the car park of the public baths in Larvik – the nearest decent-sized town to Magnusson's holiday home. Magnusson had suggested that we meet here for a sauna.

The Larvik public baths was a large sleek building, lavishly dressed in dark stone. I found Magnusson in the reception area, looking older but well rested.

'Henk, God. It's been too long…'

While I'd spoken to him by phone recently, we hadn't seen each other in decades. His face was creased with lines. We hugged, then picked up towels and headed to the men's changing area.

'So this is your life now, saunas and spas?' I joked.

He harrumphed. My fellow ex-soldier's physique had become soft. His pectorals had sunk, his chest hair was snowy white.

We closed up our lockers, grabbed a couple of water bottles, and made our way through to one of the sauna cabins. Thankfully, we had it to ourselves.

Magnusson ladled water over the stove. The steam billowed and burned my sinuses. 'That's better,' he said, seating himself on the highest bench. 'I got a response about your man.'

I looked up at him. 'From Kripos?'

'Yes. Your friend Heinrich Karremans does appear on file here.'

I waited for him to go on.

'The cabin he owns near Trondheim was broken into.'

'When?'

'Recently.'

'What was taken?'

Another man stepped into the sauna, tentatively sitting on one of the lower benches. Magnusson ladled more water onto the stove, causing it to hiss ferociously. The man, who appeared to be foreign, was soon red-faced and breathing rapidly.

'Here.' I handed the man my water bottle.

He sipped appreciatively – '*Takk*' – then left.

'Heinrich Karremans wasn't in the country at the time,' Magnusson continued. 'The burglars took just a couple of items, including a computer.'

'When was this?'

'Ten days ago. Karremans was in China, apparently. Still is, I understand from the Trondheim police team.'

I tried to work out what that meant. 'Are there many burglaries in that area?'

'A few, especially in shoulder season. The cabins are remote and closed-up. There's a drugs problem in the area, as there is in many parts of the country.'

'Odd that they didn't steal more. A computer, you say? What else?'

'I didn't see the full report. What's your interest in this one?'

The steam was searing my skin. Briefly, I explained my role in Driebergen and the team's preoccupation with Karremans.

'Do you think it's worth a trip up to Trondheim?' I asked.

'To the cabin?' Magnusson looked doubtful. 'If you were here in an official capacity...' He shook his head. 'There's nothing to see, Henk. The report has been filed, locksmiths will have been round to secure the place... What would you be looking for, anyway?'

It was a good question. 'Listen, Olaf, I've got my doubts about this team I'm working with.'

'In Driebergen?'

'Yes.'

'Why?'

I needed to be careful now. 'I know for a fact that one of them lied about his record. Said he was in the UK's Special Reconnaissance Regiment. He wasn't.'

Magnusson sat forward, elbow on knee.

'Surely he must have expected to be found out?' I went on.

'Not necessarily,' Magnusson said. 'The Brits keep membership of it a secret, don't they? What about the other team members?'

'Three of them were in regiments of some kind. But I've got my doubts about all of them. They claim to have engaged Heinrich Karremans in an online sting operation, but is that likely, given that Karremans is in China? Who in their right mind would engage in that kind of activity online there, in the ultimate surveillance state?'

'Who in their right mind would engage in that kind of activity *anywhere*, these days?'

'Hold on.'

I walked out of the heat and stepped into the plunge pool outside, gasping. For a moment I just sat there, the icy water needling my skin. *Better.*

I leapt out again and returned, dripping cool water.

Magnusson continued: 'The guy I called in Kripos has good contacts in military circles, too. Give me the names of these other team members – let me have him run them.'

I persuaded myself that these were entirely different systems to the Dutch ones, and that there would be enough degrees of separation involved. In order to make the request more reasonable, I decided to give him just the names of the core team members to begin with – Boomkamp, Vermeulen and Engelhart.

'I'll write them down for you when we get outside.'

My skin was already burning again, all the way up my back. 'By the way, does the expression *beau soleil* mean anything to you?'

'No.' Magnusson's brow creased. 'Should it?'

'Just a saying they use around the squad room.'

He shook his head. 'People say the strangest things. Do you remember that other Dutchman on our training intake?'

'Who? Johan?'

'No, I don't remember his name. But do you recall that saying of his? About not staying in any place longer than the time it takes "for the fish to start smelling", or something?'

'Cas?'

'That's right,' Magnusson said. 'He didn't seem to have received the memo that we were up in Bardufoss for the season.' He laughed heartily. 'The winter season.'

'In fact, he graduated to the KMar.'

The KMar – the Royal Netherlands Marechaussee – is our royal protection service.

'You see? All's well that ends well.' Magnusson clapped me on the back, making me wince. 'Relax now. You need to save your strength for the fishing tomorrow. It will be rough out there on the water, and that's a promise.'

*

The following day, there was indeed a powerful swell off the Skagerrak coast. We met beside Magnusson's twenty-one-foot wooden skiff in Stavern harbour. The halyards of the other boats clanked noisily as we climbed onboard. Magnusson fired up the trusty Faerd inboard engine, and off we puttered towards the offshore Svenner Lighthouse. He'd set his lobster pots near it.

The dark sea rose and fell precipitously. The Baltic currents running around the Norwegian coast keep the sea clean and ensure that the lobsters caught here are among the most highly prized in the world, especially when consumed *au naturel*. But those same currents mean that you have just minutes to live if you end up in the water. There's no waiting around for the rescue boat.

My bomber jacket suddenly felt highly inadequate.

'I just heard back from Odd,' Magnusson called over the throbbing of the four-horsepower engine. 'My contact at Kripos,' he reminded me. 'About the men on your team.'

I suppressed a comment about the Kripos man's Christian name. 'What did Odd learn?'

'I don't know yet. He's just waiting to finish his shift so that he can communicate more openly.' Magnusson himself was distracted, trying to get the measure of the currents. Long waves can travel all the way up from the English Channel, moving terrifically fast and only revealing themselves as they break over submerged rocks. It's a question of reading the ever-changing light and dark surface patterns, and feeling the sea's energy.

I was speculating about what Magnusson's contact had discovered when the boat dropped a metre or so in the water. My stomach flew into my mouth and there was a hollow *boom* before the hull rose again. The Humminbird echo sounder could only tell us what was directly beneath us; it couldn't show us what lay ahead.

The bow kept climbing skywards, the horizon slanting at an alarming angle. I licked the salt water from my lips.

'Wouldn't it be easier to buy lobster at the local supermarket, Olaf? They're in season, you know.'

Magnusson chuckled. 'What, let you Dutch rid us of our "sea monsters" once more?' He was referring to my canny fellow countrymen, who had offered to remove these creatures for free back in the seventeenth century, depicting them as a threat.

The unusual yaw of the boat was making my stomach turn.

Magnusson forced a grin. 'What's the matter, Henk? Getting

a little seasick? I thought you were made of good mariner stock. Anyway, how I am supposed to keep my Norse spirit alive, shopping in supermarkets?'

Ah yes, the fabled Norse spirit. How they like to nourish the hunter part of themselves up here. It isn't unusual for Norwegian men to go off for days at a time, alone, into the wilderness. Is that what had drawn Karremans to Norway? The remoteness, the hunting spirit?

We were approaching an area known as Rakke – an old word for the submerged rocks here. Like the coastal hills just visible on the horizon, the rocks are relatively smooth – seductive-looking, even. Excellent for setting pots against, and for trapping the kind of fish and other sea matter that make good lobster feed, lobsters being night creatures, of course.

'So how's life?' Magnusson asked. 'How's the wife and daughter?'

'Could be better,' I replied.

'Could, or couldn't?' he clarified over the strengthening wind.

'*Could.*'

'Want to talk about it?'

I shrugged and sighed, then summarised the umbrage that Petra had taken at my job. 'But it's not just that,' I said loudly. 'It feels like everything's changing.'

'How so?'

I could tell from the surface patterns that the water was moving faster. The shore was a grey line, the lighthouse ahead a needle.

'"Loss" is how I'd mostly describe it, Olaf. Loss of time, opportunity, loss of years ahead of me... loss of a pain-free existence and even a solid night's sleep without having to get up and take a piss every three hours.'

Magnusson chuckled in agreement.

'Loss of memory and mental clarity, even...'

Was it the lighthouse ahead, or a metal pole sticking out from a submerged rock? A cormorant settled on it to dry its wings, deciding the matter finally. 'And what scares me is that I'm being changed, in ways I don't like or understand.'

Magnusson said nothing, opening up a space in the conversation for me to fill.

'Petra's concern is well-founded, in part at least.' It felt good to get this off my chest, get it out in the open. 'The other day, someone showed me an image of a girl online. Sixteen years old she was. Almost forty years my junior. A third younger than my daughter. And I felt aroused.'

'Then at least you feel *something*,' Magnusson said, scanning the dark sea surface, presumably for marker buoys.

'But it made me wonder: is *that* how abusers start out? How the spiral down begins?'

Another memory, from earlier in my career: *To catch the bad guys, you must think like bad guys. Some part of you must become them...*

Magnusson was shaking his head firmly. 'For abusers, it's all about power... about getting the power they lack. That's never been you, Henk. And nothing you've shared today suggests otherwise.'

I'd been prepared to believe this about Jan Stamms, the paroled offender in Liège – about powerlessness being at the base of it all.

'But what about Karremans?' I asked. 'Surely the *Rijksbouwmeester* of Holland has power?'

'It may be that his type feels the loss of power most acutely of all, as they age. That, again, isn't you.'

'Are you sure? Think about what I just told you. I'm more and more aware of my mortality.'

'As am I,' he said. 'I've got a decade on you, remember.'

I felt bad for talking in such a self-centred way. I felt sick, too, for the first time ever in a boat. It was the unusual, persistent twisting of the hull as it cut across the currents. I could see orange and yellow marker buoys; we were approaching the pots – and the metal pole sticking out of the water.

'You can look at it in one of two ways,' Magnusson was saying, sitting up on the starboard side of the boat, one hand still on the wheel, his craggy face silhouetted. 'You can think of yourself becoming older – or becoming an elder. Of losing physical power – or gaining something in your soul. Losing physical vitality, or gaining wisdom and the ability to help others... Here' – he suddenly sat up taller – 'could you take the wheel for a moment?'

I did so, watching him roll up his sleeve and reach in for the current buoy – a white-painted two-by-four, all but submerged; it showed which way the current was running. Strongly to the starboard side, it indicated.

The waters rode up furiously around Magnusson's wrist as he felt it. I steered hard to port.

The current buoy was attached to a marker buoy by a long section of floating rope; the marker buoy in turn was anchored by the heavy lobster pot. It was important that the boat didn't cross the line of the floating rope.

'It's the two-way pull in us all,' Magnusson was saying. 'Loss, gain. Weakness, courage. It all depends what you choose to tap into. Just like with the tides –'

'Shouldn't we focus on the task at hand?' I interrupted him. The wind was getting louder. We were entering a place of converging currents.

I could feel the bile rise in my stomach. The boat was being rolled like a stick. Magnusson vomited; I followed suit, over the side, heaving it up from the tips of my toes.

*Better.*

But the metal pole was approaching fast. I needed to steer more to port.

Suddenly, one of our phones trilled. It surprised me that there was even coverage. It was Magnusson's.

'Hello?'

I was about to rebuke him for taking the call when he said, 'Odd, we're just hauling in lobster pots.' He switched the phone to his other hand so that he could keep a firm hold of the rope. 'What's that? A NATO regiment?' He shot me a warning look. 'Let's talk later, now's not a good time.'

'What is it?' I called over the wind. Sea spray lashed at us.

'They were all in the same NATO regiment – the names you gave me.'

Had Boomkamp, Vermeulen and Engelhart served together? The world tilted. 'Olaf!' I warned as we pitched down into a watery dark canyon and rode up again as fast. If we hit a rock that way, the wood-panelled hull would shatter like a toy.

'Where's the rope?' I yelled. It occurred to me that the hull might, of itself, be causing the waves to break. We were suddenly drenched, head to foot.

Magnusson had his phone in one hand, but no rope in the other.

'Where the bloody hell is it?' I shouted over the wind.

'Steer to port!' he cried, stowing his phone in his inside pocket. But we were turning the other way, in a place where the currents met, and the engine had slowed. With dread I sensed why – the rope was wrapped round the propeller.

'Don't cross the line of the rope!' he yelled. 'Kill the engine!'

'Too late!' I shouted about the rope, fighting my urge to retain the motor's power, feeling my voice rise as the water lifted us up higher than seemed possible. There was a vertiginous moment as we slunk back down, just twenty metres or so from the metal pole. I wiped the stinging salt water from my eyes. The black cormorant was still sitting there. Jesus, this was dangerous.

'We need to cut the rope,' I yelled, leaning over the stern to try to see the propeller. The underside was being lifted clear out of the water, but all I could see was tangled rope. 'You got a knife?'

'What?' Magnusson said, coming alongside. His knuckles

blanched as he gripped the top of the hull.

'Knife!' I cried out.

Another wave broke into the boat, almost sweeping the bone-handled blade from his free hand.

'If I was thirty years younger,' he shouted over the shrieking wind, 'I'd dive into that damn water and free the rope properly!' His face was dripping wet.

'No longer fit enough, eh?'

I shredded the rope on one side, then the other.

'Not stupid enough,' he replied.

I restarted the engine, barely letting the clutch out and trying to play with the pitch of the propeller as my feet slipped and slid.

'There will be some nice six-pounders left in that pot,' Magnusson complained.

'They won't be going anywhere if they're wise.'

Some rope must have remained wrapped around the prop shaft, because I could barely get enough revs out of the engine to steer us across the face of the rock marked by the metal pole. For an agonising moment, the boat was stationary, fighting the current.

Magnusson was looking at his phone. 'Odd sent me a text,' he shouted. 'About this NATO regiment. Your three men were in it in 94 and 95. NATO Headquarters in Brussels.'

Belgium, again. 'Could you hand me that phone?' My own phone had no coverage. 'I think we should call the coastguard.'

'In Stavern?' Magnusson looked shocked. 'Admit that we're in trouble out here?'

'They must be used to sailors getting into trouble on Rakke.'

'Not these sailors.' He sounded appalled. 'Are you mad?'

I gestured at the inboard engine. 'Well, you try getting more out of this beast!' Water was swilling around the bottom of the vessel.

'Just give it more revs…'

I did, adjusting the pitch once more.

Yet another wave broke over the hull. The amount of water in the boat was concerning me as much as anything now. And then a current suddenly pushed us away from the rocks. As quickly as we'd got into trouble, I was able to use it to navigate away from them. We were being swept along in the coastal current.

It took another half-hour to get close enough to the shore to be able to double back beside it to Stavern, the engine reluctant, the propeller seriously down on power. By the time we limped home, the engine was practically running on fumes, it was so nearly out of fuel.

'That's what you get when you cross the line,' Magnusson rued.

# 9

## IJBURG

THE NATO REGIMENT THAT Boomkamp, Vermeulen and Engelhart had formed part of in the mid-1990s sounded like a specialist unit. Once again, I was left wondering why Rijnsburger or the justice ministry hadn't briefed me about this. I'd gone to Norway looking for information about Heinrich Karremans (and the solace of Olaf's friendship); I'd come back with something else altogether to ponder.

Back in Amsterdam, the houseboat was empty – Petra gone, the place eerily quiet, the void all-enveloping. There was no reason to delay my return to Driebergen... apart from one other curiosity I needed to satisfy.

I jumped on a number 26 tram and rode the straight, fast line out to IJburg, where Karremans lived and worked. The series of reclaimed islands was still being developed. I wondered about the value of the contracts involved; it must have been a lucrative enclave for Karremans Architectuur. IJburg was a showcase, of sorts, for Holland's worldwide leadership in dredging. The city had fought a long-running battle against environmental interests – a majority of voters had been against the construction, but an insufficient number of votes was cast, so it had gone ahead anyway. There were now political reputations staked on IJburg succeeding, and I couldn't imagine the city fathers being too cost-sensitive at this point. All of the buildings were new, the roads and street furniture, too; even the people looked altered – toughened – by their environment, like suburban pioneers. *Welcome to the windy and watery city*, their hard-set expressions announced.

I checked the address that Stefan had given me and alighted on Steigereiland, the island just before IJburg proper. Crossing the arterial IJburglaan under rolling grey clouds, I registered just how desolate the place was. The words of Gert at De Druif came back to me: *Why do we keep building places that people don't want to live in*? There was no collar on my bomber jacket to turn up, but I'd pulled on a flat cap – partly for warmth, mostly for disguise.

The ring road hummed to the west; a line of giant electricity pylons marched through the marina-style complex of expensive houses before me. The residences here were modular, rectangular-shaped units arranged into streets built over the water. These streets were in fact perforated metal gangplanks. Most of the houses had dinghies or sailing craft moored alongside, and a personal touch, too (the odd flower box, an occasional wind chime). I was making for the cluster of structures at the far corner. That end of the marina felt devoid of life – I could see no one else around – and yet I was aware of someone else in the vicinity.

Had Rijnsburger and the AIVD already initiated surveillance on Karremans?

I stopped suddenly and leaned against a railing, glancing from side to side – a basic countersurveillance move. I still couldn't see anyone. It may have been the ever-shifting patterns reflecting off the water that had created the sense of movement.

My phone was ringing: Stefan.

'Morning,' he said. 'How was your weekend?'

'Cold and wet,' I said. 'Yours?'

'I've lost Ruiter.'

'What?'

'I was looking into the complaint by that Dutch boy, Paul

Ruiter, against Karremans. It's not just Karremans, by the way. There were several high-profile people named alongside him. All linked to that boys' home in Ghent.'

'Who else?'

'Several regional Belgian politicians. I hadn't heard of any of them, and I doubt you will have either –'

'Try me.'

'Wait, Henk, there's more –'

I turned sharply, convinced someone was nearby. But all I saw were light patterns rippling across grey shapes.

'A police captain,' Stefan continued, 'a judge and a medical examiner, would you believe it…'

'Did other foster children complain?'

'No, and Ruiter himself vanishes from the system in 1989, aged fourteen.'

'What do you mean, *vanishes*?'

'There's no death certificate. But there's no record of address, and no employment or tax records from later years…'

'You spent some time on this.'

Did that put Stefan at risk?

'I became curious,' he said.

'Did Ruiter emigrate?'

'It's not clear. Maybe. A guardian might have helped him do so.'

I couldn't ask more of Stefan. But then another thought came to mind: the parents of the victims of Robert M in Amsterdam, who'd sought anonymity for their children.

'Perhaps Ruiter changed his identity?'

'Perhaps. It should be possible to find out.'

'No,' I said. 'You've done enough already.'

'Do you want to go for that drink?' he asked. 'There's something else I hoped to chat with you about: a promotion I'm going for.'

I felt awful. 'I have to return to Driebergen today or I'll be in trouble,' I said. I definitely didn't want to do anything to antagonise Boomkamp. But I wanted to help Stefan out. 'What do you need, a reference?'

'No,' he said hastily, as though my endorsement might not be helpful. 'Just some quick advice.'

Not only was I cold, but I was also eager to get away from IJburg, and especially the immediate vicinity. I at least owed Stefan a few minutes of my time, however. 'What sort of advice?'

'Actually... it's about handling Joost.'

The tone of the conversation shifted. 'What about Joost?'

'How to approach him... never mind, this is probably best discussed over a beer. Forget it.'

'OK,' I said evenly. Was Stefan applying for a position with my old rival? 'I'll be back in Amsterdam soon enough,' I said. At least, I hoped I would – the situation with Petra permitting. 'We'll get that drink...'

I put my phone away, attempting to make sense of the conversation. Again I was struck by the sense of missing something, but what? What couldn't I recall? Unknown unknowns. *Unknowable* unknowns, perhaps. I hastened my step towards the far cluster of buildings.

Most of the houses here were glass-walled, but Karremans's home–office revealed a different kind of exhibitionism. There was a long communal table featuring a procession of workstations and anglepoise lamps; a couple of staff members sat studying their iMac screens. Black attire appeared to be *de rigeur* at Karremans Architectuur. A woman looked up at me quizzically, but I didn't break stride. Rather, I did my best to look like I belonged in this corner of the marina-style complex.

Karremans's house stood just beyond.

The sailing boat gave it away. It was a sleek, black thirty-footer that put the neighbours' vessels to shame. Unlike the floating houses nearby, Karremans's home was built on stilts, allowing it to rise up five levels. The top floor would have views on all sides.

I pulled my flat cap down over my eyes. Karremans was in China, and apparently unmarried. It meant his house should have been empty, but I couldn't take that for granted. Did he have a girlfriend, a lover?

I padded across the gangplank to his glass front door. A narrow wooden deck ran round the ground floor of the property, enclosed by a metal-cable fence. No lights were on.

I walked round the deck, feeling it creak. The residence wasn't overlooked by other buildings; there was no need for curtains or panels of frosted glass like in the other houses. There was detailing in the metal upright members separating the glass, however: the same industrial–art deco blend as in the images I'd seen in Driebergen.

I cursed my wife for having caused me to hold back mentally and not take in the details in those pictures. *God is in the details –* wasn't that a quote from another famous architect? The quote had featured in an old police training manual...

I could clearly see the room that must have been Karremans's study; it faced out north, towards the sea channel. The desk arrangement and chair looked expensive, as did the massive monitor. But there was no computer. Karremans must have un-docked it and taken it with him. Or had he?

That sense of movement again, the flash of a limb–

'Hey!' a voice called, just a few metres behind me.

I spun round to catch a young man crossing the gangplank, coming straight at me. He was swaddled in dark fabric, a hood drawn tight so that I could only make out his mouth and eyes.

'What the fuck you doing?'

'I'm lost,' I managed. 'I thought my friend lived here.'

'This private.' His accent was Asian – Indonesian, maybe.

'They all look the bloody same, these houses,' I said with fake exasperation.

He didn't take kindly to that observation. 'Who are you?'

'Simple case of wrong address, sorry.'

I pushed past him, resisting the temptation to doff my cap. I hadn't seen cameras, but their existence wouldn't have surprised me after the break-in at Karremans's Norwegian cabin.

'Get lost,' the guy said.

Was he a housekeeper, a caretaker? He looked too young. I was about to ask him when he added, 'or I call police.'

# 10

## BURNING MAN

'WHAT THE HELL HAPPENED here?'

I'd made it back to the police building in Driebergen by mid-afternoon only to find it blocked by fire trucks and crews. Red and blue flickered off the grimy yellow suits of the firemen.

I showed my warrant card to one of them. He leaned into my car.

'We had an incident at the front desk,' he explained quietly.

'What kind of incident?'

'A man set fire to himself there. Poured paraffin over his head and lit himself up.'

'Jesus.' I pulled the car over and got out. There was a hiss of rain and a rumble of thunder.

'Who?' I asked the fireman.

'We're trying to find out.'

The entrance to the building was blackened, and dripping wet from the fire hoses. Smoke hung in the air, along with the smell of burned plastic and skin. As I got closer, I saw it: the charred body, resting on its back and surrounded by hazard cones. An arm had come loose. I tried not to look at what remained of the face, and its staring white eyes.

Tommy Franks stood back from the scene, drawing hard on a cigarette. I joined him. 'What the hell?' I said. 'Who is he?'

'Christ, Henk.' Tommy shook his head. 'Apparently he was an abuse victim.'

A white-gowned evidence technician was leaning over the body, mercifully shielding it from our view.

'How do you know?'

'He told front desk. The victim, that is. He screamed at them: *You pigs were never here to do anything, never in the right place at the right time... till now. Watch!* It was all caught on camera. The bloke pulled out a litre-bottle of paraffin, poured it over his head and produced a lighter.'

I reached for my own lighter, along with my pack of Marlboro Reds.

'He got stuck in the revolving door,' Tommy said, exhaling sharply. 'By the time they managed to free him, he was already burned beyond recognition. He staggered back, hit the deck and fell to pieces.'

I was numb. 'Where's the rest of the team?'

'Inside. Convening a crisis meeting, I understand.'

I almost asked him why he hadn't joined them, but thought better of it.

'You know what strikes me?' Tommy said, exhaling hard again. 'If abuse victims are willing to do this, what else are they willing to do?'

I ground my cigarette into the wet tarmac. As I did so, I noticed a woman approaching the entranceway with a digital recorder – a journalist? It could almost have been Petra in her former guise...

'I'd better go see what's happening,' I said, making my way towards a fire escape that had been propped open with a chair. It could have used a security guard.

On my way into the building, I called ARS Nationwide. Mrs Rosen picked up.

'There's been a situation,' I began. 'I need to speak with –'

'Is this about your possessions?' she cut in.

This was bullshit. 'Yes, the chairs, sofa and damn mountain bike,' I said. 'Now could you please put me through?'

'I'm under strict instructions to wait until my manager –'

'Henk!' a voice called as I walked into the open-plan area.

I turned to face Boomkamp.

'Where in God's name have you been?'

'Amsterdam. My wife, like I told you –'

'Get in here,' he urged, ushering me into his office. Engelhart was in there too, looking down at his feet. There was no sign of Vermeulen, or Rahm.

'We've got some explaining to do,' Boomkamp said, closing the door behind him. 'SVU X-19 does *not* appear as a matter of public record.' It sounded more like an article of faith than a statement of fact. 'So how in God's name did the victim know to come here, and to do *this*?'

Engelhart didn't meet my gaze.

I cleared my throat. 'I've no idea –'

'That's not good enough,' Boomkamp said. 'The deceased man's name is Dirk Arnhem. He's from a victims' support group who call themselves The Frozen. We need better answers. We need to be doing more, Henk. We need to be helping these people!' He paused, swallowing hard. 'Instead, we're giving them such little hope that they do… *this*!' He looked at me incredulously.

Where were Vermeulen and Rahm? Thinking of Rahm made me recall the bomber case in Luxembourg – the cops allegedly causing crises in order to justify their existence and the organisational status quo…

Boomkamp stepped closer. 'Are you *with* us, Henk?' His voice had dropped. 'That's what I need to know. Can we *count* on you?'

'In what way? With the work here? 'Course you can.'

'Right, then. There's something we need to do without delay. We had a suspect here, who Ivo brought in.'

'Which suspect?' It couldn't have been Karremans. Unless he'd returned from China?

'He bolted,' Boomkamp continued, ignoring my question. 'Took advantage of the commotion out front to get away. Ivo followed him on foot and has called in his position. It's all hands on deck.'

His eyes were incandescent. He said to Engelhart, 'Get the transport ready.' I assumed he meant a van. 'The back way,' he added, 'it'll be a circus out front…'

Once the two of us were alone, he asked, 'So, what happened?'

'How do you mean?'

'With your wife? Did you get her to see sense?'

'She walked out on me.'

'Christ.' A hand on my shoulder. 'What did you do, then?'

'What do you mean?'

'Over the weekend. You didn't speak with anyone?'

'I'm not following you.'

'We've had a lot of problems, Henk. I believe you know this – information has been leaking out, and now this…'

We were walking out of the doorway, Boomkamp leading the way. The light turned off behind us. For some reason, it made me turn my gaze. Boomkamp's computer screen was showing a web page. It looked like a breaking news story on the website of one of the newspapers, I couldn't tell which.

### *RIJKSBOUWMEESTER HEINRICH KARREMANS SUSPECTED OF ABUSING –*

'C'mon!' Boomkamp snapped. 'Men are waiting!'

I felt a sharp sensation in the pit of my stomach. We walked down the long corridor, past the clean room and towards another fire escape. My ears buzzed.

'We'll discuss it on the way,' he was saying.

'Discuss what?'

We passed the door to the men's lavatory.

'Wait, I need to pay a visit,' I said instinctively. 'You don't want me pissing in a bottle in the back of the van now.'

For half a second I thought Boomkamp might follow me in there.

I closed the door behind me and immediately called the justice minister. His assistant answered.

'I need to speak with Willem.'

'Who is this?'

'Van der Pol, we met the other day –'

'It's impossible. He's not available. You're supposed to be working with Rijnsburger and the AIVD, anyway.' He paused. 'Is this even a secure line?'

'Tell the minister this is an emergency. Tell him that the situation at Driebergen is unravelling –'

There was a bang on the door.

'Wait,' the assistant said over the phone.

'What the hell are you doing, Henk?' Boomkamp called from outside.

A familiar voice came on the line. 'What's going on?' van der Steen said.

'I need to come in.'

'That's impossible.'

'Things are spiralling out of control here –'

'Trust the process,' he cut in. 'Don't communicate with me again this way. Go through the AIVD, or...'

'Or what?'

'Do you want your old problems with Joost to resurface, and other problems besides? We had a deal. This call's over.'

The door blew open. My phone was back in my pocket as Boomkamp cried, 'What the fuck! C'mon!'

He guided me out through the rain and into the dark rear space of an old KLPD van. I could just make out Engelhart driving, through a narrow section of glass at the front; Boomkamp and I had the back to ourselves. We sat on metal benches, facing one another.

'Who is this suspect?' I said.

The van swung onto Hoofdstraat; we were moving at speed. But we didn't join the A12 motorway. Rather, we were soon bumping along a dirt track. Were we heading into the forest? A very bad sensation crept into my stomach.

'Boomkamp, what's going on?'

'What's wrong, Henk? You never made an arrest before?'

Only now did I recall that there were no prison cells at Driebergen. The nearest ones were in Houten.

The van suddenly stopped; we lurched sideways along the benches. A widening rectangle of light appeared to my left as the back door opened and a silhouetted figure climbed into the rear of the van – Vermeulen, his weapon sitting prominently on his hip.

We were indeed in the forest.

'Who is this suspect?' I repeated.

The door closed again.

'You, Henk.'

The van started moving once more, heading deeper into the woods. I didn't have my service weapon with me.

'What are you talking about?'

'What happened over the weekend?' Boomkamp demanded.

Vermeulen was rubbing his wrists as if preparing for a physical encounter.

'I told you. I went back to Amsterdam, to try to patch things up with my wife.'

'But you didn't, did you?' he asked, almost jeering now. 'So what did you do instead?'

I needed to keep calm, to think. 'I don't understand where this is going.'

'Oh, but I think you understand very well, Officer van der Pol.' He let that hang there, in the bumpy gloom. We must have hit a rock, because there was a bang and the van jumped; we were heading off the beaten track.

'Do you remember what I told you, when I called you into my office the other day?'

I didn't, but I sensed he was about to remind me.

'Do. Not. Undermine. Me.' He waited, as if giving me a last chance to clear my name. 'And then I invited you to my house. My home. And you came, and my wife took your coat. And do you know what Mariella did with that favourite jacket of yours, Henk?'

I suddenly knew where that bad feeling came from. My bomber jacket — I had inadvertently 'patterned' myself, in surveillance terms. I looked for the tear in it, near the zip. It wasn't visible in the dim light.

*God is in the details...*

'We know how to do technical surveillance,' Boomkamp was saying. 'We *know.*'

Desperately, I replayed the events since that evening at the Boomkamps'. I'd been wearing the jacket all of the time, apart from when I was sleeping — or in the sauna with Magnusson... I couldn't remember what Magnusson and I had discussed there versus in the skiff. Magnusson's phone had retained coverage out on the water, so doubtless the miniaturised listening device had been transmitting there, too.

'It's time to plug all leaks,' Boomkamp was saying. He was reaching inside his jacket, perhaps to touch his gun handle, feel its reassuring solidity.

The conversations with Stefan came back to me as well, as did the one with Rijnsburger out at Leiderdorp. The time on IJburg — the encounter outside Karremans's house... even my disagreement with Petra.

*Christ.*

'There's a lot to be said about having a loyal wife, Henk. Maybe that's your problem. Or one of them, at least...'

# 11

## NIGHT TRAINING

'WHY DID YOU GO and see Karremans?' Boomkamp was asking. We were still moving, only more slowly.

'I didn't see Karremans,' I replied.

'Come now,' Boomkamp said in an avuncular voice. He spoke as if he were amused. 'That little device in your jacket not only tells us what you say, it tells us where you are.'

'OK then,' I said, folding my arms. All the while I was readying my move. I needed to exploit my ability to surprise them while I still had it. 'I was at his house, but he wasn't there. He's in China.'

'China, eh?'

The van was accelerating again, and I used that momentum to throw myself to the back. I'd seen the inside of the rear door when Vermeulen got in; my hand landed just above the handle, bracing myself. Vermeulen was on top of me, but my speed in the bumpy darkness had caught him off guard.

Boomkamp was banging on the side of the van. 'Stop!'

Before Engelhart could react, I'd yanked the door handle and the door swung out. I did all I could with my arms to break my fall, landing on the forest track with Vermeulen on top of me. The heavy Belgian winded the life out of me, but protected me from Boomkamp's aim.

I reached back and up for Vermeulen's hip-holstered gun. He'd had the same idea of course, but again I had the benefit of surprise. My hand clasped his trigger finger and I squeezed with all my might; the weapon jumped with a bang and Vermeulen's grip slackened. He curled up in a ball, shot in his lower body.

The rear door had closed again, Boomkamp taking cover. It gave me a moment to try to wrestle Vermeulen's gun from him, but no luck. Engelhart would be edging down the side of the van, ready to fix me in his sights.

I got to my feet, bent double, and ran into the dense forest, hearing cracks of gunfire at my back.

*

The bomber jacket was moss green, and maybe that's what saved my life. I'd no doubt that both men were expert shots, having served together in that NATO regiment. If I were to stay alive, I needed to be better than them, exploiting my own training in those northern Norwegian forests.

But the odds were against me. There were two of them (three, if Vermeulen recovered). They surely knew the terrain they'd taken me to, they had the advantage of communications, and they potentially had the ability to call in support. The key factor was their level of motivation. From my experience, most fights come down to one question: who wants to win most?

My breathing was heavy and becoming ragged as I wove between the dense fir trees. The rain hissed; thunder occasionally rumbled. It helped soften my progress, the saplings snapping less sharply, the mulched leaves damping my footfall.

When I sensed I'd got sufficiently far from them, I paused to catch my breath, which was condensing. The temperature was dropping. Night would come soon, which was good and bad. Darkness might help me seek cover, but without a den or shelter I'd be in for a worryingly cold night.

I slipped my jacket off, ripped open the fabric beside the zip and found the device – no bigger than a thumbnail, including its battery. I dug a hole in the ground, buried it and kept moving.

A hundred metres further on, I stopped again to check my phone. It showed one bar of coverage and almost no battery life. They'd brought me to a dead zone.

There was one thing I immediately needed to satisfy myself about, so that I could gauge the extent of the threat they posed. Unwilling to use my voice in case it carried across the cold air, I thumbed a text to Stefan:

*The boys home in Ghent (re. Karremans). whats its name?*

While waiting, I tried to use the phone's compass, but was having trouble calibrating it.

The phone vibrated with Stefan's reply.

*Beau Soleil.*

So there it was. Boomkamp, Vermeulen and Engelhart were connected to the boys' home where the notorious abuse had occurred.

What did it all mean? How did their time together at the foster home link to the NATO regiment they went on to serve in? Whatever remained unclear, it showed me – as nothing else could – the extent of their rage and revenge-lust.

I texted Stefan again about gunshots in the forest north of Driebergen, and how he should alert the police there...

*Your message failed to send.*

Perhaps Boomkamp had already alerted them, declaring me a fugitive suspect and persuading someone at Driebergen to monitor my phone. It would be illegal without a warrant, but that didn't seem to have stopped him elsewhere. Had he leaked the Karremans allegations to the press? Nothing could be ruled out now.

The phone screen was blank anyway, the battery dead. I threw it as far as I could, back the way I'd come. The phone snapped a sapling as it landed. I heard something else. The machine-gun rattle of a woodpecker, and...

'Fan out,' Boomkamp's voice faintly commanded.

Had they found the transmitter? If so, they had my tracks.

There was no sun overhead to find direction by. My internal compass told me I was moving south – back towards Driebergen – but I couldn't be sure of that.

*Keep moving*, a voice inside my head urged. *Cover ground.*

A path appeared amid the underbrush: again, it was good and bad. Faster, yet more easily followed.

I decided to take it and began jogging at a steady pace, regulating my breathing and being careful with my footfall. Only now that my adrenaline levels had dropped did I register the repeating sharp pain down my right-hand side. From where Vermeulen had landed on me?

I was betting that the path would take me back to civilisation. Not quite, as it turned out: within a couple of hundred metres I emerged in a clearing... a small lake fringed with reeds; an old, broken-down, single-storey house. Had it belonged to an estate? This whole area had once been a wilderness-playground for Holland's landed aristocracy.

In the open of the clearing, the rain fell insistently. The thunder rumbled on. I walked slowly around the water, peering through the rain-pitted surface, seeing a silvery flash in the depths. It hadn't been completely abandoned.

But the building had.

I stepped over the sill of the entranceway, which was missing its door. The thatched roof had caved in, the supporting beams shattered by a combination of weight, damp and termites.

There was evidence of a makeshift fire – long ago abandoned – and corroded tins of food. A cracked mirror remained above the original fireplace. Glaring back at me, my eyes appeared huge – belonging to someone else entirely, intensely alive. They startled me.

The cottage resembled the kind of prop used in my military training. If that was true for me, it had to be true for Boomkamp and Engelhart. I had to try to put myself in their boots – to anticipate the moves of my pursuers. They were armed, coordinated, and trained to storm a structure such as this one, should I be hiding inside. I'd managed to surprise them once, leaping from the back of that van; they'd be hell-bent on preventing me surprising them again.

Reluctantly I left the shelter, wincing from the pain in my ribs as I stepped back into the rain. They couldn't be far away, and over that *knock-knock* of the infernal woodpeckers – louder, more resonant now – I heard movement.

I crouched down.

Yes, something was moving in the forest. Was it them, or an animal?

There was no time to find out. I crawled forward on all fours towards the water's edge. Lying beside it, I rolled gently in.

I was already wet through, but the cold was shocking. My idea, if I could even call it that, had been to hide with my head above water among the reeds. It was the last place they should have looked for me. Perhaps I'd hoped that the cold would anaesthetise the pain in my ribs, too. But my ribs contracted, making the pain intense. Within minutes I'd be dead from the cold, anyway.

I couldn't rely on them passing through the clearing quickly. Through the reeds, I couldn't even see them approaching.

Numbly I clambered out again. I was dangerously cold and starting to lose the power of structured thought – starting to feel more and more like a hunted animal. My only salvation lay in the darkening sky, making it harder for them to see me – assuming they weren't equipped with night-vision or thermal-imaging kit, in which case I was finished.

I clambered across the muddy lakeside like some amphibian creature, with two instincts: to dirty my jeans, and to make it look as though I'd fallen into the water. Ripples were still washing against the shore.

In this manner, I made my way for three or four metres,

looking up every few seconds for any sign of them. I sat up, my eyes darting among the gloomy branches and underbrush. Then I stood and ran, crouching, towards the line of trees. I couldn't feel my legs; I could only see them pumping beneath me. It was as if I were looking at someone else's lower body. I was dripping but the path was already wet and soft; I wasn't leaving a trail.

The first tree I found, I climbed ravenously, my hands grappling for ever-higher branches. I forced myself to slow down, to prevent the trunk and branches from shaking. That way, I managed to get four or five metres above the forest floor, into dense foliage. I made my legs level along a branch, having tested it for strength. My muddy jeans blended in with the branch, and my green jacket was lost in the leaves – the tree made an effective hide. The twin worries now were my adversaries' powers of observation, and the cold seeping into my broken bones.

Why hadn't Boomkamp or Engelhart arrived yet? They knew my direction of travel; I'd struck out on a clear path. Had they waited for backup? But it was unlikely – they'd have a lot of explaining to do, even if they managed to persuade others of my fugitive status.

Were they taking care of the fallen Vermeulen?

There was a crackling sound that might have been a small animal. As it came closer, I spied a human moving cautiously along the track: Engelhart, alone, his weapon in a two-handed grip.

My plan was to jump down on top of him. Only, now that he'd arrived, I saw that my mind had tricked me again. The distance to the ground risked a bad landing. Engelhart's palpable sense of alertness and purpose told me that I wouldn't get a second chance – maybe not even a first one.

He crept forward.

The woodpecker rattled away at my nerves.

Upon entering the clearing, he made, cautiously, for the

broken-down building. Then he saw the muddy trail leading to the water's edge.

He looked around him, and for a second I felt sure he would peer up into the hide and spot me, but instead came a whisper of radio static. Hastily, he muted the two-way radio clipped onto his lapel.

He started walking around the lake, interrupting his circuit to stalk over to the abandoned cottage. After a minute spent inspecting the inside, he returned to the water's edge. He was staring intently at the reeds and vegetation fringing the lake as he circumnavigated it. I knew exactly what he was thinking: *Something doesn't feel right.*

Soon he'd be on the far bank – looking directly back at my elevated position. That wouldn't do – I needed to keep him looking down. I had no better idea than to throw my cigarette lighter into the nearside of the lake. It was made of battered metal, dulled from use; I was betting that the light wasn't strong enough for it to reflect as it flew.

Again I hesitated, owing to the numbness of my throwing arm. I was half-hoping that Engelhart would give up on the clearing and look elsewhere. But I knew he could sense my presence. I practised a couple of flicks of my wrist, keeping movement to a minimum.

I was ready. Hand trembling, I clasped the lighter, aimed, and flicked it towards the lake. It landed with a soft plop on the nearside of the water. The sound could almost have been a fish rising, but Engelhart knew the oddness of it immediately and fired his weapon.

*Crack, crack.*

Where was Boomkamp? Probably trying to radio him.

*Finish the clip*, I willed Engelhart.

Of course, he knew not to do that.

He came round to the source of the ripples, staring into the water, his back to me. I wouldn't have a better chance. My heart thumping, I gripped the branch hard, and slid underneath it so that I hung by both hands. I hoped that this would reduce the height of my fall.

As I readied myself to let go and run at him, the branch gave way at the trunk with a shattering snap. I landed in a crouching posture. Engelhart had swivelled and fired reflexively into the tree, at the source of the noise. My crouching run propelled me towards him. He swung his arm round and fired again, at my lowered torso, missing… just. My fist met his nearside temple with all the force of my body's weight and momentum; it must have felt like a blow from a lance. His eyes rolled back into his head and dulled.

I thought I'd killed him. But then he staggered back into the water.

Quickly I waded in after him; I managed to catch his gun as his slackening hand released it. He twisted round and crashed into the water, and there he floated, face down, his jacket billowing at the back.

I'd been prepared to kill him – certainly to let him die. It wouldn't have been the first time that I'd have let a man drown.

Only, I couldn't do that.

Whatever Engelhart had done, he was still a policeman. We'd have to work it out, or my conscience would also be the loser.

I left the gun on the bank and jumped in, reaching around him – ready to haul him out, part of me fearing that he'd played a trick and lured me in to try and drown me. But he came out of the water limply, and it was only when I got him bent double that he spluttered and shook from his depths, shuddering back to life.

I pulled his two-way radio off his lapel; it was wet and useless. So, too, was his phone, which I fished out of his inside pocket.

I picked up the gun and sat beside him.

His eyes fluttered open, dark pupils roving between me and the surrounding trees. Perhaps he thought he'd died or entered some nightmare. I slapped him hard across the face.

'Don't go to sleep.'

He stared at me.

'Call to Boomkamp.'

His body began to shiver.

'Call out to Boomkamp!'

He didn't respond.

'What else have you got?' I went through his pockets more thoroughly; there was a folding pocketknife.

On it was engraved: *Beau Soleil Boys' Home Scouts*.

He looked blankly at me as I weighed the knife in my palm.

'Let's go.' I left his redundant possessions in a little heap by the lakeside, like an offering to the gods of the forest. 'Get up.' I prodded him in the small of the back with the gun's muzzle.

As soon as we'd rounded the lake and re-entered the cover of the trees, he stumbled off the path amid low branches.

'What the hell are you doing?' I said. 'Get back on the path. I'll shoot.'

But he knew I wouldn't. I'd saved his life once; he knew that I wouldn't kill him now. My hand was trembling. The cold and the pain were getting to me, more than ever.

Engelhart had stopped, dead still, facing away from me. It gave me a chance to listen. There was a faint murmur – the sound of traffic on a main road?

Suddenly, the top part of Engelhart's shoulder vanished into a dark-red mist.

The muffled sound of a gun report blended into rolling thunder; I was horizontal again – on the forest floor – as the second shot blew apart Engelhart's skull.

'Jesus, Boomkamp!' I screamed. 'Stop the madness!'

'It's not Boomkamp you need worry about,' came the calm, strident voice of Tommy Franks through the trees. 'Not anymore.'

# 12

## THE SWITCH

MY SEARCHING GAZE SWEPT the fir trees. The starkly vertical, black trunks blurred as if viewed through a zoetrope, creating that flickering sensation in the inner eye.

Was Tommy Franks part of Boomkamp's inner circle after all?

If so, why had he appeared to be such an outsider? Was it a cover?

The rain hissed down. I forced my eyes to focus.

Why had Franks killed Engelhart? Had he done so by mistake, while trying to kill me? It suddenly felt like I knew nothing at all.

I crept back to the edge of the clearing. The lake, the building… and a movement beyond: blurry brown, like a fast-moving fox – was that him?

I pulled out the clip of Engelhart's muddied gun. There were four 9mm rounds left. I drew back into the trees and waited, frozen in place, making myself as small and still as possible.

The minutes stretched by. The familiar noise of the woodpecker was replaced by the haunting hoot of a tawny owl. My eyes adjusted to the dark. My clothes were damp and the forest was only getting colder. The cigarette lighter had meant fire and warmth, but the cigarette lighter lay at the bottom of the lake.

I looked up at the tree canopies; they spiralled darkly and my vision swooped back to the forest floor. Where was Franks lurking? The pain down my right side was overwhelming. So, too, the sense of fear. Not just of Franks's marksmanship – there was also a primal fear, permeating all parts of me, of my own animal instincts and where they might lead me now.

*Keep moving.*

I struck back out onto the path, where my progress was unimpeded and hence noiseless. Earlier in life, in Africa, a safari guide had taught me how to spot animals, even at night.

I saw a heaving and subsiding form lying among the trees. I stepped back off the path and crouched down.

Was it Franks, lying in wait?

Only... why? In my last conversation with him, amid the firemen, I'd asked him where the rest of the team was. He'd said, *You know what strikes me? If abuse victims are willing to do this, what else are they willing to do?*

I tried to find meaning in that. Perhaps there was none. Perhaps this was all just senseless bloodlust. All I could assume was that he was better prepared than me to wait this out. Better prepared with warmer, drier clothes, more ammunition, and a more accurate firearm...

I reached for a rough-edged stone and hurled it into the forest. It crashed to the ground. At first... nothing.

Then – 'Help' – a ragged voice escaped the heaving form in the undergrowth. The voice was Boomkamp's.

Quietly, I crept over to where he lay fallen.

His eyes widened. 'Henk,' he croaked.

'Shh.' I put my finger to my lips.

His face, neck and shoulders were dark with blood. He was shivering.

'Did Franks do this?' I whispered.

'Someone... came out of nowhere. I thought it was you.'

I crouched. 'Keep your voice down.' I took my jacket off and wrapped it over him. It was damp, but all I had to offer. 'What have you got on you?'

'My gun…'

'A phone?'

'Yes.' He grimaced with the effort of trying to reach down. 'Hip pocket…'

I did it for him, finding something small and cylindrical.

'Not that pocket,' he said. 'The other one.'

There I found his smartphone.

'What's the code?'

He told me.

I unlocked the phone and dimmed the screen. It had battery power but no signal. 'I need to find coverage,' I told him, 'and get help.'

'Go that way.' He nodded in the direction I'd been travelling in. As he did so, he grimaced, baring his bloodstained teeth. The wound had caused blood to rise up inside him. I thought of trying to fashion a compression bandage but I couldn't see where the wound was, and getting him to a nearby hospital was the clear priority.

'What about Gunther?' he said.

'He's gone.'

A small cry escaped Boomkamp's mouth.

'Shh,' I urged. 'Where's Vermeulen?'

Boomkamp didn't answer my question. Instead he said, 'We did what we could. We knew each other from a young age, you know…'

I nodded. 'At the boys' home, in Ghent.'

'Do you know what went on there?'

I hesitated, torn between finding a signal for the phone and hearing this.

'They got us drunk on cider, passed us round like pieces of meat, Henk. Filmed us.'

'You formed a pact,' I said.

107

He stared directly up, through the treetops to the dark heavens above, not denying it. 'We did what we could.'

'Who were they? The people passing you round?'

'Powerful people. Karremans wasn't the only one.'

'There were complaints, made by Paul Ruiter.'

'Ruiter.' His eyes closed.

'You knew him?'

'Knew... know.' Boomkamp took a moment to breathe. 'He went back to Belgium, would you believe it? To Liège... changed his name to Jan.'

'Wait... not Jan Stamms?'

The paroled sex offender who begot Operation Guardian Angel...

'Others are gone,' Boomkamp said. 'Wiped from the earth.'

'By who?'

He didn't answer. 'It comes down to who you meet in life. I wish I'd met a man like you earlier, Henk. I had a guardian who took me away from Beau Soleil, only to abuse me himself. So, you see...' His voice trailed off.

I looked up and around. Where was Franks? Why hadn't he returned to kill?

'Keep an eye on that Magnusson, by the way. Up in Norway.'

I looked sharply at him. 'What did you say?'

'He's one of them.'

'What are you talking about?'

'We looked into him, too.' His voice had gone faint. 'He's a downloader.'

'That's impossible.'

Had they come to suspect *everyone* as abusers, outside of SVU X-19? 'I need to get that phone signal,' I said angrily.

'Wait, Henk. In my hip pocket, there's some medicine I must take.'

I reached in and found the small bottle.

'What is it?' I couldn't see the label.

'Please.' He gestured for it.

He screwed the cap off and had thrown the liquid down his throat before I realised. Numbly I tried to scoop it out of his mouth with my hand, to turn him on his side, but he'd already gone limp.

'Did what we could,' he repeated, his voice a haunting whisper.

# 13

## STANDING IN SILHOUETTE

AT FIRST, I THOUGHT that I was dead. Slowly, the white room came into focus and the bottom of the hospital bed outlined itself. So too did Wim Rijnsburger – standing at the far side of the room. He came over, his bloodshot eyes peering at me.

'Where am I?'

'Zoetermeer,' he replied.

The AIVD head office?

'Am I in hospital?' I asked aloud.

'Of a sort.'

'What happened?'

'You had a pneumothorax.'

'Say again?'

'Collapsed lung.'

He nodded at my right ribs.

'Plus acute stress,' he added. 'A full physical and psychological breakdown, in fact.'

I moved my legs under the bedclothes. The pain throughout my upper body made me stop. 'I've lost weight.'

'Yes, three kilos. Are you able to talk about what happened?'

I looked up at the ceiling, recalling my last moments of consciousness in the forest. The phone call, the wait, the men arriving... I must have passed out once I knew I was safe. It's funny what the physical body will endure in the name of survival, until it no longer needs to.

110

'I was with Boomkamp before he committed suicide. He *is* dead?' I looked at Rijnsburger.

The secret service man nodded. 'We concluded that he poisoned himself after shooting the rest of his crew. We just need it confirmed – that you shot Boomkamp in self-defence.'

'Only I didn't,' I said. 'You mentioned the rest of his crew – Vermeulen as well, then?'

'Yes.'

'It was Franks who killed them all.'

Rijnsburger looked down at a clipboard in his hand. 'You've mentioned this before, talking in your sleep here. The psychiatric nurse noted it.' He set the clipboard aside. 'Henk, Tommy Franks wasn't in that forest.'

'Yes, he was. I heard him speak.'

'Did you, though?'

I sighed and sank my head back into the pillow. 'It was him.'

Rijnsburger was silent for a second.

'Rest,' he said. 'I'll come by and see you in a day or so.' He picked up the clipboard again and patted me on the shoulder with it. 'We'll talk.'

As he left, a nurse poked his head round the door and asked, 'Are you able to see one more guest, Mr van der Pol?'

'Who?'

'Your wife.'

'Please.'

Petra appeared in the doorway, her pained eyes meeting mine. 'Can I hug him?' she asked the nurse.

'Better not to.'

She sat beside me, taking my hand and wrapping hers around it. And another kind of healing began.

*

I joined Petra at her cousin's house in Delft, just fifteen minutes from the AIVD building in Zoetermeer. Cousin Cecilia was a lively, bright woman. My time there was mostly spent sitting in an armchair in the conservatory that she'd recently had built.

It called to mind Boomkamp's wife Mariella, now widowed. She'd been visited more than once by the secret service about her own role in abetting illicit surveillance, the needs of the state coming before her grieving.

All this I learned upon returning to see Rijnsburger, who was eager to finish my own debrief. This time we sat in a battleship-grey meeting room. The blinds were drawn; the light was artificial.

'We took DNA from Boomkamp.'

It was standard procedure with any suicide.

'Any matches?' I asked.

The DNA would have been run against a data bank. At least *some* of those who the police didn't manage to catch alive were unable to live with their guilt...

'One, yes. A crime scene in Norway.'

'Heinrich Karremans's cabin in Trondheim? The break-in there?'

Rijnsburger handed me a photo. It showed a starkly beautiful house set in a snowy wilderness; the fenestration was instantly familiar.

'Did you find anything else up in Norway?' I asked.

I was thinking of Magnusson, and Boomkamp's final comment about him – which I couldn't bring myself to believe.

Rijnsburger looked at me quizzically. 'Such as?'

'Never mind. So Karremans was exonerated?'

'Karremans was not a suspect. Some of our friends in the fourth estate are eating humble pie.'

Perhaps he was referring to the online newspaper article I'd seen in Boomkamp's office, when leaving it for the last time.

'What about the other members of the team? Franks and Rahm?'

'They've gone home. SVU X-19 is history. Your mission there is over.'

He paused, giving me a chance to say something. I remained silent.

'Everything will be organised differently. It has to be so,' he said. 'There will be a new central child-exploitation team' – he paused now for emphasis – 'here in Zoetermeer. New structures for national and international coordination involving Europol and Interpol, joint centres of intelligence and expertise, new victim-identification task forces and cybercrime initiatives, even inroads to the big internet companies…'

He paused longer, again giving me a chance to speak.

I didn't.

'The question remaining is what happens to you, Henk. Where you fit in now. The minister is keen that we find you a home.'

It all sounded right, but I was left with the distinct impression that something was very wrong – some person, or group of persons, who'd gone unpunished.

'*Beau soleil*,' I murmured. I could still hear Boomkamp saying those words, lying there on the floor of the forest, baring his bloodstained teeth.

'What?' Rijnsburger asked.

I was about to offer an explanation, but changed my mind.

\*

It was a short distance from Zoetermeer to the Ministry for Security and Justice. Van der Steen had time for me. As I was shown into his office, I wondered what his motives were in agreeing to meet now.

'You've lost weight,' he said.

'Without any time spent in the police gym. A miracle.'

He chuckled. 'Drink?'

'Still or sparkling? No thanks.'

I grimaced as I lowered myself into the chair he offered. We were sitting once again at the round glass table strewn with papers. The work of government went on.

'I've read Rijnsburger's report,' he said, his steely eyes fixing on mine. 'It remains for me to add my thanks – and those of the ministry – for a job well done, in testing circumstances.'

'I appreciate you saying that, but there's something else we need to discuss.'

'Your job?'

'There's that. There are four things I wanted to bring up, in fact.'

'Oh?'

'First, I don't know how much Rijnsburger's report went into the histories and motivations of SVU X-19's core team members. For what it's worth, my reading is that Boomkamp, Engelhart and Vermeulen sabotaged the Stamms case because Stamms himself was abused at the boys' home that they'd all been put into – that's where their anger and solidarity originated. You're aware of this?'

'A gift that kept giving.' He corrected his answer: 'Yes, it's too bad.'

'The question being, how many other suspects did Boomkamp and company release in their pursuit of the abusers at that foster home?'

'Maybe we'll never know,' the minister replied meditatively. 'After all, Boomkamp, Vermeulen and Engelhart are no longer with us.'

'But other people are very much alive. Did Boomkamp's widow have anything to say about the matter?'

He opened his mouth to speak but there came a rap at the door. His assistant's head poked in: 'The PM wants a brief chat with you in ten.'

It didn't sound like an invitation. Van der Steen nodded his acknowledgement, then turned back to me. 'You said you had several points. Let's get them out on the table.'

'OK... Ghent – the boy's home in question: will the file be reopened?'

'That's a question for the Belgians.'

'Is it, though? When we last sat around this table, you mentioned a suspect and kingpin in the Amsterdam area. Well, that kingpin is alleged to have abused boys at that care home in Ghent, and elsewhere, and he's very much Dutch.' There was no need to mention Heinrich Karremans by name. 'Jan Stamms – one of his alleged victims – is Dutch, too. Stamms changed his name. You're aware of all this?'

Van der Steen sighed impatiently. 'We're making a lot of organisational changes, Henk. Are you aware of *that*?'

'Rijnsburger told me about working with Interpol, Europol and the rest.'

'Well then. We're adding new prosecutorial resources, too, here in The Hague,' he went on, glancing at his watch. 'We're adding capacity, Henk. Look, I'd like to find a proper home for you now. Clearly you have a knack for getting to the heart of things, and our law enforcement agencies need that more than ever with said changes afoot. Have you considered the *Rijksrecherche*?'

'Internal Investigations?' I almost laughed.

He held up an appeasing hand.

'I need to return to Amsterdam,' I said more fiercely than I'd meant to. 'I need to get well, and save my marriage.'

'Fine, so tell me what job you *do* want. You mentioned four things. I've counted three: the SVU X-19 core team members, the Ghent boys' home, Karremans...'

I leaned forward, even though it hurt my ribs to do so. 'Tommy Franks,' I wheezed. 'You warned me that at least one member of that team was rotten. It turns out that they *all* were, only in different ways.'

'Henk, I don't have time for this. Where are you going with it? What are you implying?'

'I'm not implying anything. I'm inferring that Tommy Franks may have been there in Driebergen to sabotage the saboteurs. Where is he, by the way?'

The minister sighed exasperatedly. 'Back in the UK.'

'Well, we know what's been going on in the UK of late – the institutional child abuse cases coming to light… lots of important people must be worried over there. Are we dealing with something similar here? We also know that individual members of the Night Market paedophile ring were based in the UK –'

'Henk! Rijnsburger's report covers the salient points!'

'Right,' I said, 'but keep in mind that Rijnsburger downplayed Franks's role on at least two occasions. Once when I was recovering in hospital, and he suggested that I'd totally imagined Franks killing the other men in the forest – only I hadn't. Then there was the other time, when we had a meeting in Rijnsburger's van and he told me that Franks had lied about being in a British military regiment… Perhaps that last titbit was intended to make me question Franks's credibility. Well, it had the opposite effect, in the end. Franks looks like an expert dissembler now.'

'Are you calling into question the analytical abilities of the AIVD, even?' van der Steen asked incredulously.

'Not necessarily. But I'd be happy to help you with any ongoing enquiries, so to speak.'

He nodded curtly. 'I'll take that under advisement.'

'Or talk to Rijnsburger's boss?'

'Don't push it, Henk.' He stood and gave me his tightest smile yet. His assistant was waiting at the door, signalling that the prime minister was about to come on the line.

'You said the SVU X-19 case would change me,' I concluded. 'It did.'

He patted me tentatively on the shoulder. 'Leave things with me. Expect to hear soon about a new police role in Amsterdam, and how you might remain… *useful* to the ministry.'

\*

Two days later, I was opening up the houseboat on Entrepotdok. Nothing much had changed in the neighbourhood while I'd been away. The knick-knack designers and start-up kids were going about their usual business. The water around the boat looked perfectly calm.

I unlocked the cabin door and made my way down the steep wooden steps into the darkness. The air was sour. I opened the curtains and a couple of windows, letting cool air circulate.

It was good to be back in Amsterdam. Petra had popped over to the Albert Heijn supermarket on Sarphatistraat to pick up some milk and other essentials. I savoured the moment of familiar stillness, registering the reassuring creak in the boat's timbers as other vessels passed by.

I padded through to the galley, turned the heating on and checked that everything was in its rightful place. A silver tankard that sat above the drinks cabinet; the gun case that was locked up, just as I'd left it. In the bedroom, Petra's jewellery, all there. The hatch at the back, secure. My home computer in the aft space (you couldn't exactly call it a room)… yes, it was all present and correct.

In the bathroom, I found paracetamol – the last strip from an old blister pack I'd forgotten about. I pushed the loosened pills into my mouth, washed them down with water from the tap, and then stared at myself in the mirror.

Another vessel passed by, rocking the boat more. I relieved my aching bladder, flushed the toilet and stepped back into the main space.

'Jesus!' I managed, my heart hammering against my ribs.

He was standing in silhouette, in my usual spot beside the porthole.

'Hello, Henk.'

# *Part V:*

## Choke Point

# 14

## THE RETURN

Frank Hals had died aboard a blazing ship. Only, apparently he hadn't.

It was no trick of the light. His head was there in full silhouette against the window. He'd gained weight but still he had that electric, battle-ready presence.

'This is a blast from the past,' I managed. 'I thought you were dead...'

A long pause. 'For a moment back there, I thought so, too.'

I eyed the front door of the houseboat; Petra could be back from the shop anytime. 'Did you not think to knock, or call ahead?'

He shrugged. 'The door was open.'

Hals was a local hood who'd grown tens of millions of euros' worth of cannabis in the hull of a clipper ship moored at the far end of the harbour. He'd got into a spat with another hood – a spat facilitated by me – and his clipper had gone up in flames. At the time, I'd been more concerned with finding the 'proof of life' of a kidnapped bureaucrat in Brussels than seeking Hals's 'proof of death'; now the bureaucrat was presumed dead and Frank Hals's face was a metre in front of me, very much alive. Things evolve.

'Are you not going to offer me a drink?' he asked.

We'd first met at demonstrations in the early 1980s, protesting the displacement of people around Amsterdam as businesses and city government took over. But as my life had found a fair current with Petra, so Hals's had drifted off course. He'd built up a chain of coffee shops, becoming defensive about his investments...

I circled around him towards the galley – and my gun case.

'What are you doing here?'

In 2008 he'd gone to court accused of cultivating marijuana for resale. A notoriously sharp defence attorney had argued that the entire crop had split from a single plant thirty years before, and that this one plant had originally been acquired for personal use. One of the witnesses at the trial was never seen or heard of again.

'Are you looking for this?'

Hals held up my handgun and took a step closer to me. 'People know people, who know people. And some of them are wondering what conclusions you've drawn from your time down in Driebergen.'

A thump resounded through my chest. How could Hals have known what I'd been doing there?

I needed to buy time.

'Just back up there, would you Frank? And put that gun down.'

He was weighing the weapon in the palm of his hand. In the dim light, I couldn't see whether the slide stop was off.

'I suppose it wouldn't do to have another accident aboard, would it?'

'Why don't I fix you that drink?' I said hurriedly. 'Jenever?'

'For old times' sake? I think not, on reflection.'

'You haven't told me where you've been,' I said from the galley, fixing drinks anyway. My fingers trembled as I pulled a plastic tray of ice from the freezer. 'I'd like to hear the full story.'

'I'm sure you would.'

He wheeled me round by the shoulder. Ice skittered across the wooden floor. Next thing I knew, Hals had a hand between my legs and his vice-like fingers were squeezing, hard. I tried to reach round, but my upper body was pinned by his other arm. His strength was extraordinary.

'Here it is in a nutshell, Henricus. I've come to like dry land... reclaimed land.'

Every nerve ending in my body screamed as the grip between my legs tightened. My breath sharpened, my vision blurred, and a dreadful, sick feeling engulfed me. I tasted it on my teeth.

'There's a lot of money tied up in the buildings around this harbour. More, even, than in those coffee shops I once ran.'

I tried to say something but had no breath.

'There's a system.' His own breath was sour, putrid. 'There are interests to respect.' Heinrich Karremans? 'People who you really shouldn't mess with this time...'

Who'd tipped Hals off about my time in Driebergen? Someone inside the police – the security services, even? I couldn't think. The pain was bright, like light, through my lower body, ribs, head.

'Stop,' I managed to wheeze at the point of passing out.

He did so. I collapsed onto the floor, registering the door handle turning...

'*Hoi*!' Petra called.

I tried to warn her, but my voice had gone completely. My eyes watered.

'Henk?' came my wife's uncertain voice.

Hals's rough-skinned face hovered above mine, peering up. The darkness of it contrasted with the light above. My thoughts reeled. The darkness of the Dutch Masters was owed to them starting off with a black canvas and adding back the light; the image blotting my vision was the *Girl Dressed in Blue* – a stolen version that had been harboured aboard Hals's ship. Verspronck's young girl in her Sunday best... the suspicions swirling around Hals and underage girls had been there for years...

'Henk!' my wife's voice called out as she clattered down the steps.

There were too many pieces on the chessboard already, and I'd only just arrived back in Amsterdam.

'Frank Hals!' she cried, surprised.

'Petra,' Hals responded, standing up. 'It's been a while.'

'Jesus!' She knelt down.

'I'm OK,' I said hoarsely.

'I came to visit and found him collapsed on the floor,' he lied. 'It was a good thing that I was passing.'

'Water,' I managed.

'I'll take it from here,' my wife said. She went to get a glass, slipping on a cube of ice and regaining her balance just in time. 'Christ!'

'I should be going,' Hals said calmly. 'It was a good thing I managed to catch you, Henk. Wish I could have seen you in easier circumstances.'

'All right Frank,' Petra snapped. 'I'll take it from here!'

She raised my head and carefully poured cool liquid between my lips. Above us, the door opened and closed. I gasped.

'What happened?' she asked.

Where to begin?

'I thought that man had died in the harbour during the big fire there?' she said.

'I thought so, too.' My face screwed up as I got to my feet. I was aching in so many places that I could no longer distinguish the sources of pain.

It was only after she'd helped me to the sofa that I managed to say, 'Do you remember that racket the authorities here were running, exchanging cheap energy from foreign countries for certain favours? Diamonds, high-class escorts and the like?'

'Didn't all that vanish with Lottman?'

The kidnapped bureaucrat had been the one orchestrating the scam from Brussels.

'Not entirely. The Amsterdam police gifted a Verspronck painting to the Norwegians, but the deal went bad. The painting was stolen back by Frank Hals before his boat went up in smoke. Somehow Hals must have escaped, and laid low since.'

Petra did a double take. 'Hals was in league with the Amsterdam police, to steal a priceless artwork?'

'Yes, with Joost. I'm sure of it.'

I knew what I needed to do now.

'An original Verspronck, harboured on Hals's boat... *burned*?' Her mouth was agape.

'We thought so at first. But in fact, no – the painting itself later showed up in a locker at Schiphol, as a rolled-up canvas. Joost handled the recovery personally.'

She shook her head in disbelief. 'Why did Hals come here?'

I didn't want to get back into my time in Driebergen and the child abuse that I'd investigated. Everything was telescoping together, though. Had the range of favours offered to foreign diplomats included underage sex?

'Hals is a mystery to me,' I said, avoiding her question.

My wife sat on the sofa's arm and placed a consoling hand on my outstretched leg. I was already planning ahead – who I needed to speak with, and what I needed to do.

# 15

## RIJKSRECHERCHE

THE JUSTICE MINISTRY AGREED to fast-track my application to the *Rijksrecherche*, as the National Police Internal Investigation Department is known. The idea of investigating fellow police personnel didn't sit easily with me, but it was a role that I'd already played in Driebergen, and the justice minister himself had suggested it during our debrief.

Sometimes we don't pick our place in the world – it picks us. What was it that my dad once said? *God will put you in the right place, even if you don't know it at the time.* At least it would give me leverage over Joost, I determined. And more than anything, I needed a warrant card in order to carry on my enquiries.

Kelly Verhagen was a no-nonsense recruitment coordinator who received me at Amsterdam's main police station early the next day. 'Do you need help?' she asked, collecting me at reception. I was limping.

'I'll let you know,' I said. 'What do you have in store for me?'

I put her in her late twenties. She barely looked old enough to be appraising an ageing horse like me, but I kept that thought to myself.

'Just a couple of tests and an interview.'

She carried a translucent plastic folder, almost certainly containing my file, and led me up to the third floor and down a corridor.

'Here.' She gestured for me to enter a cramped meeting room.

I grimaced as I sat at the small table.

'Can I get you anything? Water? Coffee?'

'Black coffee would be great.'

'Okey dokey,' she said.

It was one of my stock phrases. I couldn't help but smile.

'While I get that, you may as well make a start on this.' She pulled a sheet of paper out of her folder and placed it on the table in front of me.

I eyed the series of questions. 'What's this?'

'Anyone being considered for Internal Investigations is required to sit a moral compass test now.'

'A what?'

I read the first question:

1. *Your dog is sick. The vet says he needs an operation that will completely cure him but costs 5,000 euros.*
*(a) Do you pay?*
*(b) What if it's your cat?*

'You've got to be kidding me.' I looked up at her. 'Who wrote these? The multiple-homicide squad?'

Maltreatment of animals was a known indicator of psychopathy.

'Whoever wrote them, it wasn't me,' she said breezily. 'The sooner you start, the sooner you finish.'

2. *Your best friend is driving; you're in the passenger seat. He is careless going around a corner and hits a dog crossing the street. No one sees, and there are no marks on his car. He does not turn himself in – what do you do?*

'Need a pen?' Kelly asked.

'No,' I replied, suddenly lost in thoughts about my friend Johan. He'd shot a Hungarian racketeer, and Joost strongly suspected as much. How would I go after Joost from within Internal Investigations if he could dredge that up at any time?

*One step at a time, Henk…*

'You might as well take the other test.' Kelly whipped out three pages stapled together.

*A. What do you consider to be your greatest strengths?*

I flipped to the other pages.

*B. And your weaknesses?*
*C. What accomplishment are you most proud of during your lifetime?*

The blank space on the third page stared back at me.

'Is everything OK?' she asked.

'You've got to stop asking me that. You're starting to make me feel infirm.'

'I'll bring you that coffee. There's no time limit, by the way.'

Twenty minutes later, I put my pen down. I hadn't written much, but hoped that it counted. Kelly collected up the pages, glancing at my final answer. 'That reminds me,' she said, writing something on a form of her own.

'What?'

'I forgot you had a daughter.' She smiled approvingly.

'So, what now?' I asked.

'You need to see the police psychologist.'

'What psychologist?'

'Sonja Brinkerhof.'

'I don't know her.'

'She's not available today, but I'm sure you'll hear very soon. You should receive a letter –'

'No, this is all supposed to be fast-tracked by the justice ministry. Where is she? How can I get hold of her?'

Kelly paused, and pursed her lips in an evaluative gesture. 'Wait here. Let me see what I can do.'

*

Sonja Brinkerhof was a university professor who worked for the police part-time. I took a cab over to Willemspark, where she lived, and asked the driver to drop me two streets away. It gave me the chance to smoke a cigarette and reflect on the last time I'd been here. A stone's throw away, a Norwegian diplomat had lived – and then died, when that Verspronck painting had been stolen back by Frank Hals's crew. Crime and respectability have always been close neighbours in this city.

I ground my cigarette out on the pavement, opened a low iron gate, and walked up a stone path to the front door of a house that had been converted into apartments. It was an imposing address for a university professor.

I rang the bell and stood back, glancing up the facade at the glowing lead windows of her top-floor residence.

I was bang on time. Still, it surprised me when the door buzzed open without me needing to announce myself to the intercom. Thankfully there was a lift, albeit an old-fashioned and slow one.

Finally, I arrived on the fourth floor. Across the parquet floor of the hall was a door, ajar.

I knocked and pushed the door further open, revealing a high-ceilinged room with bright chandeliers and a Bechstein baby grand piano. A big-boned woman with grey-brown hair appeared. She was my age, maybe.

'Sonja,' she introduced herself. 'And you are Henk? I'm short of time, as ever. Please.' She gestured for me to follow her through to a living room, with leather sofas positioned around a stone fireplace. There was a distinctly old-money feel about the apartment.

'I have to leave in half an hour,' she said, 'but let's see how far we get. Willem asked me to make time.'

By 'Willem', I assumed she meant van der Steen. As she opened up a file in her lap, I experienced a vaguely uneasy feeling – that perhaps I'd underestimated both her and this interview.

'I'm going to be open with you,' she said. 'The work of the Internal Investigations department is crucial, as I'm sure you're aware. If the public loses confidence in our police men and women, then the state itself is in danger. So, we need to satisfy ourselves that those being considered for the *Rijksrecherche* are rock solid, morally. They must be held to a different standard. Do you want a drink, by the way? Glass of water? I read about your accident…'

'No, I'm fine, thanks.'

She nodded appreciatively; clearly she was keen to get going. 'Different people have different ways of going about this,' she continued. 'My background is in family psychology. I try to understand people through their key relationships, which are, I believe, a mirror to their personalities.'

Was that true? While I resisted the notion, I saw validity in it.

'Let's start with your wife,' she said, pulling a cap off her fountain pen.

'Petra?'

'Yes. How long have you known each other?'

'Over thirty years.'

'And where did you meet?'

'Here, in Amsterdam.'

I knew she was trying to get me talking.

She glanced at her folder. 'This was after you left the army?'

'Yes.'

'You were doing what, at the time?'

'I was… deciding what to do with my life.'

'Before going into the police?' Her downcast eyes narrowed.

'That was quite a gap there – two years, if I understand correctly?'

I needed to be careful. I'd been rudderless for part of the early eighties.

'Can I be honest?' I said.

Her dark-brown eyes looked up. 'Please.'

Quickly, I composed the response in my mind. 'I decided that before I did anything else, I needed to meet someone. My wife, that is. I didn't have the most stable upbringing. Other ex-servicemen were rushing into this and that. My feeling was that, without a real foundation in my personal life, I'd ultimately fail at whatever I tried.'

I wanted to keep the image of a young Petra in my mind's eye, but my thoughts involuntarily went to Manfred Boomkamp – how he'd lain in the forest near Driebergen, shot up, baring his bloodstained teeth. He'd said, *Sometimes it comes down to who we meet in life, Henk.*

'Go on,' Sonja prompted.

'That was the important thing,' I said, composing myself. 'As I look back on things, it was the people who didn't do that who ended up struggling most. Friends who remained single… or worse, married to the wrong person.'

I seemed to have said the right thing, because she smiled as she wrote something down.

'Johan Bakker?'

I blinked hard. 'I'm sorry?'

'Your army colleague. Weren't you his best man?'

She'd certainly done some digging.

She prompted: 'He's divorced now, isn't he?'

Shrugging nonchalantly, I said, 'I just got lucky that I met Petra when I did. Of course, kids change everything.'

'Yes,' Sonja said neutrally as she looked again at my folder. As she perused a couple of loose pages, my gaze swept her calm apartment.

She turned another page and I glimpsed the answers to the test I'd sat that morning. My answers must have been scanned and emailed to her, then printed off; it was like I was looking down on myself from the chandeliers.

She eyed her watch. 'So how would you characterise your relationship with your daughter?'

I thought about it. 'It can be a challenge at times, I'll admit. But could I imagine life without Nadia now? No, it doesn't bear thinking about...' I checked myself. Sonja Brinkerhof's apartment was *too* calm; there were no photos, no evidence of young life. She didn't have children – or young relatives – was my guess.

Her family psychologist's brow was crinkling. 'You were about to say something?'

'Yes,' I cleared my throat, 'about the challenges of a father's relationship with his daughter.'

Where was I going with this? I was talking too much. This was precisely the kind of trap I encouraged suspects into during police interviews. My upper chest was hot; I tugged at my collar.

'Please,' she encouraged me to continue, pen in hand.

'I think that it's very important for people to be allowed to establish their own course in life, and their own identity – to be able to do what's comfortable and right for them, that is.'

'Has this been an issue between you and your daughter?'

I tried to make light of it: 'Perhaps you should ask her.'

'I'm asking you.'

'Well, I hope I've managed to avoid that trap, through an awareness of it...'

The truth was that I'd hoped Nadia might go into law enforcement, creating a bond between us, but she'd opted instead for liberal arts, studying media at university – following in Petra's footsteps. Like many young Amsterdammers, she cared too much for material things. And I flat out didn't trust her Russian boyfriend, as Nadia knew well.

'When I consider how things went with *my* dad,' I went on, 'I'm proud that I've been present for her, and provided a reference point, of sorts.'

I wasn't sure what I was saying anymore. It was like I was trapped in a narrow corridor, and each door that I tried was locked.

Sonja's pen made a scratching sound. 'Is there anything else you want to add?'

'Sometimes,' I blurted out, 'I can't help but blame myself.'

'About your daughter, or your father?'

'My dad.'

'He left you in South Africa, didn't he? After an incident in the merchant navy there...'

'Yes. I believe it's a common experience, to feel guilt, when...' I narrowed my eyes, suddenly seeing a parallel with the victims of child abuse – a crazy thing to say, unprompted. 'I'm sorry,' I said, recovering my thread. 'Sometimes I feel I'm doing things in life to *put it right*, if you follow me. To show that, if I'm doing the right thing, then it couldn't have been my fault... back then.'

She put her pen to one side.

'And your mother?'

'Yes, that was all fine,' I said impatiently. 'We weren't particularly close, but things were cordial. Stable, rather.'

'OK,' she said. She was about to say something else, then stopped herself. 'As I mentioned, I only have half an hour. Is there anything you'd like to ask me?'

Surely the interview couldn't be over already?

'What happens next?'

'Your recruitment coordinator will advise you. Thank you for coming over to Willemspark.'

She smiled neutrally and stood up, ready to shake my hand. The sudden formality was like a slap in the face. The interview was ending too soon.

I got up with effort, refusing to let it show. 'Thanks,' I said, shaking her hand.

There was a conversational void, which she allowed me to fill.

'Right,' I said, turning towards the door. 'I can see myself out. Thanks again.'

\*

Two streets away, on Willemsparkweg – wary of crossing paths with Sonja on her way to her next appointment – I sucked hard on my cigarette.

Why had I mentioned all that guff about putting things right with my dad? It was a goal that could never be achieved. I knew that my profile wasn't the type they were looking for anyway. I'd been opened up like a filleted herring, just as she'd doubtless intended. With one fist I banged the side of a car. An alarm erupted.

Quickly I walked on. I thought of calling Kelly Verhagen, but decided against it; I knew instinctively that Sonja would recommend against me, and I needed to get ahead of events now. Instead of calling Kelly, I dialled the justice minister's office in The Hague. His assistant picked up.

'It's van der Pol calling from Amsterdam, I'm the one –'

'I remember you,' the assistant cut in. 'The minister isn't available.'

I shuddered with frustration. 'I suffered a bloody collapsed lung in Driebergen! He said I should hear soon about a new police role in Amsterdam!'

'Wait.'

Long-spaced beeps – I'd been put on hold.

'Wait for his call back.'

A click.

I wandered towards the distant towers of the Rijksmuseum in the late-afternoon gloom, still hearing that bloody car alarm. Would 'Willem' already be receiving Sonja Brinkerhof's assessment? My best bet now was surely to rejoin my old police station in a lower-profile role. It would get me back inside, in the relevant precinct – and give me access to both data systems and cases that I could use as cover…

I lit another Marlboro Red.

My old team at the IJ Tunnel 3 police station was now run by a middle-ranking cop named Bart Mulder. I knew this from occasional chats with my former team member Stefan. Mulder was a targets-obsessed bureaucrat. But perhaps there was opportunity in that. One thing I knew how to do was deliver results. Not necessarily the results asked for, but still…

I'd almost reached Museumplein when my phone rang. A withheld number.

'Van der Pol?'

It was the minister.

'I did as you suggested and applied to Internal Investigations,' I told him.

'I know – these things can take time.'

'You said you'd fast-track it. You said –'

'You need to be patient, van der Pol. Even if you're successful, there's special legal training required now for the *Rijksrecherche*. It doesn't just happen overnight.'

*Even if…*

'No special training was required for Driebergen.'

'That was different.'

'In what way, minister? In that no one else was willing to do that dirty work?'

'We needed to clean house, which we've now done.'

'Congratulations,' I said. Then, with urgency: 'At least get me my old role back at IJ Tunnel 3. I just need to get my feet under a desk.'

I thought to mention the reappearance of Frank Hals, but

knew the minister's patience was wearing thin. He was saying something about not prejudging things.

'I almost died on that assignment of yours,' I reminded him.

'All right, Henk,' he said exasperatedly, coming to a conclusion. 'Let me see what I can do.'

# 16

## CONCEALED CHAMBERS

'So, WHAT ARE YOU working on?' I asked Stefan.

This time, we'd be working alongside one another, as my new station chief, Bart Mulder, had informed me over the phone.

Stefan and I were having Sunday afternoon drinks at De Druif. Outside, clouds had gathered. A half-finished plate of *bitterballen* sat between us. We needed more mustard.

Stefan answered, 'Mulder's brought in an assistant – more like a chief of staff, in fact.'

'Who?'

'Her name's Sandra Wittgens. We suspect she's there to check up on us, only she's cute. So I'm trying to find a way to disarm her, and ask her out... maybe.' He took a hasty sip of his lager. 'What do you think?'

I laughed. 'About what?' The lights of the small bar glinted in Stefan's fair hair. 'Do you even know that she's single?'

'No ring on her finger. No mention of anyone else, and she doesn't seem to have a life outside the office, so...'

'The only thing I've found to work with women is to be straightforward with them. And that's hardly fail-safe.' I thought of my wife and my daughter. 'It's a little close to home, isn't it?'

'Is that all?'

'All what?'

'All the advice you've got for me?'

'Just don't burn any bridges, Stefan. I thought you were seeing someone, anyway?'

'I was – past tense. Look, it's not me we should be discussing here, it's you! I can't believe you're rejoining the team.'

'It's temporary.'

'It's great news, is what it is. Things have been so dull.'

'With Mulder?'

'He's like an accountant – the targets, reports, paperwork…'

Deep down, I sensed Stefan liked things that way. He'd always preferred station work to fieldwork. I wondered if he'd been interested in that chief of staff role for himself.

I held up the empty dish of mustard and caught the eye of Gert, who was drying glasses behind the bar. He nodded, signalling that he'd bring over a fresh dish. 'So, what *are* you working on?' I asked, turning back to Stefan. 'When not pining after Sandra.'

He shook his head and smiled. 'Let's see…' He looked around. The bar was quiet. 'Some small-time stuff. Moped theft is trending. Also, there's a drugs situation in the harbour.'

'Oh?' I said over the top of my inclined glass. My beer was almost finished; Stefan was barely halfway through his. He waited before explaining further, as Gert set down the fresh dish of mustard and I ordered another round.

'Go on,' I said once Gert had left.

Stefan leaned in. 'There's a nightclub called Blip.'

My eyes narrowed. 'Is that the old Icefish-class submarine? It's famous, isn't it?'

'Infamous, more like. It's been a problem since it opened – insufficient fire escapes, after-parties till noon…'

HNLMS *Ijsvis* had been Holland's largest submarine in its day. Still, it was hard to imagine it as a club. It would be cramped. Perhaps that meant 'exclusive', in the hip world of Amsterdam nightclubs…

'And now three people have died aboard it.'

'You're kidding me?'

'No. MDMA.' Commonly known as Ecstasy.

'Bad batches,' Stefan went on. 'The club's owners deny all responsibility, blah-di-blah. But it happened on their watch, so naturally their licence has come in for review.'

'Are you working with the drugs team?'

'Not yet. Word came down from on high that it was to be handled locally.'

It made sense… assuming the supply or consumption of the drugs wasn't organised. 'Has the licence been suspended?'

'No.'

'Why not?'

'Pressure, from all sides.'

'What kind of pressure?'

'Most visibly, a social media campaign to keep the club open. An online petition just reached ten thousand.'

I was amazed. Trying to get car alarms banned on our street (the bane of our nightly existence), Petra and I had barely scraped together ten signatures.

'What's so great about a rusting old submarine, which three people have now died aboard?'

'The hipster crowd are behind it. I've never been there, but apparently the acoustics are phenomenal. It's known for its techno music, hence the club's name.'

'How did you learn this?'

'Erm, from Sandra. A lot of DJs want to play there. Famous ones, from London and Berlin. The kind who will only play there and Paradiso.'

Paradiso was a storied music venue in the shadow of the Rijksmuseum.

'The city fathers are keen to keep brand Amsterdam cutting-edge, eh?'

'I guess so,' Stefan said. 'But then there are the families of the three who died. Anyway, the deal worked out was that the club's owners would pay for extra security. Four police-trained

139

sniffer dogs costing five hundred euros a night.'

'Sniffer dogs on an old Icefish submarine?' I'd known some odd cases in the harbour, but this one took the biscuit.

Just then, Gert arrived with two fresh beers. 'It'll do you good,' I assured Stefan, nodding at his new glass.

'More *bitterballen*?' Gert asked.

'We better had,' I conceded. Once we were alone again, I asked, 'Who's the owner?'

'Several people, via a holding company. The visible one is a guy named Angel Westerling. He manages the club day to day. Night to night, rather.'

I frowned in concentration, trying to remember something. 'That his real name?'

'I think it might be Angelo.'

Stefan sipped his lager.

'What's his form?' I asked.

'Westerling's? I'm still finding out. I'm due to visit him tomorrow afternoon.'

'Where?'

'He lives on Java-eiland.'

It was an extension of the Eastern Docklands, a short distance away.

'Mind if I tag along?'

'Sure. If Mulder's OK with it.'

'But will Sandra be?' I said, winking.

*

'Where are you?' Bart Mulder demanded over the phone the following morning.

'Just wrapping up a couple of things before resuming active duty.' I affected surprise: 'Did we have a meeting?'

'We need one,' my new boss informed me. 'I understood you were starting today?'

140

'Yes, I thought I'd ride along with Stefan to meet Angel Westerling this afternoon.'

'Who's he?'

'Stefan works on your team, sir.'

'No,' Mulder snapped, 'I meant Westerling!'

'He's the Blip owner. The nightclub in the harbour –'

'I know what Blip is. Who's agreed this? Listen, van der Pol, we're running a different ship at IJ Tunnel 3 these days. I know Stefan once worked for you, but things are different now, like I told you. Why do *two* of you need to meet Westerling?'

'Three people died in that nightclub. Doesn't that trump moped theft?'

'No, this is not how things work here now. I don't care if the King himself got you your job back – you and I will work out your assignments and targets, according to the grid.'

*The grid?*

The phone went muffled. Over the loud scratching sound made by his palm, I could hear: 'Sandra, what time are we both free today?'

There was some female muttering.

'Check later, then,' came his muted voice.

I adjusted the phone headset. I was passing Eindhoven on the A2.

'No, we can't move any of those…'

It was barely 10 a.m. I'd avoided rush hour and was making good progress towards Liège.

'Van der Pol?' Mulder came back on clearly, 'be in my office at nine a.m. tomorrow.'

'Yes, sir.'

\*

It was 10.57 when I pulled into a parking spot outside Lantin, Belgium's largest prison. I don't know how you design a prison to look good, but in this case the architects had excelled themselves. It was a truly dismal sight. Before me stood a long, dark concrete wall with brutal observation towers rising above the undulating landscape. In the field opposite, a herd of cows lowed beneath a tree. The grey skies threatened rain.

There wasn't enough time for a cigarette. I wrapped my arms round my ribs and made for the main entrance.

'Officer van der Pol from Amsterdam.' I held up my new warrant card. 'I have an appointment to see Jan Stamms.'

Inside, there were three dreary clusters of buildings, each enclosing its own courtyard. A guard escorted me to the building in the far cluster. I asked him if it was intentional that Stamms was housed furthest away from the entrance. He merely shrugged.

Jan Stamms was waiting for me in a light-grey interview room. His appearance was immediately disconcerting: he had large, liquid eyes, and a couple of days' beard growth.

'You can leave us,' I told the guard as I sat on the opposite side of the bare table. The guard readily did so.

'Jan, I'm Henk van der Pol from the Amsterdam police force.' I paused for effect. 'Do you prefer Jan, or Paul?'

He tilted his head. His eyes clouded over, like milk poured into tea.

'I know you changed your identity, Paul. And I know that – just as there was a concealed second basement in that nondescript house of yours in Liège, where those two boys were found – you have a hidden past, too.'

His voice was quiet. 'Who are you?'

I raised an appeasing hand. 'We'll come to that in a moment.' With my other hand I retrieved from my inside pocket a 20 x 25 cm photo that I placed face down on the table. Stamms eyed it, then me.

'First, I want to clarify my understanding: you're from

Holland, yet you ended up in a boys' home in Ghent. Beau Soleil. Is that correct?'

'How do you know this?'

I decided to tell him the truth, on the basis that it may open him up. 'I worked with a policeman called Manfred Boomkamp.'

'Boomkamp?' His eyes flashed. 'Became a *cop*? Where?'

'You knew Boomkamp at the boys' home, correct?'

He didn't deny it.

'Boomkamp died in a forest… on a police exercise. I was with him when he passed. Before he went, he told me about you, and your background.'

'Why?'

'Because of your link to the Night Market child network. The one on the Dark Web. Look, Paul, I'm going to make a deal with you. I haven't mentioned your past to anyone else. I don't know what Boomkamp might have said to others, but he was keeping many secrets himself. This conversation can remain between us – you don't talk about it, I won't either. Now, help me understand how a boy from Amsterdam ends up in a Ghent foster home like that in the first place.'

He looked like he'd gone into a trance.

'Paul,' I said sharply, trying to snap him out of it.

He blinked. 'My dad was a photocopier salesman. Worked in Holland and Flanders. It's all Dutch-speaking in the end, right?' he said defiantly.

'I suppose so,' I conceded. 'Though Liège isn't.'

'You've never felt the need to get away from things?' he demanded.

'This isn't about me,' I said, matching his defiance with my own. 'Just tell me what happened.'

My anger had the effect of calming him. He'd obtained the reaction from me that he sought.

He traced a long finger across the table top. 'We moved

around a lot… then, one day, Dad left. And Mum…'

'Go on,' I prompted.

'… just sort of gave up. So I was taken into care. We were in Ghent at the time.' He shrugged. 'That's it.'

I waited a beat. 'Back in 85, you filed a complaint against this man.'

I turned the photo over. It was a close-up of Heinrich Karremans.

Paul brought his finger to his mouth in a contemplative gesture. I'd conducted many interviews, but never seen a look that was so utterly inscrutable. It appeared that his mind was still thinking, yet he'd gone emotionally blank.

I tapped the photo with my forefinger. 'You reported him for abuse, yes?'

He kept scrutinising the image – the too-close-together eyes staring through round glasses.

'Talk to me, Paul. Boomkamp told me that they got you drunk on cider at Beau Soleil…'

'It wasn't cider.'

'So… what was it?'

His body shuddered as though he'd undergone a convulsion.

'Talk to me. Who were *they*?'

He looked very directly at me, making me flinch. 'How does this help?'

'Is it not time to bring people to justice? Who was involved? Do you recognise anyone else out there in the world now – in the papers, or on TV?'

He looked down, lost again.

'Listen,' I said, leaning forward. 'I understand the abuse cycle. We perpetrate that which has been perpetrated against us –'

'Do you, though?'

'Huh?

'Understand?'

I leant forward more, determined to retain the initiative.

'Night Market – how did you become involved?'

'Why are you here?'

'Were any other visitors to the Beau Soleil boys' home involved in the Night Market network?'

'I just uploaded, received payments...'

'You must have met others through the network, got to know them. If –'

'I've shared all I know.'

He was shutting down; I had to salvage what I could. 'You indicated that the network was based in Amsterdam. You mentioned' – I strove to recall the file I'd seen in the justice ministry, before Driebergen – 'a payment problem that needed to be resolved in Amsterdam on one occasion, correct?'

He was pressing his long fingers into the sides of his head, massaging his temples, as though willing my questions away. 'I think I should ask for my lawyer now.'

'Where in Amsterdam?'

'Who *are* you?'

'North, South, East, West?'

'Lawyer!' he yelled, deafening me. '*Lawyer!*'

There was a clank and a creak at the far end of the room as the door opened, and the guard reappeared.

My time was up.

# 17

## VELVET REVOLUTION

BACK IN THE CAR, I called Stefan to confirm our arrangement with Angel Westerling, the nightclub owner.

'Oh, I already went,' Stefan updated me.

'What?' I adjusted the headset.

'Sorry, Mulder told me to go on my own. I re-arranged it for this morning.'

There was a screech of tyres as I pulled out of the prison car park.

I swallowed back my ire.

'You didn't miss anything,' Stefan went on. 'Westerling wasn't even there.'

'He broke the arrangement?'

'Yes, we've rescheduled again. Though I did find out one thing.'

'What?'

'It's some place that he's living in.'

'Yeah, there's a lot of money on Java-eiland these days.' I picked up my speed. 'By the way, did you have a chance to check the other people involved with the holding company? The one that owns the nightclub?'

'Not yet...'

'Maybe you should.' Conscious of Mulder's orders, I corrected myself: 'If it were my case, I would.'

'I will.'

We ended the call.

As I drove back to Amsterdam, I thought of someone else I could visit in connection with Blip – someone living very near to Java-eiland…

I reached for my phone again, and scrolled down my contacts list.

*

'It's like being God up here,' I said.

The twenty-second-floor apartment had floor-to-ceiling windows. It looked north and east over Java-eiland, Steigereiland and IJburg. Beyond, the IJmeer – delicately criss-crossed with barges and their wake – glistened hazily.

Nadia came alongside me. 'I'd have preferred a view of the city, but by the time Sergei enquired, all the apartments on that side of the building had been snapped up.'

I shook my head. 'This is better. The other side, south facing, would have let in too much sun. You'd have been living in a greenhouse.'

'There are light-sensitive blinds, and the apartments are climate-controlled.'

I turned to my daughter. 'You've come a long way from the student dorm, eh?' She wore a cream sleeveless dress, a brilliant-cut diamond ring (still on her middle finger), and no shoes. I added, 'A long way from the Kriterion, too.' It was where she'd once done bar work in the university district.

'I could still fix you a coffee.'

'Same way as you did back then? I'd like that.'

I took a seat on the edge of the spacious, charcoal-grey sofa. This time, the coffee came from a Nespresso machine. The apartment had a limited range of colours – beiges and greys, mainly. The air was very still.

'So this is it – the high life. Tell me, how does a guy afford all this?' I tried to make light of the question. 'I should probably be taking notes at this point.'

She gave a short laugh. 'Here,' she said, handing me a little ceramic cup and saucer before lounging on the sofa opposite. 'Sergei's film investments are going really well. Belgium, Paris, London – it's all taking off. He's in London right now, talking to investors.'

I nodded, and sipped the inoffensive-tasting coffee.

She seemed content enough, but something just didn't feel right.

'Remind me, what kind of films are they?' Again, I tried to keep it light-hearted.

'Dad, please. Can we move on? Why can't you just be happy for me?'

'Do I look *un*happy for you?'

She made a moue. 'What brought you here?'

'You. It's been a while.'

'It hasn't been that long. How's your lung?' She glanced at my torso, still healing from the events in the Driebergen forest.

'Better,' I said.

'As if it hadn't suffered enough from nicotine.'

It was my turn to make a funny face.

We fell into a silence that wasn't awkward, but wasn't entirely comfortable, either. It still felt like our relationship was unanchored, adrift...

'Let me ask you something,' I said. 'Have you been to a nightclub called Blip? It's not far from here...'

'Oh, here we go.'

'It's just a question.'

'Then here's an answer: sure, I don't know many who haven't.'

Nadia had certainly found her way into Amsterdam's smart and fashionable set.

'Why the question?' she asked.

'You must know about the deaths from MDMA there, which

has put it on the police radar. But that's not my question. What I'm trying to figure out is how a club like that makes any money. In my day, it was the take at the bar...'

'There are still drinks. And an entrance charge.'

'But refitting an old submarine? Paying for sniffer dogs and other security measures? And then there are these DJs, flying in from London and Berlin...'

'Holland has the biggest DJs now.'

'Well, OK. But I doubt they come any cheaper.'

'If your question is, *does the club deal drugs?* – well, you'd have to ask them. But I highly doubt it.'

It didn't make a lot of sense. Maybe Blip was a trophy asset to its owners – there for prestige, rather than purely financial reasons. Like certain football clubs, maybe.

'You know that Ecstasy is only about the twentieth most harmful recreational drug, don't you? Way behind alcohol and nicotine, and far less habit-forming.'

'Who's giving the lectures now?' I said, smiling. 'Anyway, since when did you become such an authority on the subject?'

'I've blogged about it. As has Petra.'

I wished she wouldn't call Petra by her first name. 'Well, be careful, MDMA is still a Schedule One drug.' Unlike cannabis, it is highly illegal in Holland.

'Oh, don't worry, I can live without it... if you could live without cigarettes. Nicotine is much higher on the list.'

'Which list?'

'The list of harmful recreational drugs. How's that for a deal? No Ecstasy for me, no cigarettes for you.'

I had no choice but to shake on it.

*

I took the building's fast elevator back down to sea level, my ears popping as I went.

Outside, I reached for my pack of cigarettes and then scrunched them up, finding the nearest bin. It turned out to be quite a walk to the harbour, but that was OK, I was in the mood for a stroll in the bright sunlight.

And then there it was: HNLMS *Ijsvis*, breaching the surface like some giant creature. Its conning tower resembled a dorsal fin. When it was de-commissioned in the 1980s, hippies took over, stripping it of its war machinery and turning it into an arts commune. The rumour at the time was that the city wanted to compulsorily purchase it, restore it, and convert it into a tourist attraction. The city fathers focused on the nearby maritime museum instead. Little had been heard about the old submarine – until recently.

I walked closer. On the wharf beside it stood a black tour bus with smoked-glass windows. A woman with a clipboard was standing beside the open door of the coach, speaking to someone inside.

As I approached, she finished her conversation and turned to me. She was young and stylishly dressed. I almost reached for my pack of cigarettes again, then remembered what I'd done with them.

'Who does this belong to?' I asked her.

'Tonight's act.'

'A DJ has an entire tour bus?' I asked, surprised.

'Two DJs in fact, from Prague.' She gave me peace fingers. 'Velvet Revolution.'

Maybe I was supposed to have heard of them. I shook my head in bemusement. What did two guys in a luxury tour bus have to do with the 1989 Czechoslovakian uprising?

But maybe I was overthinking things.

I walked away, unable to keep myself from glancing over my shoulder at Sergei's apartment building – and the others like it – towering above the old gantries and silos. Change was certainly afoot down here in the harbour.

*

'Van der Pol,' Mulder greeted me at 9 a.m. sharp the next morning. He had thickset features and wore square glasses. We sat down in a conference room. Already at the table was Sandra Wittgens, his chief of staff, busy on her laptop.

In front of Mulder lay a printed-out spreadsheet. It looked suspiciously like the 'grid' he'd mentioned.

'I want to run through your objectives for the next quarter,' he said.

Being nicotine-deprived was hardly improving my mood.

'We're using a system called Advanced Responses Based Policing,' he continued. 'Are you familiar with that?'

'No,' I replied. 'At least, not by that name.'

'Well, you will be soon. Even our most... *traditionally* minded colleagues have come to see the value of ARBP.'

By that, I assumed he was referring to the likes of me. By 'traditionally minded', I assumed he meant 'dinosaur'.

I decided to liven things up. 'Well, congratulations on promulgating another unpronounceable acronym.' I nodded at the spreadsheet. 'I like the Advanced Scheduling System, too.'

Sandra smirked. I couldn't tell whether she was laughing with me or at me.

Mulder leaned forward. 'What it means is that we're coordinating more closely with the residents of the precinct, and responding to their expressed concerns. Making ourselves transparent and accountable regarding results.' He slapped the table. 'And that, van der Pol, is progress.'

I pressed my lips together in a contemplative gesture. 'Has police work become a local popularity contest? Is there a TV format we could pair with that?'

Mulder shook his head and briefly closed his eyes. 'Joost told me to expect this.' It was said beneath his breath – almost inaudibly – but the fleeting mention of my old boss sent a chill through me.

Mulder got on with the meeting. 'One of the most oft-reported crimes in the harbour area now is moped theft. As you know, we have increasingly affluent residents, and the value of these bikes can be anything up to ten thousand euros.'

'Ten grand, for a scooter?'

At one time, I'd owned a BMW 1200cc motorbike – which I'd sacrificed in the IJ tunnel in pursuit of a Hungarian pimp. It was the pimp's brother who had, in turn, been taken off the board by Johan...

Mulder interrupted my thoughts: 'In the case of a Yamaha TMAX, yes. *More* than ten thousand! I should know, I own one.'

It figured.

'We suspect a Moroccan gang,' Sandra interjected. 'We think they're using industrial chain cutters, and sophisticated techniques for deactivating alarms and trackers. There have even been sightings of low-loader trucks and winches, too.'

'Look, I'm sure that sorting out this bike theft is a very worthy cause, so count me in. But what about the three who've died aboard that old submarine? What's happening about them? Do their families not count, too?'

'Of course they count,' Mulder snapped. 'But that case belongs to Stefan. You know that.'

'Have you thought about involving the national drugs team, to assist Stefan with his enquiries?'

'What grounds would we have for requesting their help? They have objectives and priorities of their own. Look, there are protocols to observe.'

I wanted to mention Frank Hals – how the former cannabis king had suddenly reappeared, and why he might be a person of interest in any new drugs-related case in the harbour. The parallels, involving an old vessel, were striking. But what was also striking was the link between Hals and Joost – involving that stolen Verspronck painting – and, by virtue of his mention of Joost a few moments ago, the man addressing me now.

'I'm going to make this very clear, van der Pol. Your task is to solve moped theft. We're entering that in the grid.'

I filled my cheeks and blew the air out. 'OK.'

'Good,' he said in response to my apparent acquiescence. 'Start with a theft victim who's also a witness.'

Sandra explained: 'She surprised two suspects who were in the middle of trying to steal her Vespa.'

'Who did?'

'Jody Klein,' Sandra said. 'A landscape architect living on IJburg.'

'That's not our precinct.'

'No, but the site of the attempted theft was.'

IJburg – it was like being sent off to Siberia. But it did give me an idea.

Sandra looked at me. 'Would you consider yourself a gambling man, Henk?' she asked.

The question caught me off guard. 'I like to think that I embrace risk,' I replied.

'We allocate points out of a hundred to each staff member based on their ARBP tasks. How do you feel about all one hundred of your points going on apprehending this moped gang?'

Her fingers hovered over her keyboard, ready to fill another square of the grid.

I made a show of thinking. I knew Mulder wanted me exclusively focused on this case, and entirely removed from others.

But that could serve my purposes, too.

'Why not?' I replied. 'I'm all in.'

'Good,' Sandra said, hitting a key, smiling at me.

# 18

# TRACKING

JODY KLEIN WAS A petite woman, perhaps in her late thirties, elfin-featured and softly spoken. It was hard to hear her above the whistling wind and rattling of the cladding at her apartment on IJburg. I guessed that, like a lot of young professionals, she was displaced from the centre by Amsterdam's now-stratospheric apartment prices. Her building seemed haunted by the northerly winds.

'Let me get this straight,' I said, recapping. 'The bike was parked on Prins Hendrikkade, beside your place of work.'

'It is a Vespa, not a bike.'

'I understand that.'

As I spoke, the vehicle in question sat parked outside, in sight: a silver-coloured, vintage model with gleaming chrome-work. It reminded me of old films of mods and rockers at English seaside towns in the sixties – incongruous, given the demeanour of its owner and her pedantic tendencies.

'So, you'd been for a drink with a friend,' I summarised my notes so far.

'I wasn't going to ride it – I'd had two glasses of wine. It was raining, so I was just going to get my mini-umbrella from the luggage compartment and then take the tram.'

'Very sensible. And it was, what – nine, ten o'clock by then?'

'Nine thirty-eight. I remember looking at my watch while thinking about tram times.'

I wrote it all down. Prins Hendrikkade, which ran south-east from Centraal station, was a busy thoroughfare. It would have been quieter at that hour, and dark. Still, there would have been people and traffic in the vicinity. It gave me hope that these thieves were willing to take risks.

'So you're approaching the bike – Vespa, rather – and you notice two men beside it. Now, before you describe them, tell me how you keep your Vespa locked.'

'Well,' she said, slightly flustered, 'I, of course, have the key required for the ignition.'

'But how do you secure it? Chains, alarm?'

'I use a chain.'

'Can I see it?'

She forced open the front door against the wind, which shrieked. The noise grated on my nerves, already frayed by lack of nicotine. While she went to fetch the lock from her bike, I gazed out through the windows. Across the bright water, on Steigereiland, was Heinrich Karremans's house and architecture studio, frustratingly hidden from view behind other residences.

Perhaps this bike case wouldn't serve my purposes so well after all.

'Here,' Jody said, shutting the door behind her with a bang and handing me the chain. It was plastic-covered, functional, and no match for a strong pair of cutters.

'You don't have a tracker device or alarm?'

'A lot of people complain about vehicle alarms sounding accidentally,' she said. 'I've lived in Amsterdam for eight years, and this is the first time anyone's tried to steal my Vespa –'

'OK, OK. You've done nothing wrong. So you thought these two guys might be Moroccan?'

'I didn't say that. The man at the front desk of the police station suggested it, but those were not my words.'

'This was when you reported the attempted theft?'

'Yes, I did so straight away.'

'Let's go back to where the Vespa was left.'

Before continuing, I made a note to check any CCTV, though I knew from past experience – chasing the Hungarian pimp – that camera coverage on Prins Hendrikkade was poor, even near that fateful junction with the tunnel…

'Are you OK?' she asked.

'Fine.' I snapped out of the memory. 'Let's get back to what happened when you approached the men.'

She drew a sharp breath. 'Well, it had started to rain. And as I approached my Vespa, I saw two men crouched over it. I slowed my pace, thinking that this was odd – that perhaps I was mistaken, perhaps I had parked it somewhere else. But no, it has the distinctive mirrors. So I crossed Prins Hendrikkade, and as I got closer, I saw that one of them was wielding an implement looking like a large pair of garden shears. I knew then that he was trying to cut the chain. I was angry and afraid at the same time.' She paused, frowning.

I gave her a moment to remember that emotion. The sensation of it might come in handy in a moment or so. Finally, I said, 'Go on.'

'One of the men – not the one with the cutters – looked up.'

'You saw his face?'

'Barely. Both wore dark hoods. His face was dark.'

'Dark-skinned or in shadow?' I probed.

'I think dark-skinned.'

'What else can you tell me about their appearance?'

'His eyes were dark, too. He looked up, directly at me. Then he tapped the other man on the shoulder. They didn't even run – they just walked away, the other man putting his shears in a bag. My heart was beating very hard. I was relieved, of course, that they hadn't taken my Vespa… but then angry that I hadn't thought to do anything about it.'

'Like what?'

'I don't know. Taken a photo with my phone?'

'I'm not sure that would have been such a great idea, Jody...
What about the man with the cutters – did you see *his* face?'

'No, they both walked away from me along Prins Hendrikkade
at an angle so that I couldn't see their features.'

'Was there anything distinctive about the way they walked, or
anything else you can tell me about them?'

'I think one of them might have been wearing trainers, but I
may be imagining that. Perhaps he was just the sort of person
who I imagine *would* wear trainers, if you see the difference. I'm
sorry.'

It never ceased to dismay me how fragile witness testimony
could be, even from people as conscientious as Jody. So often,
witnesses are in situations of stress, or at least heightened
emotion, in the crucial moments. And then there is the question
of whether they are recalling actual events or memories of
imagined ones, as Jody had just alluded to. Paradoxically,
her remark instilled further confidence – in her honesty and
credibility as a witness. She was aware of what she didn't know.

'How tall were they?'

'Both were tall. Perhaps one ninety.'

'What about their build?'

'I don't know. They both wore dark clothes. Their outlines
sort of dissolved into the unlit buildings behind. It was night-
time, and raining.'

'Yes, you said.' I looked over my notes, wondering what else I
could ask her. 'The one who faced you – you said he was dark-
eyed and possibly dark-skinned?'

'Possibly.'

'But not necessarily Moroccan?' I tried prompting her. 'Could
he have been South American? Surinamese? Or Asian?'

'I just don't know, I'm sorry. His face was in shadow, and I
didn't want to make eye contact.'

'I understand. And no one else was around?'

'There were other people – cyclists, and drivers, but no one I could immediately turn to.'

'So you went to the police station round the corner.'

'That's right. I hesitated between taking the Vespa or going straight there on foot, but decided to ride, in case the two men came back for it.'

I nodded. I knew the rest: the signed statement she'd given to the new desk sergeant at IJT3, which didn't add anything more to what she'd just told me – apart from some unnecessary speculation about the two men's nationality, and the fact that this was the thirty-eighth moped theft (or attempted theft) reported in our precinct since the summer.

'Tell me, have you parked there again?'

'That same spot on Prins Hendrikkade? No! I take the tram now.'

'It's a shame for you to be inconvenienced like that.' I ran my palm over my stubble. 'I'd like you to park there again.'

'And risk it getting stolen once more? I don't think so.'

'They'll likely come back for it, that's true.' Statistically, victims of theft – even attempted theft – are far more likely to be burgled again, either because of the prospect of goods replenished on insurance, or simply because thieves work to patterns, like all of us. 'We'll take countermeasures. I'd like you to bring your bike round to IJ Tunnel 3 police station, before returning it to that same spot.'

'What are you talking about? Look –'

'I'll fit the trackers myself. One of them I'll leave in an obvious place. They won't find the second one. I know you're reluctant to risk your Vespa, Jody. I would be too. But imagine, say, that you were a single mum, and that you relied on your moped to get to work… and that this gang stole your only means of transport. How would you feel then?'

Her eyes were downcast as she considered the scenario. I

could only hope that it evoked the strong anger and fear of a few moments ago.

'We need to get these guys.'

She said it.

*

Before jumping back on a tram, I walked along IJburglaan onto Steigereiland and around the marina there. The wind whistled through the masts and halyards of the small pleasure craft, but there was a strength and cleanness to the light, too, which buoyed my nicotine-starved spirits.

At the far end of the marina sat the office–studio of Karremans Architectuur. The owner's five-storey house stood behind it, on stilts – some theory in work–life integration perhaps, though he never seemed to be there.

The studio was glass-walled. A couple of guys in uniform black were studiously hunched over their iMacs at the communal wooden table.

It wasn't obvious where the entrance was.

Finally, a curious young man got up and opened a glass door, previously invisible.

'Yes?' he asked, as if interrupted from something terrifically important.

I showed my warrant card quickly. 'There's been a lot of reported moped theft in the vicinity. We're doing some house-to-house enquiries.'

'Er...' He looked over his shoulder, rather helplessly, then back to me. 'What do you want to know?'

'Whether anyone here has been affected, or seen anything untoward in the neighbourhood.'

A couple of other faces turned my way.

'Erm...'

'I didn't mean to interrupt you. Maybe I should make

an appointment – with the manager?'

'Sure...'

'Mr Karremans?'

'Well, he's away –'

'Really?'

'Yes, in London,' he said indignantly, 'but the studio manager could maybe –'

'When is he back?'

'Did you say moped theft?' He frowned. 'Maybe you should leave your card.'

'Don't trouble yourself – the next house along may be more helpful. Thanks for your time.'

I left him looking wrong-footed and nonplussed. He would be happy to see the back of me rather than pass on word of my visit, I hoped.

Norway, China, and now London – Heinrich Karremans was certainly proving elusive. But getting closer, I sensed.

*

The number 26 tram back into town was noticeably more full than it had been on the way out to IJburg. Most of those sitting near me wore earphones and looked to be in a stupor, courtesy of their smartphones. One teenage girl had her feet up against a vertical handrail, but I let her be.

I called Stefan. 'How's it going?'

'I'm making some headway with this nightclub case,' he updated me. 'But it's hard getting people interested.'

'That's understandable.'

'Why understandable?' he asked, surprised.

My own head felt spacey from the lack of tobacco. 'Recreational Ecstasy's hardly the greatest threat to the state now, is it?'

Water and buildings flashed past, then we dropped into darkness below the ring road.

'Stefan? Hello?'

He was still there, very much so. 'I can't believe you just said that. What about the three people who died?'

'How many people die each year in Holland from lung cancer or liver cirrhosis?'

'But you smoke! And drink!'

'I quit. Smoking, at least.'

The tram rode back up into the light.

'Oh!' Stefan sounded surprised again. 'Well, tobacco and alcohol aren't illegal – MDMA is. *We don't decide the law, we enforce it*. Isn't that one of your sayings?'

It sounded familiar enough. My head lolled from side to side with the carriage's sway.

'And consider this,' Stefan went on, 'Pieter Westerling – Angel's father – is another owner of Blip.'

I sat forward. I knew that the name Westerling had been familiar. Pieter was the same generation as myself – and Frank Hals. We'd run in the same pack, more or less. A former hippy and political activist, Pieter Westerling had, like Hals, gone on to find fortune in the redevelopment of Amsterdam, and specifically its docklands. He'd also served a short spell in prison for fraud and tax evasion, I seemed to recall.

'The Westerlings own a chunk of Werf 83 – the company that, in turn, owns Blip.'

I looked round the tram, dropping my voice. 'Is that name also an address?'

'I think it references the year the company started.'

'I see.' It was the year that the submarine had been decommissioned. 'Good work.'

'I thought you just said that Ecstasy cases weren't important?'

'I changed my mind. Look into Westerling's full police record, both father and son. Also, who owns the rest of the Werf 83 company?' I checked myself, remembering once more that I wasn't Stefan's boss. 'It's just a suggestion.'

'I will. What about you?' he asked. 'What are you working on?'

'Mulder and Scully have got me working on bike theft.'

'I think you mean Mulder and Sandra.'

I'd been referencing the lead characters of *The X-Files*, popular in Holland, but remembered why it might ruffle Stefan's feathers.

'They put me onto someone who interrupted the theft of a Vespa on Prins Hendrikkade beside the IJ tunnel. It would be helpful to check the CCTV.'

'Didn't we look at that spot in connection with the Hungarian you were chasing? It was hopeless.'

'Has camera coverage got any better since?'

'Worse. Spending cuts and the civil liberties crowd... not a good combination.'

'No,' I agreed. I would have to rely on tracking the Vespa myself. Hopefully Jody Klein's insurance was up to date, and comprehensive. 'Not to worry, then. Any luck with Scully?'

'I'm sorry?'

'Weren't you going to ask Sandra out?'

'We met yesterday, actually. But just for a coffee. I don't think you could call it a date.'

'At the station?'

'No, at the café of the Maritime Museum.'

'Now *there's* progress.'

'More as I get it. Bye for now.'

We ended the call.

The tram rattled and creaked around the final corner before Centraal station. I jumped out and doubled back across the Oosterdoksdoorgang waterway to the large Saturn electronics store there.

Amid the endless aisles of consumer gadgetry, I found the section for trackers. They all seemed to work on the same principle: GPS, with software that you could download so as to map the location of the device. All of this could have been handled by the police station's technical team, but I didn't want to wait to collect the hundred points that Mulder and Scully had assigned to my goal.

I tried calling Johan, who was well versed in such technical matters. There was no reply, so I chose the most discreet-looking model I could find, bought it and a more obvious-looking variant, and then left the store, tucking the receipt away safely.

Beside the Saturn store was a sleek new Koffie & Theehuis. There was no cannabis to be found in this latest brand of coffee house… rather, clean-cut businessmen and tourists. It may as well have been a Starbucks.

For a moment I thought it *was* a Starbucks, but then found a waiter and asked him if he could spare a cigarette.

He obliged.

I poked the cigarette between my lips, tasted it, and then scrunched it into a bin beside the counter, suitably confounding the poor guy.

'I just quit.'

Outside, I looked at my watch. There were two hours to go before Jody Klein was due at the police station. I wished we'd made the appointment for sooner. My head in a fog, I returned to the houseboat to join my wife for lunch.

# 19

## BAITING THE TRAP

In PLACE OF MY usual hunger I felt stomach cramps, tinged with nausea.

'How about some soup?' Petra suggested. She had some pasta bubbling away on the hob. Her laptop was lit up on the galley table. Bossa nova filled the boat.

'No, really. Just water... and some paracetamol.'

'What's wrong? Is it your ribs and lung again?'

'In a way. I just gave up smoking.'

She stood stock-still. 'Just like that?'

I spread my palms: *It was time.*

'Oh, Henk, well done.' She gave me a hug. My ribs had only just healed; I hadn't realised how much I'd needed one. I exhaled all the air I could.

She drew back to face me, frowning and smiling encouragingly at the same time. 'For real this time?'

I nodded and smiled back. 'You can thank Nadia.'

'How so?'

'I went to see her. My God, their apartment! It looks like it belongs in *Vogue* or something.'

'Doesn't it, though?'

'I can't even begin to imagine what it cost.'

'She's lucky to have found such a well-resourced man.'

'Hmm. Anyway, we made a bet – she wouldn't take any MDMA, and I wouldn't smoke.'

My wife's frown remained, but the smile had gone. 'That's a little one-sided, isn't it?'

I assumed she meant that the agonies of withdrawal were all mine. 'Whatever brings us closer together.'

'No, I meant depriving her.'

'I'm sorry?' I said, confused.

'Smoking's unquestionably bad for you, but Ecstasy...?'

'Is illegal –'

'And wrongly so.'

This was incredible. 'I can't believe –'

'Henk, I wrote about this in depth.'

'For your blog?'

'Many hours of work went into that article, which you never read!' She paused, as if swallowing her annoyance. 'MDMA is an empathogen. It enhances sociability, communication, and closeness with others. Maybe you should try it sometime.'

I didn't respond.

'And,' she went on, 'for a world in which the younger generation is increasingly addicted to smartphones and technology, is that such a bad thing?'

'What about the side effects?'

'If it's unadulterated and taken in moderation, then the side effects are typically some pupil dilation and mild hallucination at most.'

'Let's not get into a fight about it,' I said, reaching for a chair. I blinked exaggeratedly as I sat down, seeing stars. 'I'll take that glass of water if it's still on offer.'

'Fine.'

The reality was that Petra and I belonged to an Amsterdam generation that believed in the kind of ideas she'd just mentioned. The difference being that, back in the days we met, the younger generation had been fighting for a better society. Now it was all about the individual experience, merely indulged among other people. Or so it seemed to me.

Then again, I'd joined the police. So what did that say?

'Let's change the subject.' I gulped down the water she'd handed me, then noticed her laptop again. 'What are you writing about now?'

She sighed wearily. 'The mariners' chapel off Kattenburgerstraat. It's at risk... Developers.'

'You're kidding me?' With its maritime history and rosewood pews, the mariners' chapel was one of my favourite places in all Amsterdam. 'That can't be allowed.' But my concern sounded off-key – caring about this, and not her other piece.

'There's a community meeting being organised...'

'Well, let me know how I can help. Hold on–' My phone was ringing. 'Johan,' I answered. 'What's up?'

'You tried calling me,' my friend said.

We hadn't spoken in a while. He sounded distant.

'Wait a moment.' I ascended the wooden steps and went out onto the bright deck. 'I have a question for you.'

He didn't say anything, so I jumped straight in: 'I need to track a bike that I believe a gang of thieves is about to steal. The question being, where to put the tracker so they don't find it?'

'What kind of bike?'

I told him.

He stayed silent. I filled the gap. 'I thought about the fuel tank. Isn't there a float, which the fuel gauge reads? If I could wrap the tracker in something petrol-resistant, then –'

'You won't get a signal.'

*The GPS.* 'Of course.' I wasn't thinking straight.

'If the software can't read the GPS ping, it will likely step down to GSM cellular triangulation,' he said, his voice growing stronger, more confident – more like the Johan of old... before the shooting, that is. 'What type of tracker is it?'

I explained.

'I don't know it,' he said, 'but GSM triangulation is only accurate to about two hundred metres. That's hardly going to bring you to the thief's doorstep in a city as crowded as this one, is it?'

*True.*

'The thing is, three dozen mopeds have gone missing of late,' I said. 'That's a lot of bikes to fence and move on – even smaller ones. What if the bikes are going through a chop shop? Which external parts would be left on?'

Johan was silent again. Finally he remarked, 'I don't know with those mopeds. But no part's immune to being swapped out if they go through a chop shop. You may as well stick it on the back or wherever the hell the signal is good, and hope for the best.'

'OK,' I said. I was pacing the deck, suddenly conscious that it might be annoying Petra below. I stood still.

'So, how are you?' I asked.

'Oh, keeping busy, more or less.'

'We should go for a drink sometime.'

'OK.'

I dropped my voice. 'Johan, there's something else. I need to get some information about a website. It's on the Dark Web.' I was referring to Night Market. 'Do you know of anyone who may be able to help with that?'

'A hacker, you mean?'

'Someone who could do some digging around, incognito.'

'What sort of site?'

'Underage sex.'

'Child porn?'

'That's right.'

He paused. 'Look, Henk… after everything that's happened, I'm not sure I'm your guy.'

'I understand, but maybe this will *help* with the other situation.'

'The shooting?'

'Maybe.'

'How?'

At that moment, a stark image came to me of the racketeer Zsolt Tőzsér, his face frozen, submerged in the water of that dyke north-east of Amsterdam... a silver trace of bubbles rising in the white headlights of the approaching vehicle.

I winced.

'Henk, you there?'

Joost was the key to it all. Only how?

'Yes,' I said. 'I don't know yet how it all fits together.'

'OK...' he said slowly.

'Let's discuss it in person.'

'OK,' he repeated.

Why couldn't I remember all the events leading up to Johan shooting him? Elements of the night still eluded all recall. So why didn't I just ask Johan about it, now? He was my oldest friend...

Was it embarrassment, maybe, about my failing memory?

No – something else I now saw. *Fear.*

I was afraid, of what he or I might recall.

'You're right,' I finally said, 'it's not a good idea.'

With growing unease in his voice: 'OK...'

'Let's get that drink sometime.'

We managed our goodbyes. I pressed the edge of the phone to my closed lips, reflecting again on the events of the last couple of years. When I went back down into the galley, Petra was working at her laptop, tapping the keys determinedly. I collected the trackers that I'd bought from the Saturn store, grabbed a half-used tube of superglue, and headed to the police station.

*

Jody Klein arrived at the station on her silver Vespa at 3 p.m. precisely. Sunlight flashed over its chrome and mirrors before it turned into the garage entrance. She killed the engine and pulled off her helmet.

Her elfin features looked pinched and apprehensive.

'This should be quick,' I said reassuringly, taking the handlebars. Compared to my old BMW, the Vespa felt incredibly light – like it might fly out from underneath me if I tried to ride it. I put it on its stand and eyed the various potential locations for the trackers. My gaze settled on the tan leather seat. There was a strap round the back of it.

I tore open the smaller tracker's packaging with my teeth. The device itself was round and no bigger than one of my fingernails. I unsnapped the leather strap and placed the device over the back of one of the strap's poppers; it fitted and looked inconspicuous enough. The signal emission should be fine.

I produced the superglue from my pocket. My fingers tingled. I needed to find a tobacco substitute, a smoker's methadone. Why was I fiddling around like this with trackers and glue, anyway? Who cared if these yuppies' mopeds went missing? I cursed my lack of a small vice to hold it all in place while the glue set. Perhaps I could use a heavy object to speed the process up. Not the Vespa – rather, the liveried BMW F800GS police motorcycle parked beside the garage entrance...

'Here,' I said to Jody. 'If I hold up the rear end of this bike, could you place these very carefully on the ground beneath it?'

I handed Jody the strap and tracker and she did as I asked. No sooner had I let the wheel down than a voice shouted, 'Hey!'

I knew that voice, and turned to find Kurt Larsson – a medical examiner I'd worked with in the past. Only, the jovial Swede was wearing fluorescent-yellow police gear now. 'What are you doing with my bike?' Then, as he got closer: 'Henk?'

'What's the world coming to, Kurt? You left the medical profession to join the traffic cops?'

In one hand, he held a polystyrene cup of black coffee. With the other, he clasped my own hand. 'I'd had enough of dead bodies,' he said, smiling toothily.

'Well it's good to see you again. I'm just making use of your bike for a little DIY project here.'

'Oh, what's that?'

I explained and introduced him to Jody. 'By the way,' I told her, 'if you'd like to get coffee yourself, there's a vending machine over there. It's free, and this glue still needs a couple of minutes to set.'

She followed my suggestion.

'So how's life?' Larsson asked me.

'Passing too fast,' I replied. 'You?'

'Good,' he said, patting the seat of his bike and looking admiringly over the BMW's instrumentation. 'I can't believe I'm being paid to ride this thing all day.'

'I didn't know you were a biker,' I said. 'I would have suggested going out on a ride sometime.'

He picked up the discarded packaging curiously. 'You can track these from our trip computers now.'

'Oh, they work via the web,' I said. 'You can track them via any phone or laptop, in fact.'

'Yes, but that's a bit awkward if you're in a pursuit, isn't it?' He winked.

'God willing, it won't come to that.' I glanced at my watch – the glue should have set. 'Could you lift up the back wheel?'

Larsson obliged.

I snapped the strap back onto the moped's seat, then sat on it to test that the tracker was both secure and inconspicuous. Jody rejoined us.

'OK,' I said, handing her the Vespa. 'I'll walk round to Prins Hendrikkade and wait near the spot, just to make sure you're OK. Give me five minutes, then ride over there. Park it up and leave the scene as naturally as possible.'

'Should I put the lock on?' she asked apprehensively.

'Yes. Just like before. Everything as normal.'

Then I remembered about the decoy tracker. The most

obvious place I could think for it was the bottom of the luggage compartment beneath the seat. I dropped it in there.

We were ready.

'Good to see you, Kurt,' I said, walking out and waving.

'You too, Henk.'

I made my way round to Prins Hendrikkade, surveying the harbourscape and its irregular skyline as I went – the masts of the old ship moored beside the maritime museum, the copper-clad science centre built over the mouth of the IJ tunnel to North Amsterdam...

'Come on then, you thieving bastards,' I muttered to myself. 'Let's see if you can get me my hundred points from Mulder and Scully.'

As Jody pulled up on the other side of the street, my phone buzzed. It was Kelly Verhagen, the police recruitment coordinator. I didn't want to hear about my rejected application to the *Rijksrecherche* right now.

I did want to hear from Stefan, however. He'd just sent me a text, asking to meet. I surveyed Jody – looping the chain through the little front wheel, walking away – then made for De Druif.

*

Stefan was already there, up the short flight of steps from the bar, sitting and drinking a milky coffee.

'Make that two,' I told Gert.

I sat opposite Stefan. 'So what's up?' I asked.

'I did some more digging into Werf 83 – the company that owns Blip.'

'And?'

'There's a company called Cyclamen investing alongside Pieter and Angel Westerling. It's Middle Eastern.'

'Where in the Middle East?'

'The Emirates.'

'Hmm.' There was money pouring into the harbour area from all four corners of the globe. Still, this felt significant. A sheikh from the Emirates had been implicated in the favours-for-energy racket. Or was I seeing patterns where they didn't exist? *Look for patterns long enough, and you'll find them anywhere.* Who'd said that?

'Henk, are you OK?'

Through the windows I glimpsed a young couple leaning over the canal's railing, smoking. The canal waters looked unusually still. Like the dyke in which Zsolt Tőzsér had died...

'Henk!' Stefan prompted.

'Yes. Have you told anyone about this?'

'I updated Sandra,' he replied.

My coffee arrived, and we waited for Gert to leave again. I watched him go back to the bar. There were packets of cigarettes beneath it.

'Do you want me to leave you alone?' Stefan was asking.

'No,' I replied. 'Sorry. What did she say?'

'Sandra? Not much. Merely that I appeared to be veering off course with the case. It's supposed to be about drugs, after all.'

I thought about that. Her reaction seemed understandable.

'But that's not all,' Stefan went on. 'I looked more deeply into Pieter Westerling's past. There was a lot on the system. Fraud, tax evasion, drugs... and this.'

He slid a document over the table towards me. It was an old police complaint form. 'A boy at a foster home near Breda filed a complaint against him.'

My heart thumped. Breda was near the Belgian border.

It was a while since I'd seen one of these old forms. The date showed 17 October 1993. I must have filled out hundreds over the years on behalf of alleged victims of various kinds.

'And consider this,' Stefan said, pointing to the name of the complainant, 'Jurgen Straeffer is now a doorman at Blip.'

I studied the complaint form. 'This was never taken further, I'm guessing?'

'No,' Stefan replied. 'Only, why not?'

I shrugged. 'The relationship between an abuser and his abused is never straightforward – if that's indeed what happened here.'

'But why would the alleged victim end up working for the alleged abuser, at Blip? It doesn't make sense.'

'It might, if Westerling felt he needed to make things right with him. Or buy his silence, maybe. Who knows?'

'There's more,' Stefan said. 'There's another complaint against Westerling, by a young girl – right here in Amsterdam.'

He slid another police form on top of the first. It was more recent. Much more recent: last year.

Stefan leant in. 'This time, the victim's name is redacted.' In place of the complainant's name was a band of black ink. 'Why?' he asked.

'Why what – the redaction? Youth victim… privacy.'

Stefan flushed, like he should have known that.

The address of the alleged offence was Keizersgracht 840.

'What is that?' I asked, pointing at the address.

'What?'

'That address – Keizersgracht 840.'

'I don't know,' Stefan replied.

I entered the address into my smartphone. It was almost on the Amstel river, and looked to be a private residence – an expensive one, judging by the location.

I realised that I had froth from the coffee on my upper lip and wiped it away. 'Have you said anything about *this* to anyone?'

'Not yet.'

'Nothing to Mulder?'

'No,' he replied.

'Don't.'

Stefan paused. 'Look, Henk… this is my case. You've told

me enough times: you're no longer my boss.'

'Fine. Then work it as you see fit. But if I were you, I would work the drugs angle, the club in the harbour, like you were asked to. Everything else – the alleged child abuse, the Middle Eastern investments – I suggest you forget, and file back where you found it.' I slid the reports across to him. 'You haven't told anyone else?' I reconfirmed.

Stefan paused again, as if choosing his words carefully. 'I thought I was doing you a favour by passing these on?'

'OK, I'm sorry.' I held up my hands. 'And I'm grateful to you for sharing these. I just don't want to see you end up...'

'What?'

'Like me.' I exhaled sharply through my nostrils, making them flare. 'At odds with everyone. My advice is to focus on what's working for you. Focus on Mulder, and Scully.'

'Well I most definitely don't want to end up with amnesia,' he joked. 'One of these days, you'll get Sandra's name right.'

With the lighter tone, I took my leave. I walked out into the late-afternoon sunshine, aware that things wouldn't stay light for long.

# 20

## MOONLIT DRIVE

BACK AT THE BOAT, Petra was still working on her article about the mariner's chapel. The title read: *AT RISK!*

'I'm going to go deep on this one,' she promised as I pecked her on the cheek.

My hands, arms and feet were tingling. Giving up smoking had left me in a state of nervous exhaustion – anxious yet lethargic. I thought about making a doctor's appointment, or at least visiting the Albert Heijn on Sarphatistraat to get some pain killers, but instead retreated to the sofa.

My head was throbbing; I was shivering. I lay down, replaying the conversation with Stefan. Eventually, I managed to doze off.

Next thing I knew, it was night. My mouth was bone dry and there was an audible buzzing sensation.

At first I thought I'd developed tinnitus. Then I reached for my phone: it was sounding an alert for the tracker app, telling me that Jody Klein's moped was on the move.

I swung my numb legs to the floor, and found and booted up my laptop, sitting with it on the leather sofa's edge.

Petra wasn't in the galley. She must have gone out, to the shops maybe.

The tracker map launched on the screen. It was still showing the location on Prins Hendrikkade where Jody had left the Vespa. I realised that I was looking at the location of the decoy tracker. The thieves must have found and discarded it.

175

I opened up the map for the second, more discrete tracker. It showed a short red line, indicating that this other device had moved into the IJ tunnel.

For what felt like minutes, nothing happened. Then the red line started again, on the far side of the tunnel – heading north on the S116. It passed the intersection with the S118 and proceeded up through Volewijkspark.

At the next intersection, a few hundred metres further on, it turned east onto Nieuwe Purmerweg and then north again onto Waddenweg. I didn't know these streets, nor this part of North Amsterdam. The progression of the worm-like line was slowing as it turned in on itself – into what looked like a dead end…

I accessed the same map on my smartphone, removed my gun from its case, and grabbed my jacket and car keys, locking up the boat as I left.

*

I knew from that break in the red line (through the IJ tunnel) that I'd miscalculated. But only now did I gauge the depth of my miscalculation. It was obvious, really: the GPS could only send a signal while out in the open. As soon as the bike was indoors – in some lock-up, chop shop or hiding place – I'd be relying on the much-less precise GSM triangulation, as Johan had warned.

Jody Klein's Vespa was quite possibly lost for good, already.

I drove north through the dark tunnel, emerging at the other end and following the road up through Volewijkspark, the regularly spaced sodium lights hypnotising me.

I cracked the window open to allow in a cool breeze. It was after 11 p.m., and the traffic was light. I took the next exit ramp onto Nieuwe Purmerweg, following the tracker, then turned left and found myself approaching what looked to be a social-housing estate – several fat blocks of brick and concrete, facing back onto the S116. A full moon hung in the sky behind the estate.

North Amsterdam was a blue-collar area. It was socially cohesive – the ethnic minorities here were relatively well integrated. Crime levels were no higher than in the city centre. Whoever had taken the Vespa had hardly led me to a no-go area.

I killed the engine and got out of the car. The housing estate felt safe, spacious and green – confounding my expectations of where moped thieves might hide their loot. The map on my phone showed that I was in the right area. I paced around a low-rise parking garage. Inside it were a few mid-range cars, a van – nothing suspicious.

There was no one around, nobody to ask.

In the housing blocks themselves, lights were on, but there was no pretext for calling on any one apartment in particular. In some indefinable way, it felt more eerie than if I *had* been led into a no-go zone. I looked around once more: why here?

I was about to call it all in to the relevant North Amsterdam police precinct when my phone rang.

It was Johan.

'I've been thinking about our conversation earlier – you wanting to find a hacker for that site on the Dark Web. You said it might help with the shooting… how so?'

'Leave it, Johan. It was a bad idea. I'm sorry that I troubled you with it.'

'Just tell me the name.'

I sighed, still eyeing the angular corners of the housing estate's forecourt. The flat surfaces were lit with pale moonlight. 'It's called Night Market.'

'Doesn't mean anything to me.'

'That's a good thing.' I changed the subject: 'You know I fixed that tracking device to a Vespa, which I thought might be stolen? Well, it *has* been stolen, and there's no GPS signal. I'm in North Amsterdam trying to make sense of the last readable location.'

'It's likely indoors.'

'That's what I thought.'

'Be patient. Perhaps the tracker will be on the move again to a different location.'

'I hope so. If not, I need a new plan altogether.'

I thought of Mulder and Scully's grid.

'Take care.'

'So long.' I ended the call impatiently.

I walked one last loop of the low car park, then drove away.

Minutes later I was at the south end of the tunnel, turning onto Prins Hendrikkade. I pulled up beside the spot where Jody had left her Vespa. It definitely wasn't there. I put my hazard lights on. There was a case for searching for the discarded decoy tracker to see if I could lift fingerprints. But even with a GPS fix, that might take hours. I could see at least one rubbish bin and a couple of storm drains...

I thumped the steering wheel, put the car back in gear and pulled a U-turn, skidding onto IJ, passing the police station and speeding down Valkenburgerstraat, into Waterlooplein. At least I was back in familiar territory. I passed City Hall, crossed the Blauwbrug bridge over the Amstel, and then took a sharp left, heading along the riverside.

I came to a halt on the north side of Keizersgracht, pulling into a parking spot at a forty-five-degree angle to the canal. Directly opposite was Keizersgracht 840, where Pieter Westerling had allegedly abused the unnamed girl.

I cut the engine, found my flat cap in the car's glovebox, pulled it on and exited the vehicle. Number 840 was indeed an expensive-looking residence – an old merchant's house with six storeys of brick and dressed stone. I walked over an arched bridge towards it.

To my left – at a right angle to Keizersgracht – flowed the wide

Amstel river. Its rippling surface was silvery in the moonlight. There, too, was the Magere Brug – the famous 'Skinny Bridge' with its little drawbridge, built by two sisters living on opposite sides of the river… or so the old folk tale went. And on the far bank stood the Royal Hotel. It was here that a sheikh from the Emirates had beaten a high-class escort into unconsciousness.

I felt a tightening sensation in my upper chest. It wasn't just the non-smoking – call it an old mariner's premonition. A discreet plaque next to the doorway of 840 announced it as *The Silver Key*. There was a camera intercom.

Why *had* the girl's name been redacted from the complaint form? Solely for reasons of privacy, or for some other reason, too?

I drew back into the street, looking up the face of the building. Lights were on inside but the windows were screened by heavy drapes. Something – a movement at the edge of one of the drapes, maybe – caught my attention, but too peripherally or quickly for me to register what. Somebody looking down on me, perhaps?

I returned to the car.

Once inside, my phone buzzed. It was Petra.

'Where are you?' she asked. 'I got back to the boat to find it empty.'

'I had to track a suspect. Long story. Where were *you*?'

'I went to the mariners' chapel.'

'Oh. Why?'

She paused. 'To pray.'

'Really?' This didn't sound like Petra.

'I just felt the need. I also took the opportunity to get all the details of the planning application. For some reason they weren't available online.'

Planning applications were affixed to the buildings in question.

'What did you learn?'

'It's a big project. The consulting architect is Heinrich Karremans.'

That didn't surprise me. Karremans Architectuur must be involved in scores of developments in the area. It did give me an idea, however. 'Sounds like an angle worth looking into…'

My wife had been an investigative journalist for *Het Parool*, after all.

'Oh don't worry,' she said. 'I will.'

I didn't want to bring up the child abuse issue, but I felt a sudden sense of hope that she might be able to learn something about the man Jan Stamms had identified as an abuser…

'When will you be back?' she asked.

I watched a dark Mercedes approach the door of 840.

'Not for a little while,' I replied, straining to see. A bulky driver had opened the rear door of the car, shielding the passenger from view.

'I won't wait up then,' Petra said.

The front door of 840 opened and then closed again, the driver returning to the Mercedes. I didn't catch the person entering the house.

'OK,' I responded, before realising that Petra had hung up.

\*

After my earlier nap, I didn't feel sleepy. Each time I blinked, lurid squiggles appeared behind my eyelids. I shook my head hard. Even if it took all night, I would wait for someone to emerge from 840 Keizersgracht so that I could get a frontal view.

I reclined the car seat, pulling the cap down over my eyes. I thought to place the ignition keys on top of the dashboard, so that any passing cop might think I'd had too much to drink and was sleeping it off.

At some point, the lights went out on the arched bridge over

Keizersgracht, then on the Magere Brug. They stayed on over at the Royal Hotel, however.

My hands were shaking. I grabbed the steering wheel, my trembling fingers lit pale grey by the moonlight. I considered returning to the boat and the warmth and familiarity of my bed. Then the squiggles again, and something described itself behind my eyelids: it was a white feathery shape, pointing down and to the left... Was this what I'd glimpsed earlier around the edge of the drapes, in the house opposite? A feather, clasped in two little female hands – the bottom left corner of the *Girl Dressed in Blue*?

Surely I was hallucinating. I was almost certainly seeing patterns where none existed now. I rubbed my eyes vigorously and looked up, catching the door of 840 opening. Someone appeared, hazily outlined against the dim interior of the house.

I blinked, to focus. The man's outline and gait were instantly familiar.

No, I wasn't hallucinating – the man was Frank Hals.

I exited the car as quickly and quietly as possible and crossed the dark bridge over the canal, my face lowered.

But by the time I'd reached the far side, he'd already vanished again, into the night.

# 21

## PURSUIT

DAWN HAD COME SLOWLY, following a fitful sleep back at the boat. As soon as it was light, I returned to Keizersgracht, parking further along the canal. I walked back to 840.

The house was quiet, the drapes closed.

The discreet plaque had gone. It was early, but I rang the bell anyway.

No reply.

I rang it briefly a second time, then retreated to the other side of the canal.

I don't know how long I stood there, watching and waiting for some sign of life. The edges of the drapes in the windows appeared to be playing tricks on me, twitching.

Where was Frank Hals living now? I'd looked previously on the police computer; he no longer appeared.

There was a lightness in my head, like bubbles were rising through it. Also a buzzing, coming from my phone: Jody Klein. I pressed answer and returned to my car.

'So they took the Vespa,' she said.

'Yes, as planned.'

'You've been able to track it though?'

'Yes.'

'And so... what happens next?'

'Enquiries are ongoing. I'll let you know as soon as I have something.'

I ended the call and made my way back to the boat to drop off the car. Then I proceeded the short distance to the police station on foot. I entered by the garage.

There, I grabbed a black coffee from the vending machine. Kurt Larsson rode in on his bike, the engine burbling loudly inside the enclosed space. He saw me and gave a throaty blast. I waved to him and went into the main building.

The way up to the squad room passed by the ground-floor interview rooms. Through one of the small windows, I caught sight of the back of Stefan's fair head. I stepped closer, getting a look at the person sitting opposite him: big guy, maybe in his late thirties, pitted face... Had Stefan brought in Jurgen Straeffer, the doorman at the nightclub?

On what pretext?

'Henk,' a voice from behind me called. Mulder's. 'How are you doing on the moped case?'

'You're the second person to ask me that in almost as many minutes. Don't worry, I'm sure your VMAX will be safe.'

'It's a Yamaha TMAX,' he corrected me. 'And I'm not worried.'

We had the stairway up to the squad room to ourselves. I took a sip of coffee. My phone was buzzing again.

'Well?' Mulder said, leaning on the stair railing. 'Have you turned up anything?'

It was the tracker app. Jody's Vespa was on the move again.

'I'll know soon enough.'

I retraced my steps past the interview rooms. Shouting came from the one Stefan occupied; it was the other man's voice. But I couldn't stop to find out what was going on. The tracker was moving south on the S116 towards the city. Re-entering the garage, I stared transfixed as the red line extended towards the IJ tunnel – towards the police station – then paused at the intersection with the S118.

It was turning, before the tunnel – heading west.

I'd parked my car beside the boat, ten minutes' walk away. *Stupid*.

Larsson was still clambering out of his biker gear.

'Kurt, I need your bike.'

'What?' he said, his face fish-like with surprise.

'I've cleared it with Mulder.' Before he had a chance to argue I said, 'You remember that tracker I fitted to the lady's Vespa? Well, it's on the move.' I showed him the map display on my phone. 'Now, how do I get this onto the bike's trip computer again?'

Two minutes later, I was speeding down into the tunnel. The crash helmet was slightly too small and pressed against my temples and forehead, but it felt good to be back on a BMW motorcycle – like being reunited with a trusted friend. The engine was an 800cc – smaller than my old one had been, and more nimble as a result. I found the switch for the rear-mounted orange flasher, which flickered wildly in the tunnel. That, and the bike's distinctive white and blue livery, soon caused cars to swerve aside.

I roared through the tunnel and accelerated up the incline towards the S118 intersection, indicating and peeling off to the right, up and around. I was moving quickly, gaining on the tracker, which the trip computer showed to be five hundred metres ahead.

I searched the greenery and open spaces beside the road for reference points. I'd lived in Amsterdam for over thirty years, yet struggled to recall these streets. It was a green and grey blur, until I veered onto Mosplein. There, the two sides of the S118 split around a brick church with an exposed bell that flew towards me; the most direct path took me left, the wrong way down a one-way section of road. An oncoming van swerved from my path.

I braked. The front wheel twitched as I negotiated a dog-leg turn back onto the correct side of the road, where the right-hand side of the S118 rejoined the left.

The tracker was still five hundred metres ahead.

I accelerated hard again, past car dealerships, an electricity substation, a sign for the ring road...

The computer gave three hundred metres. I strained to see the outline of a moped and rider.

There was a squashed cylindrical building that looked like it had been dropped from outer space. On the opposite side of the road, I glimpsed a flock of cranes marking out the waterfront, which the tracker was moving towards.

The tracker was slowing. I was two hundred metres behind it when it turned south onto Ms. van Riemsdijkweg, towards NDSM-werf.

There! A flash of silver as he turned, then he vanished from sight once more, behind buildings.

I slowed and turned too, onto NDSM-werf. It had been one of the city's most important shipbuilding yards in its day; now it was home to a hundred or so artisanal studios, MTV's European head office... and a skateboard park, among other things. It was a 'creative hub', or so its promoters claimed. But to me its new purpose was a pale imitation of the old one. I was reminded what a vast site it was, removed from the beating heart of the city, just visible across the water.

I could see the silver Vespa – glinting on open ground. Where was it going?

I decided to ask its rider. As I approached, he looked over his shoulder. He wasn't wearing a crash helmet – rather, a hood. I could tell immediately that he was North African.

I came alongside him and pushed up my visor. 'Get off the moped,' I ordered.

He came to a halt, planting his feet either side of the Vespa. Jody had guessed right: he wore trainers.

'Who are you?' he said.

It struck me that I was in plain clothes – unusual for a police motorcyclist.

'I ask the questions. Documents, please.'

He stared at me challengingly.

I dismounted and quickly removed the keys from his ignition.

'Hey!'

'Your ID and licence.'

Nothing.

'OK then, let's start with your name.'

'Who are you?' he repeated.

I showed my warrant card. 'Name!'

'Erik.'

'Full name.'

'Ibrahim.'

'Erik Ibrahim?' I confirmed.

He didn't deny it.

'Address.'

He remained silent.

'Where do you live?'

'Nowhere near here.'

I was about to arrest him on suspicion of handling stolen property when instinct took over. I pulled my phone out and angled it towards him.

'What the fuck!' he cried, vaulting off the tan leather seat. He ran astonishingly fast towards one of the derelict buildings. I tried to follow, but only for a hundred metres or so… I couldn't leave the two bikes.

Returning to them, breathing hard, I checked my phone. The photo was good enough.

Then I stared at the moped. Or more exactly at the leather seat, to which the tracker was affixed. I stepped closer and lifted it up, revealing the small luggage compartment beneath. All the while, I was vaguely aware of him watching me, from the cover of the buildings.

Inside was a white plastic bag containing bright-blue pills, with question marks pressed into them.

I looked up and around. Graffiti marched aggressively across the derelict buildings. Crazily scudding clouds reflected in puddles, on the empty ground. Where was he?

At least Jody Klein's Vespa was safe.

I reached for my phone again to call the situation in, regretting that I hadn't tracked Erik Ibrahim for longer.

*

'He's a courier of some kind, I'm sure of it.'

We were in the squad room. I was sitting on the edge of Stefan's desk, my arms crossed.

'How many pills?' Stefan asked, his forehead furrowed.

'Several hundred. Maybe more.'

'That's a little too much for personal consumption.'

'I'd hope.'

'Could he be dealing?'

'He could, but why steal the moped? And what about all the other moped thefts? Also, what was he doing in that part of North Amsterdam, where the bike was kept overnight? There must be other people involved.'

'I think you should tell Mulder. Maybe it *is* time for the national drugs squad to get involved.'

'Maybe,' I said. 'What about you? I saw you interviewing someone earlier. Was it Straeffer?'

Stefan nodded.

'What happened?' I edged further up on his desk, trying to get more comfortable. Sometimes I felt an ache between my legs, ever since Frank Hals's visit to my boat.

'Not much. I asked him about the three people who died – whether he knew them. He didn't share anything.'

'It sounded like a lively conversation.'

'It was. I also asked him about his relationship with the owners. Westerling in particular. He became defensive.'

187

'Hmm. And then you let him go?'

'There was no justification to hold him.'

I picked a piece of loose thread from the seam of my jeans.

'Do you think the cases might be connected?' I asked.

'How?'

'A bigger MDMA ring – using mopeds to move the merchandise around the harbour. There's a lot of money in these new-built apartments… a lot of potential clients…'

'It's a theory. But do the facts fit? I vote we let Mulder and Sandra decide.'

I'd expected Stefan to say this. I pulled out my phone, and brought up the photo of Erik Ibrahim. 'This is the moped rider. Could you do something with it?'

Stefan had been an expert in image recognition when we'd worked together before.

*Times have changed,* his expression said.

I nodded balefully.

He sighed and said, 'Hand me the phone.'

'Good man.'

\*

When I returned to the boat for lunch, I found a printed trip itinerary on the galley table.

London City Airport.

The following day.

The toilet flushed. A moment later Petra appeared from the lavatory, smoothing down her skirt.

'Leaving me?' I asked wryly.

'Oh,' she said, surprised. 'You're back…That trip is for my article. I'm interviewing Heinrich Karremans. He's in London, working on a project. Doesn't sound like he's returning to Amsterdam any time soon, so…'

'Does *he* know that you're interviewing him?'

'No, but he's due to speak at a public meeting in London tomorrow evening, so I thought I'd take my chance. Flights are cheap.'

I considered this turn of events.

'What's he working on over there?'

She produced a glossy brochure from underneath a sheaf of papers and handed it to me.

The front cover showed an aerial view of London's Docklands. I recognised the stubby pyramidal tower with low cloud (or was it smoke?) hovering over its summit, the lazy bend in the river nearby... On the opposite bank sat a digitally rendered office block with softer edges – not nearly as tall as the pyramidal tower, but broader, longer, and labelled *Newfoundland Wharf.*

'It's a former public-housing block,' Petra commented.

'A taste of things to come in Amsterdam?'

'Not if I can help it,' she said, taking the brochure back.

'Perhaps I could join you. It's been a while since I've visited London. It would be nice to take a short break.'

'You've only just started your new job.'

'I'll find a professional reason for being there.'

I took her in my arms. She smiled, and whispered conspiratorially into my ear, 'Perhaps you could be my research assistant.'

'Your intern?' I said, growing more aroused by the second.

'It's an unpaid position, I'm afraid,' she said coyly.

'Perhaps there would be other rewards...'

I was tempted to try and lead her towards the bedroom, but it was in the middle of the working day. Still, I was relieved that Frank Hals's vice-like grip hadn't left lasting damage.

\*

Thirty minutes later I was sitting in a conference room at the station with Mulder and Scully.

Sandra, rather.

'This is serious,' Mulder said, his forehead creased.

Stefan had found the rider I'd photographed. His name was Tarek Hosseini, not Erik Ibrahim. He lived in Kolenkitbuurt, which sat on the westward fringe of the city – just inside the ring road. As inner neighbourhoods went, it was the closest Amsterdam got to a trouble spot – almost all social housing, inhabited mostly by immigrant families. Hosseini's record showed a classic pattern of drug convictions and related petty theft.

'We'll need to get the locals involved,' Mulder concluded, looking at Sandra.

I understood him to mean the local police precinct.

'Why?' I asked, baffled. 'Why can't we bring him in here first and sweat him?'

Sandra shook her head firmly. 'That precinct has done a lot in terms of community relations. They need to handle this their way.'

'We can certainly hand him over,' I said, 'once we've quizzed him about his criminal activities in *our* precinct.'

'No,' Mulder said emphatically.

'I don't understand –'

'There's a community leader there called Tammy Goss, who has close links to the media,' Sandra said. Then she seemed to lose patience with the explanation. 'We'll give you something else to work on.'

'But the amount of MDMA found on him suggests organised –'

'We're going to involve the national drugs team,' Mulder informed me.

I restrained myself from pointing out that I'd suggested this in the first place. 'What do you want me to do, then?'

'Gather all the evidence for the moped theft and recovery,' Mulder replied. 'Be ready to turn it over to the relevant teams once we've identified people to liaise with.'

'Okey dokey,' I said, sitting back.

'There are plenty of other cases that require attention,' Sandra said with a wink. 'Don't worry, we'll reallocate your hundred points.'

# 22

# THE RAID

I WASN'T WORRIED, BUT I was resolved on taking one additional step.

Outside, the sunlight was bright and sharp. I drove over to Kolenkitbuurt, where community leader Tammy Goss ran an 'urban farm' that sat in the shadow of the A10 ring road. Google had informed me that Tammy was an American, from Baltimore, who'd lived in Amsterdam for the last twelve years. Google also told me that she had her own video channel on YouTube that attracted more than eighty thousand viewers.

She was easy to spot. She had a mass of curly, fawn-coloured hair, and wore brightly patched dungarees. As I approached her, she was giving instructions to what appeared to be several volunteers.

'Tammy,' I called out.

She stopped talking and turned around.

'I'm Officer Henk van der Pol,' I said, showing my warrant card. 'Could I have a quick word?'

'Irina, why don't you give them their feed?' she told the girl in front of her. Beside her were two long henhouses; the clucking and squawking almost drowned out the ceaseless traffic sound of the ring road, but not quite.

'No appointment?' she said, walking away from the others, who eyed me warily. 'What's the meaning of this?'

'I hoped to get your advice, Tammy. There's a man from

this neighbourhood who's been stealing mopeds in another precinct.'

'Your precinct?'

'Yes. We suspect the thefts are organised and drugs-related.'

'Based on a stolen moped?' she asked sceptically.

'Yes.'

'Go on.'

'We don't want to cause any problems, given the good work you're doing out here.' I made a point of looking around admiringly.

She softened a little. 'It was a derelict site till this time last year.'

'I'm interested to hear more about it.'

She paused, then said, 'We made a contract with the neighbourhood families: we'd get permission and funding to develop the site, if they helped build and maintain it.' I sensed that she'd given this spiel many times. 'We acquired the chickens on the condition they fed them and cleaned the henhouses.'

I nodded, remembering once noticing the previously derelict site, while driving round the ring road at dusk. 'It was a pretty scary place before, wasn't it? This is quite the transformation.'

A toddler, held by a crouching woman, appeared to be entranced by a chicken strutting across a pen.

'It was a neglected space,' Tammy corrected me, 'and an uncomfortable one at that. Yes, it could be intimidating at night. But it's also close to the shops and the main walking routes through the neighbourhood. So we've turned it into a place of community self-empowerment.'

'How many locals take part?' I asked, eager to win her cooperation.

'Increasing numbers,' she replied. 'Many of these families originate from rural Morocco and Turkey. They've expressed interest in keeping small cattle, just like they keep in their home countries. So we're now looking at goats – sheep, even.'

Much as I tried to understand, it mystified me. 'Don't you have difficulty reconciling that with the need for cultural integration?' I asked. 'This is Holland, not the Atlas Mountains.'

She turned to face me, her hands finding her hips. 'Why do you think about integration that way? You're saying people here should be denied their animal husbandry traditions just because this country is flat?'

I didn't understand her perspective, but nodded all the same. 'You're right.' I looked beyond the site to the ring road and the surrounding buildings – the repeating patterns of mundane, four-storey apartment blocks. My gaze shifted back to the clucking wildlife in front of us.

'Wasn't this the promise of your generation?' she added, easing the tension. 'A better society… not just for some, but for all?'

I answered her question with my own: 'Does this sort of thing happen back in Baltimore?'

She laughed. 'Baltimore's a *li*-ttle different.'

'I'll say. We've all enjoyed episodes of *The Wire*.'

'Baltimore has its fair share of problems, but the underlying issues are the same. Think of it like epidemiology: apathy and casual violence, spreading among communities in the same way as infectious diseases. We're just looking to institute break points.'

It was a good break point in itself, to return to the subject of Tarek Hosseini. But before I had a chance to, Tammy said, 'The future of this city's soul lies in projects like this one.'

Important though it was to build a rapport with this woman, some part of me bristled at a foreigner defining the soul of my city for me. We Dutch were now reckoned to be a minority in Amsterdam, in terms of raw population percentage.

'Tammy, do you know Tarek Hosseini?'

She narrowed her gaze. 'I don't think so. Who's he again?'

'The man I mentioned. He lives three streets from here and

was found with several hundred pills of Ecstasy in the luggage compartment of a Vespa, which he stole from a thirty-six-year-old female landscape designer.' *And no amount of chickens, goats or sheep changes that*, I left unsaid.

'Why are you telling me this?' she asked sharply.

'Like I said, we think both the drugs and moped theft are organised –'

'Then hunt the organisers, not the organisees – if such a word exists.'

I kept quiet.

'Find the people telling Tarek what to do.'

She may as well have said, *Do your job, officer.*

'If only it were that simple.'

I watched the chicken lift its feathers; I could tell that the toddler was in awe of it, and wanted to get closer. What the child seemed unaware of was its razor-sharp beak, and the sideways glare of its eyes.

I walked away, leaving behind another investigative dead end.

*

I'd driven most of the way back to the station when Johan's call came in. 'Are you free to talk?' my old friend asked.

'Very.'

'That website you were looking into on the Dark Web –'

'Night Market?'

'Yes. I found out something about it.'

'I suggested that you left it alone.'

'Yeah, but you also said it might help… Do you want to know what I found out, or not?'

'Of course.'

'The site's been taken down.'

My chest deflated. 'I'm not sure how that helps, Johan.'

'I found out the name of the guy who got it taken down. He's one of yours.'

'A cop?'

'Yup.'

'How did you learn this?'

'He's from the UK, actually – a cop called Tim O'Farrell – from the London Metropolitan Police.'

The name said something to me. Maybe it was just the reminder of Tommy Franks, who had also been a policeman with London's Met – or so he'd claimed.

'Johan, how did you find this out, when even *I* didn't know?'

'An online forum.'

'What kind of forum?'

'Probably better you remain in the dark. I had someone else look into it for me. Anyway, do you know this O'Farrell guy?'

'Nope.'

Assuming Johan's information was correct, who had this London cop been working with on the Dutch side? It could have been any number of internationally oriented bodies that had sprung to life post-Driebergen...

'Never mind then,' Johan said sombrely. 'What about that moped you were tracking? Did you find it again?'

'Yes.'

'And?'

'It was a wild goose chase. A wild chicken chase, even.'

\*

I was still craving nicotine as I entered the station. Inside the squad room, I found Stefan, his feet up on a waste paper bin and his hands interlaced behind his head. He was the only one there.

'You're looking remarkably at ease,' I said.

'Nothing to do. The nightclub case has been taken away from me.'

'Oh?'

I looped my jacket over the back of my chair and sat down heavily.

'Though I *am* meeting Sandra for a drink.' His eyebrows shot up and down.

'I thought you'd met her for a drink already.'

'That was just coffee.'

'Fancy a walk?' I said. 'Let's celebrate your success by getting an ice cream cone or something.'

Anything to get my taste memory off nicotine.

'Bit late in the season for ice cream, isn't it?'

We walked out of the front of the station, along to Prins Hendrikkade, and sat on a wall overlooking the harbour. The sun was still bright. Now we could talk freely.

'So, how come the nightclub case got taken away from you?' I asked.

'Mulder brought in the national drugs team.'

As expected.

'Are you completely off it?'

'More or less. I was about to pay Pieter Westerling a visit, but Mulder instructed me not to.'

I watched a gull wheel against the blue sky, its wings immobile.

'Where does he live, out of interest?'

'North Amsterdam.'

'Whereabouts?'

He told me. It was close enough to where Tarek Hosseini had taken the Vespa the previous night – but, like everything now, it was inconclusive. I inhaled deeply, breathing in the marine air. The sunlight reflected blindingly off the water, making my eyes blood-dark when I closed them.

'It'll be interesting to see what Joost does.'

My eyes snapped open again. At first I thought I'd misheard Stefan.

'I'm sorry?'

'Mulder is coordinating the involvement of the drugs squad with Joost. I wonder how he'll play it.'

It felt like the ground had disappeared from under me.

'Why Joost? He's in The Hague now. How do you know this, anyway?'

'Joost and I are in touch.'

Terra firma suddenly turned to terra jelly.

'Why?'

'Joost took an interest in me. Don't you remember how he asked me to join the Lottman kidnapping team down in Tilburg?'

'Yes, but —'

'What's wrong?'

*You were working for* me *down there, providing intelligence* on *Joost*, I wanted to exclaim.

'We stayed in touch,' Stefan added, unaffected by my growing concern.

'When was the last time you talked to him?'

'A day or so ago. We talk every once in a while.'

I shook my head sharply, wishing the entire situation away now, specifically my conceit in believing that I'd been mentor enough to Stefan.

'Have you talked about me?'

It was the wrong question to ask. Too defensive. Suspicious, even.

'Er, not really…' He tried to make light of it. 'But don't worry, you weren't forgotten while away in Driebergen!'

Stefan and I had talked about Karremans while I was there. So that was indeed what Frank Hals had meant… *People know people, who know people. And some of them are wondering what conclusions you've drawn…*

'You look surprised,' Stefan said. 'I tried to tell you about it that day...'

'What day?

'Just the other week.'

'When?'

'You'd just gone to Driebergen. Had you returned to Amsterdam for the weekend? I think you'd come back from a trip to Norway... Anyway, I did bring it up.'

Now that he mentioned it, I vaguely remembered Stefan calling me while I was visiting Karremans's place on IJburg...

'I asked you how to approach Joost about a promotion I was considering putting in for,' he prompted. 'You were busy at the time.'

I remembered being cold and uncomfortable that afternoon on IJburg, and needing to get back to Driebergen...

Stefan went on: 'Joost was approachable enough about it, anyway.'

'What promotion?'

'Oh, it doesn't matter. After chatting to him, I decided against going for it. He didn't think it was a good idea. Said something better would come along. What have you got against him, anyway?'

'Who – Joost? Why d'you ask that?'

He shrugged. 'Just a feeling I get. That you blame Joost for things.'

If only Stefan knew.

'Let's change the subject,' I said tersely. There was nothing I could tell Stefan now that might not get back to my nemesis, inadvertently at least.

We sat for a few moments longer, then returned to the station in silence.

\*

I was feeling a sensation of slow-motion collapse as I returned home to the boat that night. Was it even possible to be demoted from bike theft? Policing litter, perhaps?

A discarded pack of Marlboro Reds sat beside the water's edge on Entrepotdok. I kicked it in. A young neighbour out walking her dog shot me a disapproving look.

But back at the boat, things were looking up a little. Petra had cooked *zomerse stoofschotel* – summer stew with vegetables. A bottle of red wine stood open on the table.

'What have I done to deserve this?' I asked, pouring two very full glasses. 'Or are *you* feeling guilty about something?' I arched an eyebrow.

'Perhaps I was hoping we could pick up where we left off this afternoon,' she said, sidling up to me.

I caressed her back, then helped dish up the stew.

We sat down.

'*Proost*!' Smiling, we raised our wine glasses, and began eating.

'I met a woman this afternoon who you might find interesting.'

'Who?' Petra said, mid-mouthful.

'She runs an urban farm out in Kolenkitbuurt, has her own –'

'Tammy Goss?'

I narrowed my eyes. 'Yes.'

'I interviewed her last month.'

'Oh.'

'Don't worry,' she gave me an underlook, 'it hasn't featured on my blog yet – you haven't missed anything.'

I smiled. 'It got me thinking about things – how things were, back in the day. You know, how we really hoped to change the world... Where did all that go?' I sighed and reached for my wine glass.

'They have an expression in France, don't they? *Mettre de l'eau dans son vin.*'

'Meaning?'

'Mellow.'

'Hmm,' I said, draining my glass. 'I had in mind doing a couple of jenever chasers.'

Petra chuckled. 'Maybe it's a good thing we're going to London.' Then she made a bridge with her hands, resting her chin on it. 'Things haven't turned out so badly, have they?'

She was wearing a low-cut top, and the candle's half-light revealed her cleavage to particularly pleasing effect. I was set on resuming where we'd left off earlier when my phone rang.

'I'll turn it off.'

But as I pulled the device out to do so, I saw that the caller was Mulder.

'Actually, it's the boss. Hold on...' I pressed accept.

'Henk?'

'Yes.'

'Sorry to disturb you at night.'

'What's up?'

'I just thought you should know that the national drugs team went to do a preliminary search of the nightclub in the harbour.'

'The submarine?'

'That's right. They found MDMA.'

Why did he think that I needed to know this now?

'They also found your daughter there.'

'Nadia?'

Petra shot me a look.

'It's OK,' he said. 'She just received a caution – this time. This is all off-grid.'

*Off-grid?*

'We look out for one another,' he added.

Neither of his last two statements was comforting.

'I just thought you should know,' he concluded. 'Good night.'

# 23

## CHOKE POINT

I GRABBED MY COAT and my warrant card. My hand hesitated in front of the gun case. I'd had a large glass of wine.

'Where are you going?' Petra demanded.

'I have to check something. I'm sorry, I'll be back shortly.'

'What's happening? Why did you mention Nadia?'

'It's fine, I'll be back soon.'

'Tell me!'

I explained, and finally she let me go.

It wasn't fine, however. As I walked down Entrepotdok towards the harbour, Nadia wasn't taking my calls.

I paced through the darkness and soon came to the submarine, the slick-black shape contrasting with the glittering surface of the dark water. Its conning tower loomed stealthily. Velvet Revolution's tour bus had gone.

A couple of people were milling around: frustrated club-goers, by the looks of it.

'Tonight's event is cancelled,' announced a big guy at the mouth of the gangplank. Tied between the railings was police tape.

'Who are you?' I asked him.

'Security.' The man drew back to appraise me. He wasn't Jurgen Straeffer. 'Who are *you*?'

I showed him my warrant card. 'I need to see yours.'

He showed me a card for a private security company. I didn't recognise the firm, but it wasn't uncommon for the police to outsource security to private contractors. 'Drugs team told me to keep it secure,' he said.

I nodded, then strode past him, stooping under the tape.

'Hey,' he said, 'show your warrant card again, I'd better note your name.'

*

The old Icefish-class submarine had been stripped down to its shell, with only essential piping and electrical wiring remaining along the highest circular point. It looked like the wiring had remained unchanged since the hippies inhabited it thirty years before. Gone was the artwork, though – dark fabric blanketed the walls. Metal flooring spanned the widest point, but the club still looked surprisingly small when empty. Down the sides ran plush leather seating, and directly ahead rose a DJ booth, like a pulpit.

Illuminating all was the submarine's original red lighting, designed to encourage pupil dilation – enabling submariners to find their night vision fast after raising the periscope, thereby minimising the time that the periscope protruded above water. Everything about a submarine is designed for stealth.

There was no one remaining from the drugs team; I called out, and got no response. Beside the steel entry door stood a folding table. On top of it sat a clipboard with a register attached, a box of thin rubber gloves, and a separate box of bootees. I didn't sign the register, but I did put on gloves and bootees.

After pushing the steel door closed behind me, I walked across the metal floor, past the DJ booth, and down a narrow corridor beyond. The doors had been removed, the cabins converted into VIP seating areas. The red light proved disorientating, so I reached for my phone and its white torchlight. There was no return call from Nadia – but no phone reception, either.

I stepped over a metal sill, through an open doorway and into the aft torpedo room. It, too, had been stripped. I noticed a light patch of decking where something had been standing until recently… a pill-making machine perhaps? It was impossible to say, but adjusting the angle of my phone's light, I could make out white splotches of powder – presumably from where the drugs team had tried to lift fingerprints – and also a bright-blue substance more immediately around the light patch on the floor.

I crouched down and dabbed my gloved finger into the blue substance, then touched it to my tongue: MDMA. The 'precursor' ingredient is sassafras oil, found in the jungles of the Far East – notably Indonesia, a former Dutch colony that these submarines were originally commissioned to protect.

The MDMA would have been cooked, or manufactured, somewhere other than here. This would be just a redistribution facility, supplying locals… including, apparently, my daughter.

I stood up, angrily remembering our bet.

As I did so, a loud clang resounded down the corridor.

'Hello?' I called.

There was a squeal, which I recognised to be the circular door-closing mechanism being wheeled shut.

'*Hello?*' I repeated. There was also a weird, vibrational echo.

A footstep sounded in the red-lit void, and then another. Someone had entered the submarine, and closed the door behind.

'Come on out, Henk.'

As I rounded the corner, Hals was approaching me with a gun drawn. The red light had turned his pupils jet black.

'Take a seat,' he said.

In films – possibly in books too (I don't read them) – people pointing guns seems quite commonplace. In real life, having the muzzle of a gun aimed at you forces a mental clarity like nothing else can.

'You're interfering with a crime scene,' I managed.

His face was bathed blood red by the light. So too was his bull-like physique.

'I told you that people were upset with your conclusions down in Driebergen, Henk. I took time out of my schedule to visit your home, and warn you about that. So why this, here?'

'It's a good question.'

'Well?'

My heart kept thudding, my ribs hurting once more.

'I guess I don't know how to do that.'

'What, keep away?' He shook his head.

'You think killing a police officer will help?' There was the weird echo again.

He said, 'That would be crass indeed, wouldn't it? And unnecessary. Doubtless you've left a trail of petty insinuations with the likes of your wife…'

I tried to work out what the hell he was planning to do, if not fire the gun.

'No, if ever this vessel is salvaged, I want people to find out *exactly* what you were doing here. What you did best: putting your nose in where it never belonged. Someone who simply couldn't help himself.'

There was a dull groaning sound and a juddering movement. It sounded like the submarine's ballast tanks were filling.

'All things must pass,' he said.

'It's a little late for destroying evidence, isn't it? The drugs team has already been here. They've removed equipment, by the look of it.'

He took an incredulous step towards me. 'You don't *listen*, do you?' I could feel his sharp breath through the still, stale air. The ventilation system had been turned off. 'I warned you that I know people, who know people. Christ, you don't even listen to your own words: the drugs team has *removed* evidence. Gone, for good. Don't you see?'

The hull lurched. 'So why sink the sub?' I said, my heart

hammering. 'Losing one ship in the harbour might be considered careless. Losing a second vessel...'

He shook his head again, giving up. 'It's time to cut ties.' He walked backwards. 'There's more legitimate money in this harbour now than there ever was in *fringe* activities, shall we call them. Reclamation, development, inward investment from our friends in the Middle and the Far East... we're on the cusp of a new golden age, Henk. If only you were around to witness it.' He paused. 'You could have been part of that. You could have joined me, Pieter and the others...'

'Which others?'

'You could have made a killing.'

'A legitimate killing? Isn't that a contradiction in terms?' But my words didn't even sound convincing to myself. Desperately, I tried to buy time. 'Just tell me one thing, Frank: why go to all the trouble with the MDMA? The couriers, their mopeds?'

'What trouble? Did you see *me* anywhere near the likes of young Tarek, or the woman whose scooter he borrowed?'

*Jesus* – he knew every last detail.

From Mulder? Or rather Stefan, via Joost?

The latter, I increasingly sensed.

'We all have our personal indulgences, Henricus.'

A dreadful groaning sounded throughout the hull, causing the metal floor to tremble. The ballast tanks were filling rapidly. The vessel was designed to dive fast in the event of surface peril.

'Shall I tell you, briefly, the best thing about Molly?' He was using MDMA's street name. 'This will give you something to reflect on, during your journey down.'

How deep was this part of the harbour? Deep enough to berth the biggest ships in the world at one time...

'It makes them all cuddly.' He gave a childlike shake of his limbs. 'There's a reason Molly is called the love drug.'

I recalled Jan Stamms's remark in prison, when asked about being force-fed cider at the Beau Soleil boys' home.

*It wasn't cider,* he'd corrected me.

'You'll never be right, Hals.'

'Maybe. But I'll be alive. I should disembark.'

I could hear the water thundering into the tanks, and also a muffled shout from outside; the sub lurched once more and so too did my stomach. I reached to the side for stability.

'I thought I told you to take a seat?' A steely timbre had entered his voice.

'I still have a pain between my legs. Remember? From last time we met.'

'Oh, yes.' He laughed. 'Well, you needn't worry about that now.'

He was walking sideways, crab-like, towards the exit, the muzzle of his gun still trained on me.

Another lurch, and this time I reached for the roof above me. I grabbed as many of the overhead cables as I could and pulled, hard. The lights flickered, sparked and died, plunging us into darkness; I threw myself to the side as the muzzle of his gun flashed, the bang so loud it felt like my eardrums had been stabbed.

A dull ringing remained.

And darkness.

I already had my night vision thanks to the red lights, and Hals must have had his, too... but the blackness was total, crushing.

'Shit,' he uttered.

I reached up again and pulled at the different conduits, managing to detach a section of metal piping. It dropped to the deck with a clatter. Another muzzle flash, aimed at the source of the sound; sparks jetted off the decking, giving me just enough light to see the dropped piping. I reached for it, felt my fingers wrap around the end of it, then I slunk back as another bang blasted my ears.

Stunned by the force of the reports, I tried to circle around the back of him. As the next shot rang out, I swung the piping. I was swinging at clear air, but on the third or fourth attempt I felt it sink into something semi-firm.

A groan, from his depths.

I could tell from the direction of his noises that he was falling, or crouching, maybe; I swung again wildly, and again, and again, and the impact was softer (a hand cradling his skull, perhaps?). Still, it was a good connection. The noises from his mouth suggested he was down.

And then there was just the sound of my panting breath.

I felt the end of the piping with my other hand: it was wet, with Hals's blood.

Suddenly I felt a weightless, swooping sensation – the sub was sinking. There was still a tinny ringing in my ears from the gunfire; I couldn't register the pressure change. The ballast tanks were arranged to prevent the sub from rolling, but in my stomach I could feel the vessel's descent.

I pulled out my phone. Of course there was no service. I turned on the torch. Hals's white-lit face was twisted into a death rictus. Part of his bludgeoned head appeared to be missing altogether. I waved the torch around and saw, in various places, water leaking in through old seals and flanges.

There was no way to force the main door open now, given the water pressure on the outside. That must have been Hals's intent – to entomb me this way. And he'd managed to.

A booming rocked me and caused me to topple: the hull had met with resistance – the harbour floor? How far down were we? Every ten metres equated to another atmosphere of pressure.

I was operating at my limits of knowledge about these submarines, but felt sure that there would be an escape hatch. Had Hals known that? I clattered back across the decking into the corridor, frantically searching each dark space leading off it. The water was already up to my ankles and ice cold. Even if police frogmen were sent immediately, there would be nothing they could do from the outside. The only safe way to get me out of here would be to crane the sub back up to the surface – which would take days, if not weeks.

Unless I could find that escape hatch.

Had the hippies and club decorators left it intact? It wasn't just an escape hatch I needed; the necessary precursor for any escape was a flood valve. I needed to flood the interior with water – only then would the pressure match that of the water outside. The escape hatch would be counterbalance sprung, I knew, enabling it to open outwards under its own force once the water pressure equalised. That was how these things worked at sea.

I waved the phone's torch around, desperately searching the ceiling for circular shapes. The water was up to my wobbling knees, rising fast, as old metal and rubber gave way under the increasing pressure. I was already shivering with cold in my lower body and could feel a rising sense of suffocation through my chest.

My ears popped.

There was another factor to consider: my previously collapsed lung and still-healing ribs; every atmosphere of pressure shrinks volume by half, but the reverse applies. Meaning, if I took a breath down here and tried to ascend, the air in my lungs would double in volume every ten metres. I would need to breath out, all the while, if I were to avoid rupturing my lungs… yet not exhale so fast that I ran out of oxygen and lost consciousness.

Suddenly, it seemed hopeless. I stopped and considered writing a final message to my wife. Would the phone even survive the deluge? I thought of the trip to London we had planned, and her warmth; the *zomerse stoofschotel* she'd made that evening, and the red wine we'd drunk with it… our last supper?

I thumped a metal partition wall.

It's funny where else the mind goes to in these moments.

The chickens out at Kolenkitbuurt. *Life*.

Nadia, of course. How she'd helped me kick my smoking habit. Maybe it had helped clear out my lungs a little; I had to look on the positive side.

With renewed resolve, I stumbled through to the aft torpedo room.

There, I saw it: the sheared-off trunking that would have been available to pull down in order to create a clear channel of water for ascent. It signified the escape hatch, though my torchlight was fading and unable to make out anything in the gunky darkness overhead.

But to the left, I could just see a circular protuberance: the flood valve, surely. I reached up, straining for the feel of circular metal – *there* – and wheeled it open. The water came in with a *whumph*.

The shock of the cold was total. Very soon the water was to my throat. I bobbed my way across to position myself under the escape hatch, unable to see anything. The oxygen was disappearing and spots of light prickled my vision. They could almost have been nitrogen bubbles, or the warning of them – yet another risk of ascending too fast. I took a final sip of air in the last remaining space, filling my lungs to bursting point, and was then immersed, my head buffeted by the tumultuous water.

Already I felt the 'air hunger' – that tightening sensation of lack of breath. My right hand couldn't feel anything above. I pushed up, my ears popping frantically. It felt like my skull was clamped in a vice. I released a trickle of precious air from the side of my mouth. My head thumped the side of the escape hatch, but was too numb to register any pain; I pushed my way free and was ascending through the velvety blackness.

I could hear the drone of a marine engine. Not immediately above, I hoped. Shapes and patterns flashed before my eyes.

For a moment I thought I'd died.

Or at least lost consciousness.

Hypothermia…

Some survivalist part of my brain knew to keep moving my hips, and my legs, and to keep evacuating my lungs, and at last I could make out dim, stippled light above. Finally I broke through the choppy surface, gasping.

I'd surfaced some distance away from the wharf, but as I rocked confusedly in the currents, I was able to make out a crowd gathered around the gangway that now led nowhere. I swam to the wharf's far end. The currents were vigorous, and mercifully carried me towards it; it was a question of not overshooting now.

I grabbed for a tyre tied there and clambered up, slipping several times on the squeaky rubber, unable to feel anything anyway. Eventually I managed to haul myself up. Water ran from my clothes.

I lay sprawled on the tarmac, fumbling for my phone.

Gone.

It would have been dead anyway. Like Frank Hals.

I forced myself upright, and eventually limped past the backs of the people looking out over the water. There was no sign of the security guard who'd allowed me onto that submarine. Remarkably, I was still wearing the bootees I'd put on upon entering it.

# 24

## LIMEHOUSE

PETRA HAD SPOKEN WITH Nadia, who in turn protested her innocence about the drugs. Given everything else that I'd learned that night, I was inclined to believe my daughter.

After a long, frank conversation with my wife – and several warming jenevers – we took ourselves down to the mariners' chapel, where we both prayed.

Only then was I ready to face a new day.

*

We travelled separately to Schiphol for our afternoon flight to London.

I wanted to catch up with a former team member from IJ Tunnel 3, Liesbeth Janssen, whose husband Marc was a fast-rising public prosecutor in The Hague. Only, she was nowhere to be seen in the motorway café on the A4 where we'd agreed to meet.

I returned to my car, which was parked on the service station's forecourt. Trucks hurtled by on the route south. A shrill ringtone split the air, and I realised that it was my new phone. I had only bought it that morning. I'd had trouble importing my contacts, and didn't recognise the phone number. Perhaps it was her…

'Henk?'

It was.

'Liesbeth, where are you?'

'Something came up – did you not get my message?'

Now that she mentioned it, there were a few that I'd missed.

'Perhaps we could just talk by phone?' she suggested.

'I would have preferred… never mind, that's fine. How are you?'

'There are a few personal things going on, actually. What's up, Henk?

'It's about Marc's work.'

'What about it?' She sounded wary.

It felt far too premature to mention Joost by name. 'I had a couple of questions about the process for indicting a public official.'

'Oof,' she said, as if winded. 'These things must go through official channels, you know?'

I did. Her response sounded numbingly familiar.

'I also wanted to catch up generally,' I backtracked, 'and see how you're both doing. But another time.'

'OK,' she said.

'Talk soon.'

I was about to end the call when she said, 'I'm pregnant, by the way.'

'Really? That's wonderful, Liesbeth! Boy or girl?'

'Don't care, so long as it's healthy.'

I laughed. That was Liesbeth: ever practical.

'Say, if you're in The Hague sometime, you should drop by the house.'

I sensed that it was her way of keeping the door open – just – on what I'd requested.

'I'd like that. Please give my best to Marc.'

'I will.'

As I put my phone away, I noticed a copy of *De Telegraaf* in front of the forecourt shop. I walked over and picked up a copy: *Amsterdam nightclub Blip sinks without trace*. It had made the front page, at the bottom. I skimmed the article, which ended on page two and quoted a police spokesman as saying that they were still trying to determine whether there had been anyone aboard HNMLS *Ijsvis* when it went down.

*

I didn't know whether it was safe to travel by air, given the changes in atmospheric pressure that my body had undergone, but it was only a forty-minute flight to London's City Airport, the captain informed us.

Petra snoozed throughout.

There was barely time for the inflight service, but thankfully they managed. I requested two miniatures of Scotch and asked the attendant to hold the ice.

Before I knew it, we were beginning our descent into the darkening, looping Thames Estuary – shrouded in mist.

I'd found a last-minute deal online for the Four Seasons Hotel in Canary Wharf, after learning that Tim O'Farrell – the London cop who'd closed down the Night Market website – worked out of nearby Limehouse Police Station.

Nothing felt too far apart anymore.

*

From the airport, we took the Docklands Light Railway to Canary Wharf station and then walked the remaining kilometre or so to the hotel. The buildings reared up around us. You couldn't miss the pyramidal tower – its summit blinked white in the mist. Bank names announced themselves in neon all around. I was fascinated, too, by the street names, which included references to the legendary sixteenth-century explorer Sebastian Cabot (if it was indeed the same Cabot). He'd discovered Newfoundland.

The Four Seasons stood at the westward-most edge of this glittering new city. Its far side faced the river. Across the water, somewhere in the darkness, was the venue for the community meeting where Heinrich Karremans would defend his plans for the remaking of Newfoundland Wharf.

'Where is it, exactly?' I asked Petra.

'Just over there, in Canada Water. Look,' she showed me on her phone.

I took hold of the device, scrutinising the map.

*

We had a couple of hours to kill before the meeting, so I decided to pay Limehouse Police Station a visit. It was only a five-minute walk from our hotel, though it felt like a different world.

I approached the screened-off front desk. A large, stout sergeant greeted me: 'Afternoon, sir.'

'I was hoping to catch Tim O'Farrell, if he's here?'

'And who might you be?'

I showed him my warrant card.

'Ah,' he said. 'Did you have an appointment?'

'No,' I replied as naturally as possible. 'I just happen to be staying nearby, on holiday. I thought to stop by and say hello.'

'Right you are, sir. Well, I'll try to get a message to the relevant person.'

It sounded vague, but security had to be a major consideration. The police station resembled the Alamo. And I recalled Johan mentioning how O'Farrell had been identified in an online forum.

'Would you like to leave your number?'

As I did so, I noticed that I had more missed calls, from one Dutch number in particular.

*Mulder?*

*

215

I walked back a circuitous route, via the river. The old goods cranes and wharves – *Barge*, *Dunbar* – felt familiar to me, as did the contrast between the wealth and social housing, cheek by jowl.

I felt at home here – as if this were my natural habitat.

I also sensed that I was being followed. Turning around, I couldn't see anyone in the mist behind me. Perhaps it was my own past catching up with me, in some indefinable way. It was a strange sensation.

I shook it away, hastening my step towards the hotel. Petra was calling.

I answered. 'Everything OK?'

'The meeting's been cancelled!'

'Why?'

'Bomb scare.'

I stopped. 'Terrorism?'

'No, a World War Two unexploded bomb, somewhere nearby. Can you believe it? Five foot long and the weight of a family car, apparently.'

'Jesus.'

'Workmen laying a foundation nearby unearthed it this afternoon.'

Ever the newshound, my wife had uncovered the story already.

'Makes you wonder how many more are out there.' This part of the Thames had been bombed almost as heavily as Rotterdam during the war. 'I'll be back soon,' I said. 'We'll think of something to do.'

But my thoughts were on the ever-elusive Heinrich Karremans. No amount of effort could get me closer to him, it seemed.

I'd barely put my phone away when it started ringing once more.

I had to change that damn ringtone.

'Petra?'

'Mr van der Pol?'

'Yes?'

'It's the desk sergeant at Limehouse Police Station, sir. The DI you enquired about wanted me to pass along a message. He said that he could see you, as he's coming off duty. There's a public house along Narrow Street where he suggested meeting, if that's convenient.'

# 25

## THE GRAPES

THE MIST HAD GATHERED in, but I managed to find The Grapes easily enough. Part of a row of seventeenth-century houses, the bar was low-ceilinged. I walked through to the back of it, looking for an expectant face, but found just a couple of older, regular-looking types.

The far end gave onto the Thames. I stared into its dark reaches, wondering how many outlaws had hidden there in centuries past.

Then I returned to the bar. As I did so, I saw him through the glass window, discarding a cigarette. The light inside caught his lively brown eyes and sandy-coloured hair. He was wearing a beige raincoat. Tim O'Farrell wasn't his real name – or at least, not the name I'd known him by.

He entered and greeted me. 'Henk,' he said. 'Fancy encountering you again, in this neck of the woods.'

My heart was beating like a bass drum.

'All a bit cloak and dagger, isn't it?' I managed.

'Precautions. A lot's happened. I'll tell you about it.'

'You've got my full attention, Tommy. Or should I call you Tim?'

'You'd be surprised by the reprisals – where they come from. Some high-level places.' He stroked the tips of his moustache. 'I retract that. *You* wouldn't be surprised.'

Part of me wanted to leave there and then. But I couldn't.

He knew that. 'Let's get that drink,' he offered. 'Pint?'

I found a quiet table. My hearing and other senses had become very acute: the murmur of the regulars' conversation, the river washing against shingle outside. Then that ringtone of mine.

*Fuck*. It was the Dutch number again. Instinct told me to take the call.

'Henk, finally. It's Kelly Verhagen.'

My mind went blank.

'The recruitment officer,' she prompted.

'Ah yes, Kelly. Now's not a good time…'

'Never is, apparently. Look, your application has been accepted.'

'I'm sorry?'

'For the *Rijksrecherche*… the tests you sat, the interview – remember?'

It felt like a lifetime ago. 'Did you say my application has been *accepted*?'

I couldn't believe it.

'One thing, Henk. The decision wasn't unanimous. A few strong voices were against.'

'*That* instils confidence.'

'Better to know these things.'

'Who was against, out of interest?'

'I can't say. But the minister had the casting vote. Sonja came out strongly in favour, too.'

'Sonja?'

'Brinkerhof, The psychologist. She said you were the most empathetic policeman she'd ever interviewed for Internal Investigations.'

I didn't know what that said about my prospective colleagues.

Franks was carrying two pints back from the bar, a pack of crisps clamped between his teeth.

'I'll call you later, Kelly.'

'Please!'

I pressed disconnect.

It was a dark beer that had a sharp tang to it.

'What is this?'

'Black Sheep.' He winked, then drank and finally sighed.

'All feels very English,' I remarked, glancing around the bar again.

'Yes. Although the place is owned by a Russian oligarch, among others.'

'It's the mirror image of my local in Amsterdam, De Druif. Means "The Grape".'

'How fitting,' Franks said, leaning in, 'because you and I turn out to be mirror images of one another, Henk.' He lowered his voice. 'Here's how it is…' and he proceeded to describe all his frustrations in trying to progress child abuse cases – the cover-ups, the wrongful use of the UK's Official Secrets Act in order to protect powerful suspects…

I sat half-fascinated, half-appalled. Eventually, the latter got the better of me.

'Franks, you killed three fellow policemen in that forest in Driebergen.'

'Only rogue cops,' he countered, forefinger raised. 'They risked blowing everything with their obsessions about that guy.'

'What guy?'

'You know very well which guy, else why would you be here in London?' He didn't need to mention Karremans by name. 'Tell me that you've never killed a man.'

'Not your way.'

In my mind's eye, I saw Hals's white-lit face twisted into its death rictus…

'Same difference.'

'Is it?' I asked.

'We're talking about a cover-up throughout the force here – and the Amsterdam one, too, I'm willing to wager.'

I was about to remonstrate, but the words never arrived.

'Night Market may have gone, but the same people remain.' His brown eyes glinted.

'What do you think, Henk?' He clinked his glass softly against mine, looking me in the eye. 'What say we slay this beast together?'

# Part VI:

The Release

# 26

## EITHER/OR

I DON'T CONSIDER MYSELF to be an either/or kind of guy. My instinct told me to join the Internal Investigations department in The Hague *and* work with Tommy Franks, though doubts remained. What had been his true motivation in slaying those rogue cops in the forest in Driebergen? They'd been trying to kill *me*, so I should have been grateful to him, only—

'Henk,' his voice cut through my thoughts.

I started, as if woken from deep sleep.

'Another?' he raised his glass.

'No, it's my round.'

I stumbled across the dimly lit timbers to the bar. The inn was as placid as before, as predictable as the river tides washing the back of it, but it all felt so different now.

Petra had texted to ask if everything was OK. I thumbed a message into my phone: *Just ran into someone I once worked with, back soon.*

As I ordered the drinks, I caught Franks out of the corner of my eye taking a call. How had he been allowed to leave Holland? Why had no incident team been appointed? Or, was I making a wrong assumption somewhere? I decided to ask him. But by the time I returned to the table with fresh drinks, things had changed again. He didn't look at all happy with the call he'd just taken.

'I need to leave,' he said abruptly.

'Already?'

'Talk of the devil: Heinrich Karremans…'

'What about him?'

'Found dead.' There was a pregnant pause. 'Do you want to accompany me to the scene?'

\*

Franks drove us across night-time London quickly in his unmarked police car, which reeked of stale cigarette smoke. Outside, the skyline had a restlessness to it – new, glaringly lit structures erupted from the low-rise sprawl. In such an old city, it had an unsettling effect.

We sped westward. I eyed Franks's dark profile, his curiously old-fashioned moustache.

'Care to elaborate on what's happened?' I asked.

'I only got half the story myself. Seems that Karremans was staying at Maritime House…' I hadn't heard of the place. Franks must have caught my puzzled expression, as he added: 'It's a hotel that recently opened on the South Bank.'

So Karremans had preferred to stay in Central London, away from the site of his latest architectural oeuvre.

'He was found alone in a suite there,' Franks added.

'And foul play hasn't been ruled out?'

'Not yet.'

'Does the death *appear* natural?'

'Let's see.'

'Who's handling the case?'

'Given who he was, and his almost diplomatic status… Let's see,' he repeated.

We were approaching a wide bridge over the Thames, from the north.

'Are we close?'

'Yep.' He pointed to a large, boxy building on the far side of the river. The hotel's name was just visible above it, in elegant aquamarine neon with an art deco feel.

'Do you have any hunches, if it turns out to be foul play?'

Franks shrugged. 'I don't know yet. But there's always the risk of vigilantes.'

'In connection with Night Market?'

'Maybe,' Franks replied. 'Karremans could even have fallen victim to another site user. Someone involved in that scene, who'd come to mistrust him…'

This sounded more like a working hypothesis than idle speculation. Perhaps Franks had read my expression once more, as he said, 'Let's not get ahead of ourselves.'

On the other side of the bridge he turned right, then accelerated again, heading west. 'One thing's for sure,' he said, changing gears. 'Karremans was a key guy in the investigation into Night Market. Without him…'

I waited for him to finish, but he didn't. It felt like he'd been about to reveal something significant, then decided against it.

I made a mental note to come back to that, asking, 'How did you get to hear about his death?'

'A contact inside the force.' He shot me a look. 'Come on, Henk, you know how it goes.'

I returned the look. 'What I know is that you wiped out three vigilante cops in the forest, Tommy. How could you get away with that?'

'And you're above it?'

Did he know about the battered body of Hals, in a submarine on the floor of Amsterdam harbour? Was that possible, or was he just making guesses? He remained as unreadable as ever.

We swerved towards the front entrance of the hotel and pulled up behind a police car with a faint screech. Franks reached for the door handle, pausing to say, 'Let me do the talking.'

*

Every hotel has its own procedure for handling a death on its premises, but central to that procedure – in luxury hotels at least – is the need for discretion. This brings both advantages and disadvantages to police investigations. It helps with the preservation of evidence, yet often hinders its disclosure.

The reception area of Maritime House was dressed in hammered copper, flush-riveted – the kind of place that might appeal to a world-famous architect, I sensed. There was a knot of men to one side. They looked serious, professional and uneasy. There was a knot in my stomach, too, tightening all the while.

'Wait here,' Franks told me, heading towards the group. I guessed that they were some combination of hotel management and plain-clothes detectives. Edging closer, I could hear snatches of conversation… 'Took his own life,' muttered one.

Suicide is the most common cause of death in hotels. Those planning to kill themselves usually prefer to be discovered by an anonymous professional rather than friends or family. This all sounded plausible in the case of Karremans, after one of the newspapers had broken the story online about him being suspected of abusing kids. The paper had in fact retracted the article with an apology, but the damage had surely been done.

Franks moved towards the lift with two of the men. A lift car arrived and they vanished into it. I ambled through to a lounge area, then the restaurant, approaching the floor-to-ceiling windows with views of the Thames – imagining Karremans making use of these same amenities, only hours before. There was a strongly nautical theme to the place: a glass case featured a pair of giant ship's binoculars… and a grey model submarine hovered above the bar, would you believe it. I tried not to see connections where none existed.

Waiting for Franks back in the lobby, I acknowledged that it was common enough for those planning suicides to pick hotels far from home… in foreign countries, even. It lent a further degree of separation between those who died and the real victims of suicide – the friends and family left behind, wondering. Over the years, Amsterdam had become a popular choice for 'tourist suicides'.

There is often a practical problem left behind, too: the repatriation of the body. Post-mortems can take weeks.

'Henk.' Franks was back, beckoning me from beside the lift car. I followed him inside, and we ascended to the top floor.

The suite was decorated in muted golds and soft greys. I walked through the entrance vestibule behind Franks, feeling a growing sense of anticipation, a compression building again in my upper chest. It would be the first and last time that I'd see the famous architect up close. There was a chemical smell and a dryness to the air.

He lay naked, sprawled on a double bed facing the windows, his pale skin saggy over his pectorals and stomach. A crime scene investigator in a blue face mask was photographing the body, his camera clicking softly. The dead man wore a scuba diver's face mask, which covered his nostrils and magnified his staring eyes.

Clamped between his puckered lips was a regulator. There was no oxygen tank on the other end – rather, a duty-free bag.

Auto-erotic asphyxiation.

I wondered why a duty-free bag, then remembered that Karremans had most recently been in China. Perhaps he'd flown direct to London from there.

'Did he have company here?' I asked.

'No sign of any,' Franks replied.

The CSI went round to the other side of the body, interested in something on the neck.

'What a way to be remembered,' Franks said.

I hoisted my eyebrows, words eluding me.

Hypoxia – oxygen deficiency – can induce hallucinogenic, euphoric states. I'd experienced something like it on the submarine not even twenty-four hours prior.

Only here, it had been used to a different effect.

'Any sign of sexual climax?' I asked.

'Come again?' Franks said.

'Orgasm,' I replied too fast, not catching his wordplay in English.

The CSI guffawed as he repositioned himself to photograph the neck and the carotid artery which – among the living – carries oxygen-rich blood to the brain.

I took a step towards the CSI. 'What're you seeing?' I asked.

He lowered his camera. 'Maybe nothing,' he said, extending a gloved hand to point out the faint marks on the neck. 'But see these indentations? The circular discolourations there? They look like finger marks.'

'Did you manage to lift any prints?'

He shook his head and brought the camera back up to his eye.

No fingerprints, yet finger *marks*.

A thinly gloved hand, perhaps? A competent assassin, but no master of his craft? Someone in the process of perfecting his trade – on those associated with Night Market?

It was all just speculation.

I stepped back to the foot of the bed. Karremans's genitals were barely discernible in the snowy hair between his legs. No sign of the death erections occasionally seen in those whose oxygen supply has suddenly been cut off; several hung at the old gallows in North Amsterdam had exhibited that macabre phenomenon, according to local lore.

But not Heinrich Karremans.

'Do you think the scene's been staged?' I asked.

Franks looked on distantly, not responding.

'It's possible,' the CSI replied for him.

'Anything's possible,' Franks said with finality. 'We'd better get out of here.' Then he turned to the CSI: 'Ta, Josh, won't be forgotten.'

Josh nodded and carried on taking photos.

As we exited the bedroom, I shot a final glance at the dead man's staring eyes. What had they witnessed here?

Outside the suite, in a corridor resembling an ocean liner's, I experienced a powerful sense of déjà vu. More than déjà vu, in fact – there were three men coming towards us, and the tall one in the middle was familiar. I dipped my head, shielding my face from view.

The tall man was the Dutch ambassador to London. Not so surprising, given Karremans's status. The case would be locked down now. Franks had got me in to see the body just in time.

The lift door pinged. Franks swiped a key card that he'd apparently been loaned by hotel management. We had the lift to ourselves.

'On the way over here,' I said, 'you were about to tell me something.'

Franks frowned, unsure what I was referring to.

'In relation to Night Market,' I prompted. 'You said something about how, now that Karremans has gone...'

*One thing's for sure, Karremans was a key guy in the investigation into Night Market. Without him...*

He seemed to remember his words, saying, 'There's only one lead left on your side of the sea now, Henk.'

'Who's that?'

'Let me see if I can get the pronunciation right.'

I waited.

The doors opened again. The hubbub of the lobby rushed in.

'Joost van Erven.'

Franks had used a hard 'J' instead of the correct Y-sound, but the name drove straight into my core like a blade: Joost van Erven, my former boss – a man I was now determined to visit justice upon.

231

# 27

## THREE WEEKS LATER

'COME IN, HENK,' THE justice minister said.

I was back in Willem van der Steen's office in The Hague. It was just down the road from Internal Investigations, my new place of work; I was commuting there from Amsterdam.

'You remember Wim?' he asked.

Wim Rijnsburger, my former AIVD handler, was sitting at the circular glass table, next to the minister.

'I do,' I said. Rijnsburger watched me, rheumy-eyed and silent.

'OK,' van der Steen said. 'Let's get down to it: we've looked at your report. You've got balls, Henk. Not even a month into your new role, and you want to indict the police force's most senior Internal Liaison member?'

'Or take a step towards it,' I qualified.

There were limits to how much senior-level support I could expect this soon into my new job, but I at least had their full attention.

Van der Steen said, 'Everything you're describing here relates back to Rem Lottman – and he's gone.'

'Indeed,' I accepted.

'So you're recommending going after Joost instead, eh?'

'I wouldn't put it quite that way.'

Joost had agitated to lead the investigation into Lottman and his disappearance. However, he'd been denied by the cabinet –

in particular by the energy minister, Muriel Crutzen, I'd later learned.

Had van der Steen also been involved in the thwarting of Joost? This was becoming complicated.

'It's going to be a question of evidence,' van der Steen was saying. 'Let's dive deeper. You're claiming that there was a scheme to reward the foreign diplomats of countries providing oil and gas to Holland on favourable terms.'

'Yes.' Surely he'd been told this by the energy minister?

'And that those rewards were distributed out of Amsterdam – facilitated by the police force. Diamonds, valuable paintings, escorts, even underage ones... Joost being implicated.'

'Right. It happened on his watch.' Joost had been the Amsterdam police commissioner at the time.

'*Our* watch,' the minister corrected me.

Rijnsburger was scrutinising me all the while. I hadn't expected the AIVD veteran to be in this meeting, and couldn't help feeling unnerved by his presence. A file on Joost in Internal Investigations, which I'd only just consulted, revealed that Joost himself had started his career in the AIVD. It made sense – it explained how he'd come to run an informant network for the Amsterdam police, which I'd first stumbled across after discovering a body in Amsterdam harbour...

Now another question was starting to surface: did Joost and Rijnsburger know one another? Were they old allies, rivals... or some combination of the two, according to circumstance?

'So, let me get this straight,' van der Steen was saying. 'You contend that Joost failed to support an investigation into a Ukrainian woman savagely attacked at the Royal Hotel in Amsterdam, because – you hypothesise – she was an escort provided to an Emirates sheikh as part of this favours-for-energy scheme. You then go on to speculate that Joost arranged for the burglary of a Verspronck painting from a Norwegian diplomat's house in Amsterdam, after the Norwegian government reneged on an energy-related agreement. A local gangster, Frank Hals – now deceased, I note – arranged for the burglary of the painting, only it went wrong, and the Norwegian diplomat died in the process...'

'It's a lot to take in,' I said, wondering how and when the minister had become aware of *Hals*'s death.

'Indeed,' the minister continued. 'And the painting was later discovered as a rolled-up canvas in a Schiphol storage locker, and misappropriated by Joost – you say.'

Something else was striking about pulling the files on Joost: being *able* to pull them. I wasn't allowed to pull my own file, nor others who'd worked for me. That would have constituted a conflict of interest. Checks and balances. And yet, in my new role, my former boss's file was freely available to me. Was I secretly being aided and abetted in going after Joost? Van der Steen knew of the grudge between us...

'Finally, you speculate that Joost may have become involved in a website catering to paedophiles. You cite the testimony of an unnamed London police detective – who you say must remain anonymous – who alleges that Joost frequented a website called' – he looked down – 'Night Market.'

I remained silent.

He sat back. 'That's quite a charge sheet.'

'They're not charges. They form the basis of probable cause, warranting the allocation of resources towards an investigation.'

'Hmm.' He reached for the conference phone and pressed a button.

'Sir,' his assistant's voice crackled.

'Get Marc up here, would you?'

'Marc Vissering?'

'The same.'

\*

Marc Vissering was a public prosecutor who'd risen rapidly to the top of his profession – and he was also Liesbeth's husband. Tall, light-eyed and youthful-looking, his clean-cut demeanour belied a killer instinct when it came to bringing cases before judges.

He arrived in the minister's office and we nodded our hellos to one another.

'Ah,' van der Steen said, acknowledging his arrival, 'we're talking about the Ukrainian woman at the Royal.'

So Marc knew all about the matter – from the minister, or his wife? Both, probably – Liesbeth had worked on the case when I'd been her team leader. At that time, Marc had also been working closely with Joost, in a prosecutorial capacity.

Were Marc and Joost in contact? It was all too much to keep track of…

'You've had a chance to look into it?' the minister asked him.

Marc nodded. 'Yes, I think I've got a reasonable sense of the dynamics here. The odds don't look good.'

'Go on,' van der Steen said.

'The victim at the Royal Hotel never came forward,' Marc summarised. 'She was never interviewed –'

'At Joost's direction,' I interjected. Joost had directed Liesbeth away from the case after she had tracked down the Ukrainian escort in question.

Van der Steen raised a palm in my direction, silencing me.

'There were no witnesses,' Marc said, continuing his assessment.

I opened my mouth to say that a maid – a fellow Ukrainian – had found the woman beaten into unconsciousness. But I stopped myself. Strictly speaking, Marc was right. There were no known witnesses to the alleged assault itself. While there is no jury to persuade here in Holland, the judges take their impartiality seriously, of course.

'If no victim steps forward,' Marc was saying, 'and there's no witness to the incident…'

It was uncannily like a remark that Liesbeth had made at the time.

*If a tree falls in the forest...*

'Given those circumstances, I don't believe that the then police commissioner could legally be considered to have acted negligently in deciding not to pursue an investigation,' he concluded.

Van der Steen nodded, accepting Marc's assessment.

I sat back, thinking about the chessboard here: who really held power over whom? Clearly the minister was the king. But as on the chessboard, his scope of movement was limited – by public scrutiny and the media, among other things. It would take relatively little to topple him, in certain circumstances.

Marc was heavily circumscribed as well, by the laws of evidence and legal procedure. Meanwhile, the police were the pawns – foot soldiers – as ever, and my elevation to Internal Investigations made me at best a middle-ranking piece, based on my extra access to files and information.

No, the piece on the board with real freedom of movement was Joost. *Senior-most member of Internal Liasion.* Somehow he'd managed to carve out a role that defied definition, even.

Van der Steen was addressing me. 'What else have you got, Henk?'

Was it wise to show my full hand with Marc still in the room? I decided that I had little left to lose now.

'The painting,' I said. 'That Verspronck, the *Girl Dressed in Blue* study – its misappropriation.' It was the most tangible element of all. 'Where did it go? Let's have Joost answer that.'

Van der Steen drummed his fingers lightly on the table.

Marc looked down.

It was Rijnsburger who coughed and said, 'In fact, I can answer for him.'

'Oh?'

'He donated it.'

'*Donated?*' I repeated, starting to sense a miscalculation on my part. 'To who?'

'It was taken from its original owners by the Germans during the Second World War,' Rijnsburger said. My stomach lurched like it had a lead weight inside; I recalled a remark by a custody sergeant at the diplomat's house where it had been stolen: *There's a question about the provenance, whether it changed hands during the war...*

'But how could he *donate* it?' I blurted. 'There are other people to consider – the Norwegians for one, and also the art insurers in London...'

'They were all consulted.' Rijnsburger put a single document down on the glass table. It looked like some kind of bill of receipt; it *felt* like the river card thrown down in a poker game – which I'd just lost.

'He donated the painting to the Nationaal Monument in Kamp Vught,' the AIVD veteran concluded.

I was speechless. My mouth opened and closed again like an expiring fish's. Rijnsburger was referring to the former concentration camp in southern Holland run by the SS. The original owners of the painting must have been sent there. It had been a transit camp for Auschwitz.

'And Joost had authority to do that?' I asked weakly, trying somehow to salvage the situation.

Van der Steen indicated that Marc could leave. The young prosecutor did so, avoiding eye contact.

The minster said, 'Whatever procedures were bypassed, no one could fault Joost for trying to return that painting to the people it was originally taken from – who didn't want any press about the matter, by the way.'

He glanced down at the report again. 'What else do we have?' He paused. 'Of course, we could have looked more closely at that gangster Frank Hals, and *his* involvement in the whole episode... only, he's no longer around.'

Rijnsburger's watery eyes were fixed on me.

The minister closed my report, dismissing me. 'Must try harder, Henk.'

# 28

## FAMILY FIRST

'WHY DO YOU NEED to know this?' my wife demanded, back at the houseboat.

'Because I have to understand what happened,' I replied. 'A woman was beaten into unconsciousness at that hotel. No action was taken. And the inaction itself was met with inaction.' I fought to contain my fast-spooling thoughts. 'You told me at the time that the man who booked the escort might not have been the same as the one who actually slept with her –'

'I never confirmed that it was a man.'

'Who slept with her?'

As a former investigative journalist, Petra valued confidentiality of sources above all else. Using that credibility, and her experience, she'd infiltrated the Royal Hotel, where the attack had taken place.

I tried again. 'You told me at the time that her client was a sheikh from one of the Emirates countries. Question being: who made the arrangement? Who paid for it?'

That might yet provide a way back to Joost...

My wife flopped back onto the leather sofa, her head lolling back, her face disappearing into the half-light. Only her neck remained well lit. It might have made a nice painting – if I hadn't still been mulling over the fate of that Verspronck.

'Let me see if the source remembers,' she allowed.

I sat down next to her, carefully. 'You're still in touch with this person?'

I'd imagined some random hotel insider – a bellhop, maintenance crew member, supplier possibly…

'Henk, please.' She turned her face towards me, her eyes alive in the darkness. 'It's bad enough that I no longer have a career. But to undermine the memory of the one I had…?'

'But here's the thing, Petra,' I said, taking her hand in mine. 'Nothing can ever be right for me – for *us* – till I've brought Joost to justice. There's too much that he's done now. Too much at stake. Too many things left unresolved –'

'Are you so sure it's about him, though?'

'Say again?'

'Well,' she said, looking up at the ceiling, or perhaps towards the heavens above. 'We all use someone else to blame at times, for what we can't explain in ourselves. I'm wondering whether that's what this is really about. Whether by bringing Joost to justice, you think everything will somehow be solved inside yourself.'

I sat alongside her, looking up too. Orange sodium light reflected off the waters of Entrepotdok and onto the varnished wooden ceiling of the boat.

'Is it about Joost, or is it about you?' she summarised.

I watched the orange patterns form, merge and then dissolve in some endless cycle.

'You may be right,' I admitted. 'There's a police psychologist who interviewed me, when I applied for Internal Investigations. I should go and see her.'

'Who is she?'

'Her name's Sonia Brinkerhof.'

'Hmm.' I knew this would meet with my wife's approval. 'I've heard that name,' she said. 'Works at the university?'

'Yes. She seemed good. Maybe she can help.'

Petra squeezed my hand. 'You agree to do that, I'll share my source.'

240

'Really?' I asked. This was too easy.

'You know him well enough, anyway. Or should do.'

'I do?' My surprise turned to consternation. I tried to imagine who it could possibly be.

'Do you agree to see the psychologist?' my wife said.

'I do.'

She paused. 'It's Sergei.'

'*Sergei?*' I did a double take, sitting up forcefully. 'As in, Nadia's Sergei? Our daughter's boyfriend?'

'Yes, Henk. *That* Sergei.'

\*

He was home when I called in at their flat in Zeeburg the following morning. It was a bright, late autumn day. He buzzed me into the building and I took the long elevator ride up to their neutrally toned, light-filled home. Nadia was out.

He wore a pair of loose linen trousers and a T-shirt with something written in Russian across the middle; his torso was impressively bulked, in spite of his advancing years.

'Can I offer you a drink?' he asked.

'Sure,' I said evenly.

'I was about to fix a protein shake.'

'A glass of water will do.'

He disappeared. I glanced around the place, looking for evidence of my daughter in photos or other personal items. I noticed a shot of them together in Paris.

'Here.' Sergei reappeared, handing me my water.

'Thanks.' I set the glass down on the coffee table. We sat. 'So, how are things?'

'Good,' he replied, smiling and crossing his legs.

I was determined not to be anything other than courteous with him. The last thing my relationship with my daughter needed was another fractious encounter.

'And you?' he asked.

'Fine,' I replied. 'I'm finally over the cigarettes.'

There was a gap in conversation.

'You wanted' – he made an unfurling gesture with his fingers – 'to see me about something?'

I wondered whether our problems came down to one of basic language – to continual, small misunderstandings about what we were trying to say to one another.

'It's more than a purely social call, yes. Petra mentioned that you shared some information with her about a guest at the Royal Hotel earlier this year. Do you remember?'

His eyes became distant as he thought.

'About a woman who was attacked there,' I prompted.

'In one of the suites?'

'That's right. She was badly beaten up.'

'A Ukrainian woman, no?'

'Correct.' My spirits rose.

'What do you want to know?'

'First, how did you become aware of it?'

I had a couple of theories, one being that Sergei had business contacts at the Royal, or whichever company owned it; the second theory – that Sergei had direct contacts among high-class escorts – I didn't even want to consider.

He paused, perhaps deciding where to begin. 'There's a company called Cyclamen.'

'Why do I know that name?'

'It's a company of some renown. It has real estate investments across Europe and the Middle East. Asia as well... It happens to be the largest builder of reclaimed islands in the world: luxury islands off the coast of Dubai, offshore airports in China...'

I remembered where I'd heard the name now. As part of a chain of linked companies: Cyclamen was one of the owners of the submarine-nightclub Blip.

'So... help me make the connection between this company

and the Ukrainian woman who was assaulted,' I said.

'We were researching the idea of a documentary about Cyclamen at the time. It sounded interesting, in a world of climate change and rising sea levels,' he explained. 'Global warming had been a theme at film festivals recently, so I saw funding possibilities, and set about researching it. Via my film company.'

Ah yes, his wonderful world of film investments. I frowned. 'I'm still not making the connection with the Royal Hotel.'

'Cyclamen *owns* the Royal Hotel,' Sergei said. 'The company is run by a group of people who include a sheikh named Yasan.'

*Bingo.* It was the name of the man we'd come to suspect of the attack: Sheikh Yasan. Ah, the small world of central Amsterdam...

'We had an appointment to see him, the day after that incident at the hotel.'

'*We?*'

'A producer of mine. A Belarusian lady, as it happens. She's very good...'

'I'd like to get her name and details, if I may. But first, tell me what happened.'

Sergei thought for a moment. 'She went to the hotel, and Yasan wasn't available after all. It didn't surprise me – she was lucky that a guy of his heft had agreed to meet her in the first place, although you can never underestimate people's desire to talk about themselves...'

'So Yasan backs out of this meeting with your producer... then what?'

'She sensed a – how do you say? – *kerfuffle* at the hotel, and started asking around on the quiet about what had taken place.'

'Go on.'

'Someone spoke out from inside the hotel.'

'Who?'

'I don't know, exactly.'

'Don't know or can't remember?'

'Both.' Sergei shrugged his bulky shoulders. 'Maybe Nadia remembers. We talked about it at the time.'

I wondered how this had then come up in conversation with my wife. The unavoidable conclusion was that Nadia and Petra discussed a good deal more than I ever knew about.

But I was losing focus; I needed to know who had booked the escort. Who had paid for her?

I reached for my notepad. 'What's the name of this producer?'

'She's gone.'

I looked up. 'Gone where?'

'Back to Belarus.'

I stared at Sergei, sensing what he was about to say before the words left his lips.

'She's left the country for good, unfortunately. Gone home.'

I knew her file wouldn't be accessible to me, either.

The list was growing.

Rem Lottman, who'd vanished overseas.

Heinrich Karremans, dead.

Was a net of some kind tightening around the collateral damage of Joost's ill deeds?

'Henk,' Sergei was saying. He pulled at the knees of his linen trousers as he leaned forward. 'Let me help you.'

Or was I seeing paranoid patterns where none existed – again? Without doubt, I needed to visit Sonia Brinkerhof, the police psychologist.

'What are you trying to find out?' Sergei asked.

My focus returned to his steady eyes. Maybe he *could* help. Maybe he had contacts, or could give me an angle on the favours-for-energy scheme. Yes, he had connections. Yet it was madness to share any of this with him. I was clutching at straws…

'Please, tell me,' he said.

'Can you get hold of this Belarusian producer? I'd like to speak with her.'

'I can try,' Sergei replied. 'Eva's still on email, maybe reachable by phone.'

'Good. Did anything else happen with the project in Eva's absence?'

'No, I tried to involve another producer, but it didn't go anywhere.' He shrugged. 'Many film projects start then stop.'

'Okey dokey,' I said, trying hard to sound relaxed. I stood up.

Sergei stood as well. 'Actually, this has turned out to be a fortunate coincidence.'

'What has?'

'You coming here today.'

'Why?'

What had he been holding back?

'Nadia and I have been together now for many months and, well…' He faltered. 'I believe in your country it is customary…'

*Oh no.*

'… to ask the father, before requesting the daughter's hand.' He gave an awkward smile. 'In marriage, of course.'

My gaze shifted to the view across IJmeer – the barges reduced to matchsticks on its glimmering surface. I tried my best to compose my thoughts, but no words arrived. What could I say?

'I really should put a diamond on that ring finger of hers, instead of the middle one.' He laughed nervously.

I looked down at my feet, and the sea of plush carpet surrounding my boots.

'Look Sergei,' I finally said, 'I'm behind whatever my daughter wants – whatever makes her happy.'

'Can I take that as your consent?'

'You can take it as a suggestion to ask her direct. It's her decision.'

'OK…'

There was another awkward pause.

'I know Petra would welcome you to the family as well,' I added.

By 'as well', I let him infer *Petra as well as me*, as opposed to *Petra as well as Nadia*. It was the best I could do.

He nodded solemnly. 'Thank you, Henk.'

*

Outside, I exhaled sharply. What had just happened? Had I really given my approval for my only daughter to marry a Russian guy I barely knew? My phone started buzzing; I welcomed the interruption.

'Henk?'

It was Tommy Franks.

'Something's come up,' he said. 'Are you free to return to London?'

'I'm sorry?'

He asked the question again.

'Erm, mind telling me what it's about?'

'Hold on.'

There was a muffling sound – he was taking his leave of a meeting or some such. Then, in a lower voice: 'I finally managed to get access to some of the Karremans case information.'

'How?'

'Never you mind.' It sounded like he was walking briskly.

'What case information, then?'

'That afternoon, before he died, he went to a place off Park Lane.'

I knew it to be one of London's more salubrious districts.

'And?'

'There's a venue there called The Silver Key. Does that name mean anything to you?'

It did: I'd noted the same name on the plaque outside 840 Keizersgracht, the merchant's house opposite the Royal Hotel

– the place I'd seen Frank Hals visiting shortly before our final encounter.

'What exactly does this Silver Key do?' I asked.

'Dunno, but it was mentioned on Night Market before the site was taken down. I think they offer events across all those countries.'

'Which countries?'

'Come on, Henk, you were in Driebergen. Holland, Belgium, the UK… Further afield no doubt.'

'Jesus.'

'Come back to London. Let's take a closer look.'

# 29

## THE SILVER KEY

I'D DECIDED TO STAY at the Maritime House hotel during my overnight trip to London. For just one night, I could afford to push the boat out.

I was sitting at the bar beneath the grey model submarine, my back to the Thames. We cops like to have a sight line towards the entrance to a venue.

It was lunchtime, and I was consulting a map of the London Underground, working out which would be the right stop for meeting Tommy Franks near Park Lane that afternoon.

Suddenly, a woman's scent arrived from the bar stool beside me.

I didn't look up.

Her arrival wouldn't have been remarkable but for the fact that there had been several empty stools either side of me.

She asked the barman for a cranberry juice. Her voice carried a hint of Russian, or it could have been a Baltic state; either way, the barman obliged and her drink arrived fast.

Green Park, I determined, putting my smartphone down.

'Are you here on business?' she asked.

I turned to her. She had light, almond-shaped eyes, and some amount of rouge on the planes of her cheeks; she was dressed in muted browns, but the soft garments did nothing to disguise her figure. At one time, I might have been flattered to imagine that she was drawn to my own physique. Being tall had been helpful that way.

'And you?' I replied. 'Are *you* here on business?'

She gave the briefest of smiles, then clamped her red lips back around the straw in her glass.

The level of the cranberry juice didn't drop. I got the sense that her drink was intended to last a while.

She stood up, smoothing down her skirt. 'In case you are lonely later,' she said, sliding a discreet, matte-black business card beside my wrist.

I looked around self-consciously, but the male eyes were on her rather than me, following her to the other side of the bar. She sat down there alone. She'd taken her drink with her.

'Another Americano?' the barman asked. His name was Francisco and he was from Bilbao, I'd learned when ordering earlier. He would have caught it all.

I widened my eyes briefly to acknowledge what had just taken place. 'I should probably take my leave.'

Turning the card over revealed that she went by the name 'Kamilla'. It was embossed in a silver, cursive script. There was just a phone number beneath.

I glanced across the bar at her, but her attention was already on someone else.

'I didn't take this hotel to be the kind of place where that stuff goes on,' I said to Francisco.

'You'd be surprised,' he remarked, leaning over the bar. 'It happens at all the best hotels across London.'

'No one minds?'

'What's there to mind?' He glanced at the card. 'A beautiful woman just gave you her phone number.' He laughed, then shook his head. 'She probably earns more in an hour than I make in a week, tips included.'

'Her tips, or yours?'

He gave a snort of a laugh, but his eyes were maudlin.

I didn't give him time to dwell on it. 'A guy I knew stayed here a few weeks ago, did you come across him by any chance?'

I pulled a photo of Heinrich Karremans from my inside pocket. Francisco tried to make sense of the image, the context; the photo had clearly been clipped from a magazine. 'I don't recall,' he said.

'Take a closer look,' I insisted.

It didn't help.

'Maybe you should ask her.' He nodded in Kamilla's direction and went to serve another patron.

'Maybe I will,' I said, putting her card in my pocket, and Karremans's photo with it.

I left a ten-pound note for the coffee and a tip and then went off to meet Tommy Franks.

*

Taking the Jubilee line from Southwark to Green Park brought me out in another world altogether. To my right was the Ritz Hotel. Opposite lay a district known as Mayfair; Park Lane bordered it to the west.

I had never seen so many Bentleys and Rolls Royces before in one place. It was as if the two car marques had sponsored the street. The rear windows of the vehicles were invariably tinted, perhaps to keep the hoi polloi like me guessing as to their owners' identities.

It took me back to a favour Rem Lottman had asked me to do, chaperoning a Ghanaian diplomat from Antwerp to Amsterdam. The diplomat and I had made the journey together in the back of a diplomatic Bentley.

As I waited, I wondered what had become of Mr Lesoto. Hadn't he been looking for a European child bride at one point?

Franks arrived on foot, a newspaper folded under his arm. He made strong eye contact as he shook my hand.

'I hope I haven't wasted your time here,' he said as we crossed the busy street, navigating our way between glamorous bumpers and grilles.

'What d'you mean?' I asked, quickening my pace to keep up. We headed up a dark side street into Mayfair.

'There's something off about this place.' He was referring to The Silver Key, apparently. 'My enquiries so far have pretty much come to naught.'

'Glad I'm here to help, then.'

We passed a sign for Shepherd Market; the area was a curious mix of opulence and the quotidian – sandwich bars, dry cleaners… even a sign pointing up some dingy steps, promising 'foxy models'.

'Where are we?' I said.

'A place in transition. Old tenants moving out – new wealth moving in. It's the most valuable real estate in the world these days. There's a few tales I could tell you about this neck of the woods, a few old slappers you probably shouldn't know about, but another time… the address we're heading to is just round the corner. Where are you staying, by the way?'

'Maritime House.'

His eyes slid suspiciously my way.

'I got to know it while here last time. It's only three stations away on the Underground.'

He seemed to accept this explanation.

'How far are we freelancing here?' I asked.

'Say again?'

I rephrased my question: 'Where's the official enquiry into Karremans's death got to? Are they aware of our field trip this afternoon?'

Franks shrugged. 'The Met now embraces the principle of flexible policing practices. I would have thought that you, of all people, could relate to that.'

I caught the acidic tone of his comment, and wondered

whether staying at Maritime House was a problem after all.

As we rounded the corner I saw the venue. It was a grand corner property: brick with gothic stone features, notably an ornate entrance way. The windows either side were dark and gloomy.

Most of the neighbouring properties were wrapped in scaffolding. The sound that the wind made on the plastic wrapping had always reminded me of sails at sea, but this location couldn't have felt more different; there was no sense of movement here. A curiously inert feeling pervaded the vicinity, as though it were a neighbourhood waiting to be lived in once more.

'For one thing,' Franks said, pausing on the opposite side of the street, 'the sign's vanished.'

'What sign?'

'When I visited last time, there was a sign saying *The Silver Key*. Beside the front door.'

It had been the same in Amsterdam, at 840 Keizersgracht. When I'd returned the next day, the sign had disappeared.

I told Franks as much.

'How did you get to know about that address?' he asked.

'A colleague found out about it by digging up a complaint against a guy called Westerling. This guy has reaped a fortune from the redevelopment of Amsterdam's docklands. Anyway, a young girl made the complaint, and the address given for the incident was the same one as The Silver Key's.'

'What became of the complaint?'

'Nothing, though Westerling has been inside for other offences, including fraud and tax evasion.'

'Not quite the same severity of offence now, is it?'

I felt the force of Franks's ire, and wondered about it. I'd seen how badly wrong things could go: the other team members in Driebergen... the ones who'd been abused at a Belgian boys' home...

The ones who'd been shot by Franks.

What exactly was his backstory?

'So how did you learn of *this* address?' I asked, my gaze roving the moribund-looking building. 'You mentioned some reference to it on Night Market. What was that, if you don't mind me asking?'

Franks tapped the side of his nose with a forefinger. *Need-to-know basis*, the gesture said.

*Bastard.*

'Let's go knock on the front door, shall we?' he said.

'What's our cover?' I asked tersely.

'Buildings Inspectorate.'

'Should we at least take a moment to get our stories straight?'

'I'll do the talking,' he said, striding across the street.

His ring of the doorbell brought no response. He looked away, grimaced, then rapped on the door with his knuckles.

'How did you know he was here?' I asked in a low voice.

'Who?'

'Karremans, of course. Was it via the Night Market site as well?'

Maybe the bell hadn't been working, as the door now opened. The man who appeared was all muscle and at least two metres tall, his shoulders and biceps straining his well-tailored suit. We were standing on the steps below, and he towered over us.

Behind him was gloomy hallway.

'Yes?' he said.

Franks flashed his badge, quickly. 'We're here from Westminster Council Buildings Inspectorate. Just making sure everything's OK.' He nodded at a scaffolding truck down the street. 'There've been some complaints about noise, and also some safety issues.'

The man stared for a long moment. 'Then talk to the owners.'

'I'm talking to you,' Franks said.

'And I'm telling you: talk to the owners.'

The door closed at a leisurely pace.

Franks stood for a moment before stalking away a few steps. I could see the man's eyes through the window.

'Well, that went well,' I told Franks.

'What nationality would you say he was?'

'Hard to say,' I replied. 'Why don't you get that warrant?'

Franks ignored my question. 'It's like entering a foreign fucking country here. Most of this area's owned by the Arabs.'

'Really?'

'They even call it the Qatari Quarter.'

It gave me an idea. 'Maybe I know another address we could call on which is relevant.'

'What address?' he said. 'Where?' We were walking briskly back towards Green Park Underground station.

'On Knightsbridge.'

It was the site of Cyclamen's European office – I'd tracked it down before coming here.

'What's there?' Franks asked impatiently. 'Come on, Henk.'

I stopped, causing him to do the same, and tapped my forefinger to my nose.

'Let me make some calls.'

He glared at me. For a moment I thought he might take a swing, but instead he asked, 'What are you doing this evening? Would you like to get a drink or three?'

'I need to make those calls. I left some people in the lurch back in Holland by making this trip.' My wife, for one.

Franks grimaced.

'By the way,' I said, 'is there a place to withdraw cash around here?'

'Plenty.' He nodded along the busy street. 'Call me,' he said. 'Doesn't matter how late.' He strode off, saying over his shoulder, 'Don't be a stranger now, Henk.'

'Nor you,' I said. 'Get that warrant!'

\*

Back at the hotel, I rang the number on the card in my pocket. The call connected to Kamilla's husky voicemail message.

I thought about phoning my wife, but noticed that I'd missed a call from Sergei while dialling the escort.

I called him back and he picked up.

'You just tried to reach me?'

'Yes, about Eva,' he said.

'Who's Eva?'

'The producer in Belarus.'

'Ah. Any luck?'

'Afraid not. She hasn't replied to my email, and the number I had for her is no longer in service.'

'Hmm. Does that strike you as odd?'

He hesitated. 'Not really. She probably just got a new phone in her home country.'

'Could you keep trying?'

'Of course,' Sergei said. 'We're family now.'

I winced as I switched on the TV and found a European news channel.

'Thanks. I have to go,' I said, ending the call.

I fished a miniature Scotch from the minibar. Then I took a long hot shower, raking my fingers over my scalp, convinced that the enquiry into the events at the Royal Hotel via Sergei wouldn't come to anything anyway. When I finally turned off the water, my phone was buzzing.

It was an unidentified UK number.

'Hello?' I said, dripping wet.

'You called earlier?' came the husky voice.

'Kamilla?'

'And you are?'

'The tall man at the bar earlier. You gave me your card.'

255

Her voice betrayed no recollection as she said, 'You would like to make an appointment?'

'Yes, it needs to be tonight, though, as I leave London tomorrow. Actually, now is good.'

She made a show of sounding busy.

I said, 'What kind of gift could I offer you for your time?'

'Are we talking about dinner, a show?'

'None of that. Just my hotel room.'

'How much time do you want?'

'The minimum.'

'The minimum is one hour.'

'Let's do that then. How soon can you get here?'

'Don't you want to know how much the amount is?'

'Of the gift? Not really. Not now, anyway.' I'd withdrawn plenty of cash. 'We can talk about it when you arrive.'

I could hear a hint of unease in her voice. 'You will need to meet me in the bar. I cannot come to your room without a key card.'

Was it to check me out again – to make sure I was safe before venturing up to my room?

'Let's just meet in the lobby, then,' I said.

She hesitated. 'I could be there by nine o'clock.'

'Done.'

As I got dressed again, I considered calling my wife. I found myself fighting a guilty feeling – but what did I have to feel bad about? There was nothing wrong with what I was doing.

I ended up lying on the bed, watching the news.

*

At 8.56 p.m., I went down to the lobby. She arrived at nine precisely. There was no hip sway, no flashing smile. *This is strictly business*, her demeanour said. Yet her attire did nothing to hide her legs: her coat ended mid-thigh, her dress went no lower. She wore high heels with bright-red soles, matching her lipstick.

The receptionists were busy checking in other guests. I escorted her past them, quickly, to the lifts.

There were two problems with my plan.

One was an awakening sensation in my lower body, which I needed to control. I hadn't been up close with a woman this young and attractive in some time. Inside the lift, her subtle perfume lent a growing sense of expectation, like the prospect of unwrapping a Christmas present.

The second issue was that she appeared to be acting independently, as opposed to via an agency. This would limit the amount of information I could expect from her, I now saw.

I opened the door to my room and she followed me in, checking it out.

'Drink?'

'Not while I'm working,' she replied, setting her slim clutch bag at the foot of the bed. She slid her coat off and lay it alongside. Her black dress was so flimsy she may as well have not bothered with it.

'I'll be back soon,' she promised, picking up her bag again as she entered the bathroom. The light and fan clicked on and the door closed behind her.

I blew air out sharply between my lips and fixed myself another Scotch. Then I found my wallet. The TV flickered away silently.

When the bathroom door opened again, she was wearing just black underwear. She turned off the light behind her and leaned against the doorframe.

'How much is it?' I asked.

'Six hundred.' She took a coquettish step towards me. 'Still dressed?' she said. 'Do you want to just watch me?'

'I can think of a couple of things. But I'm not sure whether you're into either.'

Her eyes narrowed. 'What things?'

'Erotic asphyxiation.'

I brought my hand to my throat to demonstrate.

She stiffened. 'I do not know about this service.'

I threw two fifty-pound notes down on the bed, choosing my words carefully.

'Are you aware of anyone who does?'

'Why are you asking me?'

I took a step towards her. 'Do you know any girls – or boys – who offer that service in this hotel?' I waved the rest of the money at her.

'Who are you?'

'Just someone looking for information.'

We stood for a second as she processed things.

'Here,' I said. 'Take a look at this man.'

I showed her the picture of Karremans.

Her eyes narrowed. 'Are you police?'

'Yes, but not on duty. And not from around here.'

She looked at me intently, then bit down on her lip. Reprising her seductive attitude?

I lay several more fifties down on the bed. As she bent over to scoop them into her bag, I was engulfed by a yearning for her young body.

She removed a small scent bottle from the bag.

I brought up a warning hand. 'I'd prefer if you didn't spray that in here. I don't want anyone to smell –'

Her outstretched arm swivelled. Instinctively I made to grab her wrist, in a judo move, but it was too late. My face was already wet with perfume mist.

Only it wasn't perfume.

My hands stopped grabbing, instead palming my eyeballs. There was a burning sensation, and a rushing sound in my head – the sound of panic, all my senses on extra-high alert. The door to the room was opening; it was the movement of air that told me so.

A large man. Had she made a call to him from the bathroom?

As my hands fought to restore my vision, my thoughts reeled. Why had she picked *me* at the bar earlier?

Another movement in the air told me the door was closing again behind the man. I couldn't let that happen.

My life was turning upside down like in a high-speed vehicle accident. I ran at the door – at him – and there was a deep thump as something collided with my right shoulder. It could have been a wall I'd run into.

The room swam above me.

With the distorted shapes came hurried voices, then something shattered against my head.

Stars exploded.

Head fuzzy, I rose onto all fours and roared like a cornered bull. A madness descended on me as I stumbled upright and threw a wild punch. My fist connected with something that crunched. My knuckles felt wet from the impact – cut by glass?

A light extinguished – the blue light of the TV – with a fizzing electronic sound. The hurried voices and figures started fading. Everything was darkening.

Where the hell were events taking me now?

# 30

## THEN AND NOW

*A year before…*

*My wife and I swayed along Entrepotdok in the darkness, arms loosely round each other. It had been many months since the events surrounding the drowning of Jan Tözsér at the harbour, yet I still glanced warily at the houseboat whenever I approached it.*

*The night Jan Tözsér drowned, he'd tried to break into our home and leave an incendiary device, threatening to burn us to death in our sleep. Jan's older brother Zsolt was still very much alive, as a protected police informant.*

*Petra and I stopped at the mouth of the gangplank.*

*I was lost for a second, pondering. Sometimes the questions haunted me at night, the dark squiggles of my vision forming flames.*

*'Where's your key?' my wife prompted. Her eyes were wide and unguarded from the alcohol.*

*I stooped to kiss her.*

*She pushed me away, playfully, in the centre of the chest. 'I need to pee. The key!'*

*'Erm, yes.'*

*I patted one pocket then another, and found it. We began to walk across. The planks sprung with our steps. 'Steady as she goes.'*

*Petra indulged my weak humour with a chortle.*

*'Hey,' I said, on a roll. 'What's orange and sounds like a carrot?'*

*'A parrot?' she replied, not missing a beat.*

*Which was when I saw it. A reflective metal object, placed at the foot of the door, glinting. Thankfully Petra hadn't noticed it — we'd had a few. My heart beat hard as I nudged it aside, away from the door, with the toe of my boot.*

*I let us in, and found a reason to return on my own, taking the rubbish out.*

*'Leave it till tomorrow!' cried Petra.*

*'It's beginning to rot.'*

*Something was indeed starting to smell — something to do with the older Tőzsér brother. I tore off a piece of black plastic sacking and used it to pick up the weapon by its handle. I inspected it, crouching: it was a FÉG PA-63 semi-automatic pistol. The PA-63 model had been standard issue for the Hungarian military and police forces at one time, and they still turned up on the black market.*

*But not often. They were no longer made.*

*Its distinctiveness is due to its two-tone frame. The slide, grips, trigger and hammer assembly are black. The rest has a reflective polish. Which was unusual, for military-issue weapons. The reason for the design was the relative cheapness and quick build-time.*

*The clip was empty.*

*I stood up, dizzily, looking around.*

*My old army friend Johan arrived not twenty minutes later by motorbike. Petra had gone to bed. We greeted one another and walked away from the boat, along Entrepotdok. I was checking the dark windows of the packing houses as we went. Finally, I stopped and withdrew the weapon from the inside of my jacket, unwrapping it from the shiny black plastic.*

*The FÉG shone like molten metal in the orange light of the sodium lamps. Quickly, I slipped it back inside my jacket.*

*Johan confirmed my fears: 'Hungarian, like the Tőzsérs. It's a grudge sign, Henk.'*

*'I know.' My heart thumped. 'Zsolt must have found out about the way his brother drowned.'*

*Johan and I had talked often enough about the events in the harbour that night.*

*He glanced around, checking for observers. 'Maybe we should go somewhere else,' he said.*

*I shook my head. 'I'm not leaving Petra alone on that boat.'*

*A cat arched its back on the cabin of the neighbouring vessel.*

*'Why this, now?' I said. 'Why not just kill me, if he wants revenge?'*

*Johan considered it. 'Because he wants you to suffer. The way his brother did. Drowning's not a good way to go.'*

*'I don't imagine it is. But I didn't drown Jan. I just didn't stop him from drowning.'*

*'I'm not sure Zsolt Tőzsér sees that distinction. You were the one who collided with his brother on your bike – the one who caused him to set fire to himself with that incendiary device he was carrying.'*

*I raised my eyebrows high with incredulity.*

*'That's how Zsolt will be looking at it,' Johan clarified.*

*'Then maybe we need to help him see the light. I can't go on this way, Johan. I'll go mad first.'*

*My friend swallowed hard, his Adam's apple bobbing in orange relief.*

\*

I stirred from the depths of unconsciousness. The white ceiling of the hotel room swam. A man's face was upside down, eyes wide. His mouth moved rhythmically, repeating the word 'Sir!'

His voice echoed distantly. I became aware of little shocks down the side of my face and realised he was slapping my cheek. The bang to my head must really have done something to my mental circuits, as I only remembered the escort and a man arriving. Then what?

I noticed the TV had toppled off its table.

As I pressed my palm into the carpet to push myself up, I felt glass fragments. There was a dent in the wall.

'What the hell happened?'

Some part of my brain had already worked out the need to feign extra confusion. But I didn't have to try hard.

'Another guest reported your cries, sir.' His voice was clear now. 'I'm Mr Sullivan, of hotel security.' He looked deeply concerned. 'Are you all right? Do you need a doctor? It looks like you have a nasty bang to your head. And your hand is bleeding.'

I stared at my hand. It was trembling. The knuckles were clotted with blood; glass fragments glinted.

'I'm OK,' I said, gathering myself. Mr Sullivan helped me to my feet.

'Were you attacked?' he asked.

'No.'

There appeared to be no evidence of the escort's visit, thank God. There was nothing left on the bed. No money.

'We need to determine whether to call the police, sir.'

It felt like the wrong moment to mention that I *was* the police.

'The guest who reported your cries also reported two people leaving, hurrying away down the corridor.'

'I don't remember anything about that.'

'We'll check the CCTV.'

That might show the escort arriving.

'Look, this is rather embarrassing, but sometimes I have these episodes...'

What about the bathroom? She'd disrobed there. Had she left any clothes behind in their haste to leave?

'I must remember to take my medicine,' I continued, stumbling towards the bathroom door, the blood starting to pump through my limbs.

I could still smell the perfume, which wasn't perfume. What the hell was it?

I fell back down, and out.

*

*'We had a deal,' I challenged Alderman Rem Lottman, the man ultimately in control of events. We were sitting in the 1e Klas restaurant in Amsterdam*

*Centraal station. Before long, Lottman would be gone. He was due to board a Thalys high-speed train to Brussels, where a new role in European energy and social policy awaited him.*

*I needed his help and protection more than ever, but I had only five minutes of his time, at best.*

'We still have *a deal,' Lottman corrected me, warning: 'You are not to use that recording you made. Neither you nor your wife.'*

*The recording he was referring to was of Joost, my immediate boss, describing Eastern European car thieves and trafficked prostitutes as 'thieves and whores'. Joost also stated in the recording that Jan Six – the former Amsterdam police commissioner – had supported him in the matter.*

*Lottman had played a key role in getting all these men appointed.*

*He said, 'I know how tricky those digital recordings can be – how easily they can spread around the place, once shared – like infectious diseases.' His dark eyes bored into me over the rim of his coffee cup, as he took a slow sip. 'I need to be assured of your silence on this matter, Henk.'*

*I looked around the restaurant. Parquet wooden floors, high ceilings – tall windows giving onto the frenetic tram activity in front of the station. The colours and light and bustle should have made the restaurant feel warm, friendly. To the other travellers, seated at their widely spaced tables, perhaps it did. For me, the whole scene had taken on a ghastly, gasoline-like, aquamarine hue. The harsh light flooded in. It may have been the lack of sleep, or anxiety – it may equally have been the memories of my father, and of parting ways with him in similar circumstances... Lottman had always borne a certain resemblance.*

*'I don't understand what the problem is,' he was saying, reaching into a pocket of his tent-like jacket.*

*I leaned in, jabbing the wooden table with my trembling forefinger. 'Zsolt Tözsér left a gun – a FÉGARMY PA-63 – at the door to my houseboat.'*

*'Do you know that for sure?' he asked, scattering coins on the table.*

*'It's not just the gun. My wife and daughter have both, separately, been receiving –'*

*'Henk,' he interrupted, bracing his hands against the table, ready to push himself up. 'Joost can help you with this.'*

*'Joost,' I said, seething, 'is the source of this!'*

*'Then talk to Jan Six.'*

*'Why?' I asked with incredulity. 'Jan Six is no longer Joost's boss. You've removed Six from the field of play!'*

*'Was on his watch. He still knows the players involved.'* Lottman *changed tack: 'Look, I can't help the fact that you didn't save that man in the harbour.'*

*'The man in the harbour was scum!' I hissed. 'A pimp – a trafficker!'*

*He tutted softly. 'Now now, this isn't going to get you very far, is it?' One hand retreated back into his tent of a jacket and re-emerged with his phone. 'A couple of things to note for next time, Henk. First, you don't need a separate device to do digital recordings these days – an iPhone will do.' He tapped the screen. 'Second, talking about refusing to save men because they're "scum" rather equals those indelicate remarks that Joost made about our Eastern European neighbours in the first place, wouldn't you say?'*

*Aquamarine roiled my vision. I rubbed my eyes vigorously. By the time I tried to focus again, he'd gone.*

\*

'Henk! Henk!' This time, the slap to my cheek was hard.

Tommy Franks looked livid.

'What's going on?' I said, coming to.

'You tell me!' He turned to the hotel security man, saying, 'Give us a moment.'

The security man did.

This time, there was nothing feigned about my confusion.

'Henk, what the fuck are you doing?'

I wanted to ask him the same question. Why was he here?

'We need to get you out of this hotel, fast.'

'We need to visit that suite.'

'What suite?' he shot.

'The one Karremans was staying in.'

'Why? No, Henk –'

'I'm willing to bet you'll find evidence of a struggle. Scratch marks on the wall or something…'

'*No!*'

'Check with the coroner, too. Anaesthetic delivered via an atomiser, a respiratory device –'

Stars exploded, my head thumping back down onto the floor – the shock of him striking me…

I went for his throat, and for a moment we were wrestling, panting hard, the carpet burning my knees and elbows.

'Everything OK in there?' the security man called.

'Listen to me, Henk,' Franks gasped. He was on top of me, tie askew. 'We need to get you out of here.'

'It's the same pattern. You need to find an escort called Kamilla. I have her card somewhere –'

'This isn't going the way I expected, working with you. It's not going the way I expected at all.'

I had the sense of a relapse on Tommy's part. 'You're starting to sound like them,' I said.

He screwed up his face. '*Who?*'

'Who are you, Tommy – or Tim, is it? I've lost track now.'

He glared down at me.

'I knew I was here for a reason…' I persisted.

'You'd better get the fuck out of here and back to Amsterdam. Fast. Before the diplomatic plods get involved…'

# 31

## 'SIX-SHOOTER'

*JAN SIX CAME TO see me in the end. I was walking to work, when suddenly he was alongside me.*

*I'd hardly slept a wink in weeks.*

*'Let's chat, Henk,' he said genially. He was known for that trait, but I caught a trace of pity beneath. Or was it menace?*

*I knew right then that he wouldn't help me. In his world, the strong only help the strong.*

*'There's a bar not far from here where we won't be disturbed.'*

*He took me to the karaoke bar where cops at our station celebrated good news; he was wearing the same black flowing overcoat as the last time I'd seen him there, when my colleague Liesbeth had got engaged, and when – it turned out – a major vehicle-smuggling ring had been dismantled using none other than the Hungarian informant, Zsolt Tőzsér.*

*Was the choice of bar a coincidence?*

*It was early in the day and the place was dark and empty, reeking of stale beer. Six was more red-faced than usual – like he was going to seed. His rustic features looked rougher in the sharp beam of the light behind the bar. He reminded me of an old gunslinger well past his best, his aim gone. Doubtless he was thinking the same about me.*

*'Operation Boost,' I said, acknowledging the other cause of that celebration, the last time we were here together.*

*'Good times.'*

*The owner came over. Six ordered coffee and I did the same. Then he ordered a jenever. 'You too?'*

'*Why not?*' I replied.

*We were alone once more.*

'*The alderman asked me to talk to you.*'

*So Lottman had been good to his word — whatever good that might achieve.*

'*Therefore I will,*' he added.

*Suddenly he looked furious, like some dam had burst inside. For a moment, he just glared at me — blaming me for him being out? Joost had replaced him, of course.*

*I drew back as the drinks arrived. Six waited again to continue, finally waving the owner away.*

'*We can try to protect you, Henk.*'

*He was still referring to the police as 'we'… So had they kept him on, after all? In some clandestine role, perhaps?*

'*What we can't do is end operations already underway.*'

'*You're still using Zsolt Tözsér?*'

*Six downed his jenever.*

*I did likewise as he leaned in. The fumes leaked from his mouth.* '*Vehicle theft, stolen art, diamonds. High-end prostitution. Paedophilia.*' *He listed off the types of offence that Tözsér was involved in.* '*Yes, Henk, we're still using him. He's a protected species. I couldn't cut him off if I wanted to.*'

*I meditated on his words.* '*You know, I'm sure I saw you two together, once,*' *I said.* '*At the Conservatorium.*'

*It was one of Amsterdam's finest hotels.*

'*Oh?*' *he breathed.*

'*It looked cosy.*'

*He was seething.*

*I said,* '*No doubt you're going to tell me that six hundred known criminals account for sixty per cent of the crime in this city, or some such. Well, are you, Six? Because I've heard it once too often.*'

*Only by me becoming strong would the strong help me.*

*He slurped his coffee. The speed of him regaining his composure showed either impressive self-control or a degree of bipolarity.*

*Both, possibly.*

'*Actually, it was something else I was about to quote. A saying from my old AIVD days.*'

*Vaguely I recalled something about this – about Six having started off in the secret service.*

'*If there's no man, there's no problem.*'

*I doubted he was referring to Zsolt.*

'*We had some dark humour back then.*' *He chuckled, then shook his head.* '*I think it was Uncle Joseph who first said that.*'

'*Stalin sounds about right,*' *I agreed.*

'*Well, it's good to see you've kept your sense of history, and perspective… if not exactly your sense of humour,*' *he said, getting up.*

*His smile was all bonhomie once more.* '*So long, Henk.*'

*It was the last time I'd see him, before he retired to a place near The Hague. Not far from where he'd started out, then, with the AIVD…*

*

Exiting the plane from London, my phone lit up with notifications. I strode through the long corridors of Schiphol airport, scrolling down.

There were two missed calls from an unidentified number. A return message from Sonia Brinkerhof, the police psychologist whom I'd promised I'd see. Though Sonia had a busy schedule over the coming days, she could fit me in today. I checked my watch, then thumbed a text to her to secure the time slot offered. Next, I listened to Petra's voicemail.

I immediately called her back.

'What's up?' I said when she picked up.

'Where are you?'

'Just landed at Schiphol. What's wrong?'

'Nothing. Well, this guy came to the boat early this morning.'

'You mentioned. Who?'

'*Someone* got out of bed the wrong side today…'

'Not me.' I hadn't been to bed at all – courtesy of Kamilla…

'He didn't identify himself,' she said.

I shifted my shoulder bag to my usual arm, my right, then winced at the bruise there. A groan escaped me.

'Are you all right?'

'Hopefully. What did he look like?'

'Well-dressed. He seemed official.'

'Official? How so?'

'He had an air of authority about him.'

'OK,' I said. 'So what did he say?'

'He asked if you were here. When I said you weren't, he promised that he'd be in contact.'

'Did you say I was in London?'

'I just said you were away.'

'OK…' I breathed a little easier.

I tried to think of whether it could be related to my new role in Internal Investigations – or the trip to London. Franks, conceivably? Someone from the diplomatic service? In which case, why not intercept me at the airport?

'I trust you picked up some English liquorice in London?'

I tried to match her lighter tone: 'I'm going one better – I'm following through on my promise already.'

'Which promise?'

'Seeing Sonia Brinkerhof.'

'I'm impressed. Though I'd expected nothing less, after revealing my source.'

*Yeah, a fat lot of good Sergei did me,* I felt like saying.

But I didn't.

\*

Sonia Brinkerhof saw me in her apartment – the same place she'd interviewed me for the Internal Investigations role a month ago. I drew solace from the knowledge that she'd gone on to endorse my candidacy for the *Rijksrecherche.*

'Please,' she gestured, glancing at the plasters on my knuckles as she showed me through to her stately living room.

I sat down on the worn leather sofa. 'We're meeting in a purely personal capacity, correct?' I'd called ahead to go over the terms and conditions, yet still felt the need to confirm this. 'Our meeting has nothing to do with my new police role?'

'You don't need to say that. I'm first and foremost a family psychologist, not an informant.'

Her remark throbbed with irony.

'So, how do we do this?'

She glanced at a carriage clock on the stone mantelpiece. 'I have to leave at two o'clock, as mentioned.'

'Understood.'

'Why don't you start by describing in your own words what it is you want to resolve?'

'OK,' I said, crossing my legs protectively, and considering where to begin. 'I've been having some flashbacks lately. It's to do with... an incident, which occurred a year or so ago. A series of incidents, in fact. They...'

How to describe them, without implicating Johan? Could I tell her that someone I knew killed a man – and that I'd witnessed part of the incident but couldn't remember how it happened?

That was the truth of it.

She waited, pen in hand.

'I guess what I'm trying to say is, things built to a head, and at the crucial moment, I don't remember what took place.'

She made a brief note. 'You think that you're suffering from a memory blockage, in other words?'

'Yes. Only I wasn't knocked out or anything like that. It wasn't... that. It's just, for some reason, I don't seem able to recall events as well as I'd like to.' I corrected myself: 'As well as I *need* to.'

'And this is causing you problems, in the present?'

I gave a cathartic exhalation. 'Yes, in ways I don't even understand. It's like this hole inside.' I grasped at my chest. 'A missing part of me...'

A shudder, from the depths of me. Sonia reached for a box of tissues, but I waved them away.

'It's affecting my relations with my wife... and my daughter, and her fiancé...'

Perhaps she remembered me describing my family in our prior interview, as she said, more softly now, 'Do you want to tell me what you *do* remember?'

*The flash – illuminating the shell casing flying from the Sig... Johan's outstretched arm moving towards Zsolt's heart... I try to look away, only to hear the second gunshot explode low over the dykes of Waterland, forcing away my gaze further, to the hamlet nearby... A dog barks, distantly.*

How could things have come to that? However hard I tried, I just couldn't remember...

'Could we try this a different way?' I said. 'Could you explain the different options for recalling something like this from the past?'

'Generally, in these sessions, it's me who asks the questions,' she replied. 'But, OK, since we're short on time – the good news is that this event is in the relatively recent past. The bad news is that, depending on the extent of the trauma involved – and it seems clear that trauma *is* involved – that may be irrelevant.'

'How so?'

'All of our memories are theoretically available to us, from our earliest age. All are theoretically there in our subconscious. The conscious "remembering" mind is only a very small part of our mental being.'

I canted my head.

'If it were a trivial memory, the conscious mind might have simply tucked it away, in which case it would only require a relevant prompt or trigger.'

The word choice made me wince.

She caught it, I was sure – she was too damn perceptive. 'If it's something you're ashamed of, or afraid of, then the memory may be misshapen, so that you recall only the memory of an erroneous memory. Or nothing. The hole of which you speak.'

'OK,' I said slowly, uncrossing my legs. 'So –'

'The trick is to bring it to the surface consciously, and *care*fully. The memory is buried for a reason. Uncovering it could entail a very strong psychic release, which might overwhelm you.'

'So…?'

'Three choices – one being mental reconstruction, which you could theoretically do on your own.'

'Without you?'

'Everything here is confidential, up to the point that I have a legal obligation to report something to the police. I'd hate for you to place me in that position.'

'What if it involved a friend?'

'Same difference.'

I recalled a question from the test I'd had to sit for my new role: *Your best friend is driving; you're in the passenger seat. He is careless going around a corner and hits a dog crossing the street. No one sees, and there are no marks on his car. He does not turn himself in – what do you do?*

Sonia had seen my answer – along with those for every other question. She waited for me to nod my understanding before continuing: 'What about your dreams?'

'What about them? I don't remember them either. I wake, damp with sweat, only aware that I've had a nightmare.'

'Not being able to remember your dreams is usually a sign that your conscious mind isn't ready to confront the dream content.' She paused. 'So there are very few options left. This simplifies things. I would suggest hypnotherapy –'

'Being *hypnotised*?'

'Yes, but that's potentially most dangerous of all. I

273

don't practise it myself, and there's no one I could reliably recommend...'

'So what does that leave?'

'Find the trigger. Have you tried talking to your friend? Properly, and carefully?'

# 32

## WITHOLDING

*Driving back from a welcome day trip to Petra's cousin in Delft, I narrowed my eyes in concentration. We would decamp there yet, if I had my way.*

*The eastbound Amsterdam ring road was dark and sticky with rainwater.*

*'What's wrong?' my wife asked again.*

*Joost wasn't returning my calls, but that wasn't the problem – Joost's lack of interest came as no surprise at this point.*

*I couldn't pinpoint the source of this new anxiety…*

*'Fatigue, maybe,' I replied.*

Chronic, *I could have added.*

*She patted my knee and I eyed my watch. I was due to catch up with Johan in an hour's time.*

*'Good thing we're almost home,' she said, withdrawing her hand.*

*'Yes.'*

*Vehicles swished by in the fast lane.*

*'Should we drop in on Nadia?' I asked.*

*Petra turned to me. I glanced across at her features, whitened by the oncoming headlamps. 'Where?' her eyes flashed in the reflected light and dimmed.*

*My gaze returned to the road, carrying with it a white impression of my wife's face. Dimly I saw the vehicle edging past in the left lane, its engine rumbling.*

*'The Kriterion?' I suggested. 'Doesn't she work a late shift on a Sunday? We could stop by and say hello.'*

275

*It was mud-spattered, open and high-sided — like a refuse truck. Come to think of it, I'd seen it before…*

*'Are you worried about her again?'*

*'Not especially.'*

*'Come on, Henk.' I sensed her making a moue. 'I know that look.'*

*'I —'*

*Passing Schiphol, seven kilometres back.*

*'Huh?' she prompted.*

*A windblown dark head appeared over the side of the truck, then a hand…*

*'Jesus!'*

*I swerved, sending Petra's head bobbing left, almost colliding with mine. The object released bounced off the top frame of the windscreen with a metallic bang, the glass quicksilvering.*

*There was no road ahead anymore, only milky light patterns.*

*Petra had her head in her arms. I fumbled for my hazards while braking, hard, hearing a skid, a horn blare. Time stood still as I waited for the bang of a front or rear impact… I slowed and veered right, coming to a juddering halt with a grating sound as we ran into the concrete motorway siding.*

*We were stationary.*

*Short, shallow gasps escaped my mouth. I fought to catch my breath. The hazard lights flared orange across the spider's web of broken glass.*

*'Are you OK?' I turned to my wife.*

*She was sobbing and shaking as I tried to cradle her.*

*Still I kept waiting for the bang.*

*Instead came flickering blue.*

*It was a piece of breeze block that had been hurled our way, the traffic cops eventually determined, after analysing the fragments embedded in the windscreen frame.*

*By the time that determination was made, far worse would have happened.*

\*

276

'Christ, Johan, it's good to see you,' I said, clasping his forearm. I guided him to a candlelit table at the rear of De Druif. 'It's been too long.'

'Yes, it has,' he said.

I caught the accusation in his words.

'Please.' I gestured for him to sit.

I signalled to Gert to bring our usuals, making a pen-stroke gesture to ensure that it went on my tab.

'What's up?' Johan asked.

'I thought it would be good to catch up. It's been too long.'

He nodded thoughtfully. 'I'm hearing something else,' he said. 'Something you need.'

I looked across at the darkening canal outside. There were no boats; the water looked unusually still.

'OK,' I said, arriving at a decision. 'You're right. I keep thinking back to that time' – there was no need to spell out which – 'and what happened.'

'You think I don't?' Johan asked, astonished. His pale eyes were as alert as they were distant. 'Christ. All the times, Henk, that I kept searching for some comfort – that there wouldn't be repercussions, with the police… or worse!'

I banged the table. 'And I gave you everything I could! If there was anything more I could have given you, do you not think I would have? But –'

He sat back and crossed his arms as our beers arrived. I nodded my thanks to Gert, who made to leave again but then turned and said, 'A man was in here earlier, looking for you, Henk.'

'Oh?' I glanced around the bar. 'Who?'

'Didn't say.'

'Well, did he leave a message, or a number?'

'I don't think he wanted to be remembered. But I thought you should know.'

Johan's eyes flickered between Gert and me, and I caught something there, too.

Suspicion? Anxiety?

'I'll be at the bar,' Gert said, leaving us.

'So what is it you want to know?' Johan demanded.

'What happened...'

Something was terribly wrong.

'I shot the man.'

'Yes,' I said, recalling the Hungarian lying submerged in the dyke, like in a watery open coffin. 'But what led up to that event? My memory's... gone.'

'Huh? It's simple. I had the gun, you didn't. You told me to shoot him, in the head and the heart. So I did.'

'But –'

'I take full responsibility for my actions,' Johan was saying, his voice increasingly laced with accusation.

What was he withholding?

'Let go of it,' he concluded, 'as I learned to. The hard way.' He stood up, jostling the table and slopping the beers.

Again I fumbled for the associated memory, my palm wrapped around my hot forehead.

'So long, Henk.'

And with that, he left.

I called Gert over. 'What did this guy earlier look like?'

'Hmm...' he thought. 'It's not so easy to describe people, is it?'

If I had a fifty-euro note for every time a potential witness had trotted that line out, or similar...

'Attire?' I prompted. 'Height?'

'Smartly dressed, organised-looking. But pretty anonymous, too...'

The same man who'd been to the boat earlier, as reported by Petra?

'Oh, there was one thing,' Gert said.

'What?'

'He made strong eye contact. Not sure he meant to. Tough to forget, though.'

*

Who was he?

I was so preoccupied by the question that I missed three calls from Petra – I'd set my phone to silent while in the bar.

The mist was thick on Entrepotdok as I paced the short distance back to our houseboat. Its dark outline looked wrong, bouncing in my field of vision as I lengthened my stride.

The darkness… why no lights on?

I fumbled for my phone. By this time I was running, and the phone fell from my hand. My other hand, slick with sweat, sought haplessly to catch it; the phone flipped and fell, landing beside the water.

Its screen wasn't cracked, mercifully. Rather, it was lit up and vibrating, almost over the edge.

*Petra.*

I grabbed it and answered.

'Henk, thank God! Where've you been?'

'De Druif, with Johan… Didn't I mention that?' I was sure I had. 'Where are *you*?'

'Nadia's.'

'Sergei's?'

'The same.'

'Why?'

I stopped ten metres from the boat.

'Someone came by again.'

'Who?' I asked, my heart hammering. 'The same man?'

'I don't know, I didn't answer the door.'

'Why not?'

'Just a bad feeling. I don't like being there anymore.'

*Not again.*

I walked silently over the gangplank. 'Hold on, Petra.' I removed the phone from my ear and looked around, listening intently. All I caught were creaking timbers, quietly lapping waters – a distant shout, the faint traffic noise on Sarphatistraat. The familiar.

'Sorry,' I said.

'Henk, what the devil is going on?'

'I don't know...'

I unlocked the door and entered the cabin, descending the steps warily. Turning the galley light on revealed nothing.

'Petra?'

But she'd gone.

'Henk.' Sergei's voice came on the line.

*Christ.*

'Do you need help?' His voice struck an appropriate tone of concern, but I caught a trace of triumph beneath.

'I can manage, thanks. Is my wife –'

'Because we're family now, and where I come from, that means that we look after one another.'

I felt my chest and throat tighten. 'Just put my wife back on the goddamn phone, will you?'

He did so.

'I'm here now if you want to come home,' I said, reaching for the clay bottle of jenever.

With that, I ended the call.

I found my usual spot beside the porthole, setting the full glass down on the little shelf I'd fixed up there. Staring out into the watery darkness, I tried desperately to remember.

*

'There he is,' Johan said in a low voice.

I stared at him as he walked down the dark street.

Between him and his almost-identical brother, I'd observed that gait often *enough: it was definitely Zsolt, the informant.*

*We were sitting in my car, just one of a row of anonymously parked vehicles on a nondescript street in Zaandam, north of Amsterdam.*

*'Should we wait for him to get inside his apartment?'*

*My gaze swept the quiet, suburban scene. In the three hours we'd been sitting there, I'd spied no sign of a security detail – personal or police-provided. 'Let's go now,' I said, instinctively. 'You ready?'*

*We pulled on our gloves and Johan quickly began soaking a handkerchief with the chloroform, spilling some on the seat between his legs.*

*'Christ, careful!' I said.*

*Chloroform sounds like a cliché from a bad action film, but it has the beauty of being fast-acting and self-regulating: victims knock themselves out fast, and nothing worse. I wanted Zsolt to remain alive.*

*'Ready,' Johan said.*

*We reached for our door handles. Barely had we exited the vehicle before Zsolt broke into a run. He hurtled down a lane behind his apartment block, but my longer stride allowed me to gain on him easily.*

*I grabbed him by the shoulder and wheeled him round. He had a serrated knife in his hand now, but not the resolve to use it first time; the contrast with his brother was striking – Zsolt the brains, Jan the brawn. My contempt for them both rose up through my oesophagus.*

*I clenched my right fist and jabbed him square on the nose. He yelped.*

*The knife dropped as he clasped the crunched cartilage, blood leaking through his fingers.*

*'That's for almost fucking getting my wife killed on the motorway.'*

*He bared his teeth, sucking in an agonised breath; Johan forced the handkerchief over his mouth. His eyes widened as his air supply ceased. Blood bubbled with the ineffectual nasal breathing, and red spittle flew as Johan pressed the handkerchief harder.*

*I held his head. He gasped and tried to bite Johan's fingers, but the glove protected them, until finally Johan loosened his grip and Zsolt collapsed back against a plastic dumpster with an alarmingly loud clatter.*

*Still I couldn't see anyone else.*

*'Hold him,' I told Johan, ''till I bring the car round.'*

*By the time I'd backed into the dark alleyway, Zsolt was limp. I opened the rear doors. Johan picked him up by his feet as I quickly dragged him onto the back seat by his arms, having found some sacking to lay down first. A lot of blood was leaking from his broken nose.*

*I cuffed his wrists and ankles with plastic grips.*

*We sat in the front of the car as though nothing had happened. Both breathing hard, though.*

*Still I couldn't see anyone. Calmly, I put my seat belt back on and began driving east out of Zaandam.*

*We'd barely covered a kilometre before he kicked and moaned.*

*'Shit,' Johan said.*

*'Is the dosage wrong or something? We can't take him into the city like this.'*

*Another kick, harder this time, against the rear door.*

*A taxi passed by us, the driver staring ahead.*

*'Where do we go then?' Johan asked with panic in his voice. 'I arranged —'*

*'Never mind what you arranged. Do you have more chloroform?'*

*'It's gone.'*

*'Christ, Johan!'*

*He looked paler than ever as the ring road's lights glided over his stolid features. Then I saw a helpful blue road sign.*

*'We'll take him to Waterland,' I said. 'No one will hear us there.'*

# 33

## CAPTAIN HENK

'Well this is cosy,' I said, entering Sergei's apartment. The lighting was low; a familiar bossa nova song played in surround sound. The green hue of my wife's drink suggested chartreuse, which she rarely succumbed to.

'Henk,' Sergei said, stepping forward. 'Join our little *borrel*.' He used one of the Dutch words with no easy translation, though he'd apparently understood its origins. 'I have chilled jenever.'

'I'm sure you do. Where's Nadia?'

'Erm… working late, I believe. But I like where you're going – we should make this into an engagement celebration.'

My daughter now had a job with an 'online fashion-lifestyle hub', whatever the hell that meant. We'd barely spoken since she'd been caught with MDMA on her aboard the submarine-nightclub.

'Well at least let me take your jacket,' Sergei said.

I preferred to keep it on. 'I have to be elsewhere too, I'm afraid.'

I met my wife's challenging stare and said to her, 'Describe the man who came to our boat earlier.'

'I told you,' she responded, tersely. 'He seemed official. Why don't you ask at your work?'

'All that journalistic experience,' I said. 'I'm sure you can give a better description that that.'

Her jaw clenched as she held back from speaking.

'You hadn't seen him before?'

'No!'

He wasn't Joost, clearly. But it could have been almost anyone – one of Frank Hals's old henchmen, even? No, that hardly connoted 'official'…

'Look, Henk,' Sergei said, stepping bulkily between us. 'Maybe I could help?'

*If you know a London escort called Kamilla, then I'm sure you could*, I almost said.

He continued: 'Petra mentioned the situation with Joost.'

'Oh?' I said, shocked.

'These favours, for energy –'

'What the hell else did she fill you in on? Our sex life, perhaps?'

'Henk!' Petra shouted. 'Sergei is offering to help!'

'How?'

'I know people,' he said, raising his own voice. 'In energy. Russia was involved, too.'

'No it wasn't!'

'It wasn't *in the end*,' he qualified, 'but discussions still took place, before.'

I exhaled hard, shaking my head in bewilderment.

'How do you know this, Sergei?' I demanded. 'Just who is your so-called contact?'

'Henk!' my wife reproved me once more, setting the chartreuse down and striding over. 'Your problem is with Joost.' She yanked me away from Sergei. 'Just go and see the man, for fuck's sake, and have it out with him – not with your family!'

It was a moment of piercing clarity, a shaft of internal illumination – the best idea I'd heard all year. I reached for my phone, and in my contacts found Stefan's number. Joost had forged a mentoring relationship with my old team member, after all.

'Stefan?'

'Henk?'

'Where the hell is Joost these days?'

\*

*We'd made it as far as the remote hamlet of Ransdorp, with its brick church – squat-looking, huddled against the night sky. The full moon bathed the surrounding dykes with a silvery gleam. I cursed the low flatness, the sight lines it afforded.*

*Zsolt was still kicking at the door, every hundred metres or so now, his groans getting louder. His moaning was joined by thudding and rattling as I drove off the road, as far away as I could get from other vehicles and human habitation.*

*I killed the headlights. We were off grid, with no easy way back, the road getting ever narrower. I'd never felt more hot and anxious; suddenly I pulled over and cranked open the window. The still dyke alongside gave off a brackish, putrid odour. The moonlight lent the car bonnet a sheen. Beneath, the engine clicked as it contracted.*

*Once my breathing had evened out I said, 'You need to go get your Sig.'*

*'What?' Johan turned in his seat; it creaked sharply.*

*'Your gun, Johan.'*

*A loud moan came from the back.*

*'We discussed this,' Johan said, his features pinched.*

*I tried to think – not about what we'd discussed, rather what we needed to do next.*

*'Anything could happen now,' I said, recalling our army training. 'Someone might find us here. We need to be prepared for all eventualities. Take the car.'*

*'But –'*

*'Do it now. Don't worry about our friend, I'll stay here with him. Drive back to yours, get the weapon, and be back here soon as you can. It won't take long.'*

*I jumped out, strode round the back of the car and pulled Zsolt from the rear seat. He landed on the peaty soil like a sack of baby potatoes.*

*His silvery-looking eyes glared up at me.*

You – *his accusing look said, as clear as the moonlight above –* you killed my younger brother...

*Johan got in the driver's seat of the car. The engine started again and he began reversing back up the track, the tyres slipping in the soft earth. Johan's head was out of the window, bent away from me to see behind. He'd kept the headlights off, thank God. A single dark vehicle snaked along the main road.*

*Otherwise, all was quiet.*

*All was still.*

*Apart from Zsolt.*

*'You'll die,' he managed to say.*

*'Really.'*

*Blood was still leaking darkly from his nose.*

*I had the physical sensation of sinking into the swampy terrain.*

*'You fucking shit,' I hissed, booting him in the ribs. 'I didn't kill your fucking brother. He killed himself, after he tried to burn me to death!' I booted him again. 'And my wife.'*

*He curled into a ball, a silvery-black embryo.*

*The smell, the swamp – there was something primordial about it all. I knelt in the damp softness. My clenched fist hovered above his face with a consciousness of its own, seeking its target...*

*'Stop.'*

*Seeking, wanting...*

*'You want information.' His mouth bubbled blood.*

*'What information?'*

\*

Joost spent his days now on a small island in Zeeland, off Middelburg – an hour and a half's drive south of The Hague. The more I thought about him – while driving down there the following morning – the less I understood about what had become of him. About his police role. His life…

The satnav gave a misleading sense of proximity as I approached his address. In vain I searched for a house.

The land either side of the causeway had narrowed to strips of dun-coloured heather. There was a sparkle of frost. Wind generators beat the sky, breaking the distant, dark horizon. Modern, slender versions of the windmills that would have been here for centuries – visual references sunk into my subconscious.

And sea, of course.

Zeeland.

\*

Stefan had mentioned that Joost recently suffered a heart attack, but my adversary's physical condition still shocked me. His physique had always been scrawny, only now it seemed to have shrunk, reminding me of a walnut.

'Henk,' he said wheezily, at the door of the sea cabin. 'What in God's name are you doing here?'

I'd half-expected Stefan to have forewarned him; it was gratifying to sense that he hadn't.

'Just passing,' I replied. 'Thought I'd look you up. Old times' sake.'

A gull cawed above.

He eyed me. He'd lost none of his disquieting, evaluative stare. 'You'd better come in.'

He led me into a sparsely furnished living room with a picture window onto the sea. Binoculars stood vigilantly on the windowsill. There was a distinct 'old man' smell, a green upholstered chair, and a trolley alongside for wheeling an oxygen tank…

'Bane of my life,' he said about it. 'The sea air's supposed to help, mind.'

'Does it?'

He shrugged. 'Do you want coffee?'

'Thank you.'

As he moved slowly into the kitchen, I eyed the wooden-walled room. There were surprising books: classical fiction, and others about nature, the area...

No evidence of a female presence.

All the signs of solitude.

'Last of the pot I made earlier,' he said, reappearing with a mug.

I sipped. It had a bitter, singed taste.

'Well sit, man!'

I did so, crouching forward, the cup at least warming my hands. You could freeze herrings in here.

'Just passing, eh?'

'In a manner of speaking.'

He pulled a blanket over his knees and took a shot of oxygen. I thought of asking about his heart attack, but couldn't think what to say. He'd had one. End of story.

'Not exactly on the road to anywhere, is this, Captain Henk?'

The form of address woke something inside me. It was a long time since he'd conflated my old army rank with my first name. Indeed, I hadn't heard it since the start of the long train of events that had now brought me here.

'OK,' I admitted, 'so I wasn't passing.'

'Didn't you think to call ahead?'

'Feared you might be out.'

He guffawed, gesturing at his entrapments.

'I'm haunted by some words you once used,' I said.

His old, alert gaze was back.

'At the police station' – I led us back to the previous spring – 'you were talking about the Tőzsérs, though I didn't know them by that name at the time. You said that no one had invited the Eastern European thieves and whores to come here, that there were always trade-offs... Those were your words.'

His demeanour soured. 'The words that you took to Rem Lottman, eh?'

'Yes. Only, why?'

'Why *what*?'

'Why did you say them in the first place?'

'Those were the words of... the system.'

'You *were* the system. You ran IJ Tunnel 3.'

'I ran nothing.'

I narrowed my gaze, trying to make sense of what he'd just said. A petroleum tanker had come into view behind him, on the far horizon. It was too far offshore to be docking in Holland. Maybe it was en route from Norway to some newer economy.

Joost sighed. 'I'm on the way out, Henk, in every sense. You really want to know what happened?'

For a moment, maybe two, we stared at one another.

'Well do you, *Captain Henk*?' He snapped his fingers.

And I flinched with sudden recollection.

\*

*'What information?' I demanded of the Hungarian lying in the mud.*

*'Cut binds,' he implored. 'Too tight. They slice my hands.'*

*The memory of that breeze block, on the ring road, came flying towards me through my inner vision. I blinked hard, trying to erase the enlarging, white-grey impression.*

*'How about we try doing this a different way?' I said.*

*His upper arm was bowed in a struggle to free himself; I grabbed him there and began rolling him towards the lip of the dyke.*

*'If you're so concerned about your brother, why don't you fucking join him?'*

*I recalled the breeze block smashing into the windscreen frame, and my wife sobbing...*

*'Or you can share this lousy information of yours.' I stood up, leaving him balanced on the slippery edge. 'Ever the informant, eh, Zsolt?'*

*My forced chuckle gave me a curdling sensation inside. I barely recognised myself. 'C'mon you shit, you've intrigued me.'*

*With the tip of my boot I held him on the edge. The dyke wasn't deep, but with his hands and feet bound it would quickly become his swampy grave.*

*He was exhaling sharply, irregularly.*

*'Take your time. There's another ten minutes, maybe, before my friend gets back with his gun. It's a lot like that FÉG PA-63 you left by my front door, by the way, only less cheap. Fires better.'*

*I looked around the dark landscape, registering the vague feeling of something being very wrong. Only what?*

*'I try to remember!' he cried.*

*'You're a little tease, aren't you?'*

*Some combination of rage and curiosity took over, and I rolled him in. He slid and shrieked and thrashed like a fish in shallow water trying to regain the deep; he managed to roll a complete turn onto his back once more, his silvery, agonised face breaking through the water's surface. It was his keening cry that persuaded me to drag him out again. He heaved in ragged breaths.*

*A dog began barking, distantly.*

*I knelt by his dripping ear. 'Before your brother died, I asked him a question.'*

*He was shaking, his wet eyes wide…*

*'I asked him what was so fragile that when you say its name, you break it.'*

*Shaking with cold, with shock…*

*'Silence,' I hissed.*

*'I tell you,' he said, trembling.*

*I waited. 'What?'*

*'I begin as informant, now I am more!'*

*I had that sickly feeling again, the source of which I still couldn't fathom. 'Go on.'*

*'They ask me to arrange things for people.'*

*'Who? What things?'*

*'Girls, jewels, drugs. Cars, painting.'*

'*What the fuck are you talking about, Tőzsér? Who's asking you to arrange what…* '

But my words died as I recalled Operation Boost — the high-end stolen vehicle ring, which this man had helped the Amsterdam police to infiltrate.

'*For who?*'

'*They offer these things to important people. Gifts, for favour.*'

'*To who? Who's* they*?*'

His teeth were chattering. At first, it disguised the rattling noise of the vehicle approaching.

Not my car.

Not Johan's either — a black van. I watched it approach, transfixed.

I'd noticed it before, on the main road. I'd felt its presence. The headlights were off, but as it nosed towards me, rising and dipping, they flared white. I froze like a trapped animal.

Then looked down.

He was gone. Submerged.

Heart in my mouth, I lunged for him but knew from his frozen expression in the white of the approaching headlights that he was already dead. A silver trace of bubbles rose from his mouth.

A familiar figure was running towards me.

'*The fuck've you done?*' Joost cried. He staggered. '*You killed him!*'

'*I –*'

'*Jesus, Henk, what've you done?*' He looked at me aghast. '*You're so out of your depth, you're in your own fucking undersea world! He was protected! Don't you see?*'

I started to grasp, dimly… '*He mentioned arranging favours…*'

'*He did what?*' Joost stood still. '*Where's the other guy?*'

'*Who?*' I managed.

'*Your fucking army friend!*' He looked around wildly.

'*He's gone,*' I said. Withholding was pointless now. '*He's gone to get a gun — he'll be back.*'

'*When he gets back, shoot him.*' He indicated the body in the dyke. '*Don't hesitate. Once in the heart, once in the head.*' Joost must have caught *my incomprehension, as he said: 'You make it look like a revenge attack, a Zaandam gang job. Yes?'*

*I nodded dumbly.*

*Hot tears ran down my mud-caked cheeks.*

*'Now let's get you straightened out. Jesus.' He looked around wildly. I was too numb to question what he meant by 'straightened out'.*

*'There's a disused tool shop just outside that hamlet... When's your friend getting back?'*

*I was shaking. 'Ten... maybe five minutes...'*

*'We'll have to take care of it in the van, then.'*

*'Take care of what?'*

*'Get in the van.'*

*'But —'*

*'Now!'*

# 34

## OPEN SECRET

I STAGGERED OUTSIDE, TO breathe. The light was dazzling relative to Joost's living room. I leaned against his weathered doorframe. Coffee had seeped down one leg of my jeans. Scales had fallen from my eyes.

Johan's gunshots repeated in my mind.

*Don't stop to think, just do it*, I'd ordered Johan, immediately upon his return, after pulling the dead body from the dyke.

Leaving my old army friend thinking that *he*'d killed Zsolt Tőzsér.

I hadn't known otherwise. Until now.

'You *hypnotised* me?' I turned back to face Joost, incredulous.

He was on his feet, a dark silhouette against the picture window.

'Not exactly, but you're close. It's a technique that the Dutch intelligence services developed during the war, to safeguard against officers falling into enemy hands and being tortured for information about the resistance.' He was referring to the origins of the Dutch security services, then. 'You were vulnerable and suggestible in that moment. It was expedient. It almost certainly saved your life, and that of your friend.'

'I was *brainwashed*?'

'No, not exactly,' he repeated. 'But I can assure you that they are time-honoured methods, tested in the most critical conditions that this country ever encountered. Come back inside, it's cold out.'

He shuffled around me in order to close the door. 'It's a neuropsychological process,' he said. 'Understand how hard I was trying to run those informants. Things were out of control.'

For a minute neither of us spoke. I sensed that he was giving me this time to get myself together, to reintegrate events. It was a lot to take in.

'There's work we all need to do, to recover who we always were,' he said at length.

I stared out of the window at the sea and the tanker, hovering in the distance.

Joost took a shot of oxygen. 'If it helps, Henk, by killing Zsolt Tőzsér you advanced our cause more than you could possibly have known. I couldn't control him by the end. I had him under surveillance, of course. I even followed him that night. Only he was too smart, too well-connected.'

I recalled the other night that I'd followed him, to the elite Conservatorium Hotel. He'd met with Jan Six…

But could I believe Joost now?

'You'd won a key battle in the war against the deepening favours-for-energy debacle, before even beginning.'

Was that true?

It felt like I was looking through a pane of glass, which had suddenly been rubbed clean. 'So Tőzsér was helping orchestrate those favours for energy…' I said.

'All manner of favours,' he clarified, 'from high art to young children. I got that stolen painting back to its rightful, original owners. I was the one badgering the likes of Frank Hals about the MDMA and other drugs. I was also the one harrying Heinrich Karremans and his type. I was onto that team in Driebergen, you know.'

I recalled Manfred Boomkamp, the unit's slain commander.

*Was it that bastard Joost at police HQ who put you up for this role?* he'd asked me on arrival there.

'Then how come you couldn't stop it, if you were able to do that much?'

'You've no idea how high it went.'

'Rem Lottman?'

He made a sweeping gesture with his hand. 'He's long gone. But you know that, too.'

I did.

I'd gone looking for Lottman, over the summer. To Zanzibar, under the guise of a family holiday. I didn't find him, of course. Though I *did* learn something there, now that I stopped to think about it...

'No,' Joost said emphatically. 'I'm talking about the people with ultimate power in Holland.'

'Go on.'

'How do you think Lottman was allowed to slip away so easily? That kidnapping show down in Tilburg...' He shook his head disdainfully. 'Bear in mind there were people like me pressing ministers in The Hague for inquests and enquiries. I was always being overruled.'

'By who?' I thought about the ministers themselves.

'I tried to protect you from it all, Henk.'

The justice minister?

'I even had you imprisoned in Leiden for a few days, for your own goddamn safety!'

*Could* it be?

'Van der Steen?'

It sounded extraordinary to my own ears.

'No,' Joost said. 'Think about it like a chessboard. Consider what I've just shared. Who really controls the play?'

I saw where he was going now.

'My original employers, Henk. The AIVD.'

My mind swooped.

'There's not much time,' he said. 'They're cleaning up as we speak.'

But who did he mean, exactly?

He took a final shot of oxygen, drawing my fractured attention back to him. 'Tell me,' he said, 'have you been to see Jan Six?'

\*

By the time I got back on the road, the sky and sea had darkened to a gun-metal grey. The strips of frosted heather crowded the road on the causeway. My thoughts twirled like the wind turbines.

*Alternate energy.*

The favours-for-traditional-energy scam was being eradicated from Holland's landscape. Where the hell was Jan Six living these days, anyway?

Joost couldn't help me with that. No love had been lost between him and Six when Joost took over as Amsterdam police commissioner.

How could I find Six?

First things first: I reached for my headset, and scrolled down my phone contacts. There he was.

A sharp intake of breath. 'Johan?' I said.

He'd picked up, thank God.

With a breaking voice, I confessed to having been the one to kill Zsolt Tőzsér.

Twice I needed to check if he was still there. At one point I drifted distractedly onto the wrong side of the road and had to swerve back to avoid an oncoming van. But there was a reason Johan was my oldest friend, and he let me continue with my account of everything that had taken place on the night in question.

At the end came a deathly pause.

I thought, once again, that he'd hung up.

'Makes sense,' he said eventually. 'Something had always

nagged at me, seemed wrong… When I returned with my gun, I mean. Your haste, maybe… I don't know. Neither of us was exactly thinking straight that night, were we?'

His ability to see the big picture…

'Talking of which,' he said, 'was it wise to leave Joost alone in his house?'

'How d'you mean?'

'If cleaners are at work, who might be next on their list, given what Joost just shared?'

*Jesus.*

Four minutes later I was back there. I braked sharply, the tyres locking and drifting in the sand that had blown across the road with the rising wind.

I came to a halt by his door, which was ajar. Round the side of the house ran vehicle tracks. I stared at them then entered the cabin, clasping my gun firmly.

A smell of cordite engulfed me. My vision took a second to adjust in the dim light, and at first I thought I was hallucinating.

Joost's right eye fixed me with an unswerving gaze. On his right temple, a small dark circle.

The exit wound joined with his other eye socket; a tree-like spatter of blood and other matter ran off into a far corner of the room.

I staggered backwards, reaching for my phone.

No reply from my wife.

I tried Sergei.

'Henk?'

'Where are they?' I demanded.

'Petra, you mean? Don't be upset, she's still here –'

'Nadia?'

'Yes, here… Why?'

'The man who visited the boat – the threat's worse than I thought.'

Sergei paused, making sense of my words. 'I have a gun.'

'Good.'

'If need be, I won't hesitate to use it,' he said, instilling a feeling of reassurance that surprised me.

'I'll be back in a couple of hours.'

I ended the call and backed out of Joost's cabin, trying not to touch anything. It was a crime scene now.

'Stop right there.'

I couldn't see the man, but I instantly recognised his voice.

# 35

## THE BEACH

I HAD MY BACK to him, but he could still see me. That pretty much summed up the way things had been with Rijnsburger – my handler on the Driebergen case.

Wim Rijnsburger, not Jan Six.

It made sense. Both had been in the AIVD, like Joost. But Six was likely gone – the same way as Lottman, and the rest. Whereas Rijnsburger was still very much here, wired into The Hague's power networks. Of course, he'd pretended to exonerate Joost at the meeting with van der Steen.

'Keep your hands raised and in plain sight,' he said. 'Turn round slowly. *Slowly...*' he repeated.

I did so.

He was rheumy-eyed as ever: blood in his eyes, as on his hands.

The gun was a Walther P5, same as my own.

'You'd be a dead man already, if it weren't for those jaunts to London of yours.'

'Oh?'

I didn't doubt his aim or resolve. If I made a move for my gun, which I'd holstered to call Sergei, he'd shoot.

The wind was strong, causing Rijnsburger's collar to flap.

He took a step closer.

'I'm going to pass you my phone.' He held it high with his other hand and pressed a couple of buttons. 'I'm going to explain exactly what you're going to do, on the basis that if you deviate – in the slightest – I will put a bullet through your skull.'

'So that's how the secret service structures its performance incentives these days, eh?' I joked, trembling. 'Internal Investigations has some way to go…'

He snorted. 'Did you hear that?' he said, turning. I'd noticed the black van parked there. It resembled the one I'd met Rijnsburger in once for a crash meeting, while I'd been working in Driebergen. It was the same driver, standing beside the open front door. He had a gun, too, and was making good eye contact.

Anonymous, official-looking? Was this the man at the boat and De Druif? These agents were known for nothing if not their ability to make you feel special.

He nodded silently in response to Rijnsburger's words, not taking his eyes off me.

Heavy raindrops landed on the crown of my head. Gulls cawed above as if waiting for carrion.

So Rijnsburger, the real rogue operator, had ensured that one of the hapless mavericks – Franks and I – took out the rest of the Driebergen team. It was Franks who'd done so in the end, of course, but we'd both played our part – both served our purpose on the chessboard.

Both been Rijnsburger's cleaners.

The mind works fast when confronted with the muzzle of a P5.

'I've brought up the phone number of the man you know in London.' He set the mobile down on the ground, a couple of metres in front of me. The guy beside the van covered him all the while.

'Five things,' Rijnsburger continued. 'I want you to press the dial button. Then tell him that you're back in London, that you've discovered something significant, and that you want to meet. Finally, that you will text him the time and location of the meeting from this number.'

I wouldn't be doing any texting afterwards if I made that call. And there was no doubt that Tommy Franks was next on his list.

I thought about the moves I could make here. If Tommy picked up and I pretended to leave a voicemail, allowing him to ask me questions, then *maybe—*

'*Don't* try to leave clues for him,' Rijnsburger warned, reading my thoughts. 'Stick to the script, or —'

'What, Rijnsburger?' I interrupted, taking a step towards him.

I had nothing left to lose anymore.

That was his oversight.

I readied myself to go for my gun. I'd been in the army, after all. I just needed one distraction, to occupy both of them. Could I cause a gull to dive on us? Hardly.

No, it had to be some more basic method of surprise...

As I stooped for his phone I said, 'In which scenario *won't* you shoot me?' I lunged, reaching inside my jacket.

Rijnsburger grabbed at me with his free hand. 'Don't,' he simply said.

The driver hastened around to the front of the van, in order to get a clear shot at me. But I'd foreseen that, too, and this time I didn't fail with my judo move: I had Rijnsburger's wrist high up behind his back, spinning him round to face his driver so that he formed a shield. But he was both hefty and agile – he'd managed to kick away my gun, which I'd dropped. I could see the driver edging towards it.

Rijnsburger was trying to do too much at once. So was I. We shimmied and grunted as we wrestled, seeking all the while to gain advantage, shifting our weights in ways that might throw the other off balance. Soon he would figure out a means of turning me towards his driver's aim.

I clasped my hand over his – the one holding his own gun – and felt for the trigger guard and his forefinger. I squeezed, then again and again. Three loud bangs, causing geese to honk. One of the shots hit the driver, somewhere around his middle. He was down on the ground, surprised, as if he'd heard something he didn't understand.

But he was still alive, his gun pointing our way.

The sight of the driver down summoned something new in the secret service man. He backed me forcefully against the wall of the cabin, winding me. As he pushed away, my flight instinct took over. I dipped my shoulder, ducking through the open front door of the cabin, slamming it shut behind me and reaching for the hasp. Five shots rang out in succession, blasting holes in the door.

Inside the cabin, options were limited. Did Joost have a gun? He still lay there, staring.

The front door banged and bowed, admitting light at its edges. Rijnsburger would kick it in at any moment. I removed my jacket, wrapped it round my hand and used it to bash in the picture window, which shattered loudly. I'd barely dislodged a large shard from the bottom when the front door flew open. Over I went, through the now empty window.

Scrambling among shattered glass, I retreated round the side of the cabin, away from the van and driver, breathing heavily. Blood was running down my leg into the sand and lichen. I couldn't tell if I'd been shot or sliced by glass. Too much blood.

Rijnsburger's footsteps moved cautiously across the floorboards inside the cabin, approaching the window.

The boards creaked.

'All right, Henk,' he said. 'You're unarmed, and we have the location to ourselves.' I wondered if he'd ordered the causeway closed.

He walked leisurely back through the cabin and out of the front door. I could just about hear his soft footfall coming round the side of the building. He ignored his driver's gasps.

'I cleared my schedule today – there's really no hurry,' he called out.

I shuffled back to the far outside corner of the cabin, ready to jump either way, depending on which side Rijnsburger reappeared.

Only he didn't.

The van door slammed. My guess was that he'd removed all the weapons from the scene – all but his own – and locked them in the van. Had he reached for a fresh clip, a new gun? I'd counted a possible eight rounds fired from his P5, which chambered nine...

I looked down the bleak beach, contemplating escape options. No cover, no other houses, no one around.

Only flatness.

'It's something I needed to do anyway,' he continued.

As I tried to make sense of his commentary, the smell of petroleum spirit found my nostrils.

'We need to take this house to the altar.'

It was an unusual notion of sacrifice, and not one I recognised from what little I knew about the secret service, its ceremonies and folkways.

With a whoosh the cabin was alight. The black smoke soon followed, pulled horizontally down the beach by the wind. The cabin was made of wood – within minutes it would burn down to a collapsed, charred mess, Joost's body cremated beyond recognition. Me exposed.

The work of immigrant vandals? Perhaps that's what he would blame it on. I didn't doubt that he had a plan, a story. Some other front.

There was no choice but to run for it, so I did.

*

The trick was to stay away from the road, which Rijnsburger could drive along in the van. So I did the only thing I could: I ran down the beach and onto a sandy promontory. My legs functioned, but not well. Instead of my usual, easy stride, I experienced a sensation like a vehicle rolling on oval-shaped wheels; my right hip dipped alarmingly. My knee and hip ached, my toes squelched in my boots. The blood there…

The south-easterly winds were moaning, pushing me towards the choppy sea. When I glanced back over my shoulder, the cabin was all but gone.

Rijnsburger was following. I caught the dull glint of his gun, swinging. Heard my name called.

I had a couple of hundred metres on him. There was little chance of him hitting me from that range with the P5 – even if he stopped to take careful aim – but my heart sank as I saw the sandy promontory separate from the land, a dark finger of water dividing it from the road and the causeway.

The promontory dissolved into sea, less than a kilometre ahead.

The crack of gunfire spurred me on.

I kept scanning for some indication of life – of help. I thought I heard a dog bark, only where?

I looked behind. Did Joost have a dog? No, I'd have noticed it, surely…

Rijnsburger was now jogging at a steady rate, his legs rising and falling evenly, sand blurring his feet.

Still, I had my phone. Pulling it out, I saw that I had a bar of coverage and fumbled for my most recent calls. Another gunshot told me to keep moving.

Johan picked up.

'I went back,' I panted, 'you're right.' A breath. 'They killed him.'

'Who – Joost? Slow down.'

'No option.' A breath. 'After me.'

'Where the hell are you?'

'Nehalennia-eiland.' A breath. 'Heading north-west.' Wheezing. 'Along the beach.'

*Crack.*

A faint whistling noise, distinct from the wind, told me he'd come very close with that last shot.

The phone slipped from my hand as I tried to sprint.

Johan was two hours away, in Amsterdam. Rijnsburger was a hundred metres behind, gaining, and the end of the promontory was in sight.

It wasn't a promontory – a spit, rather.

Longshore drift, forcing matter down the coast. Could that help me? I didn't see how.

The light had changed, was playing tricks. The spit dissolved into a watery silveryness where the clouds broke and a white beam filtered down. The vertical light shaft appeared fantastical in comparison to the dark, stormy clouds surrounding it.

I staggered onward, lowering my gaze to my wobbly feet, negotiating the mini-ravines carved in the sand by eddies and undertows.

There were no trees or obstacles to hide behind, not even a lone boat. I had the sense of turning transparent, like some marine spectre. Could I swim for it?

Surely I was a dead man.

I couldn't feel my feet anymore, and increasingly had the sense of hovering over the flat wetness. In contrast, Rijnsburger's shoes slapped the sand hard, and the sound seemed to multiply. Like horses' hooves at my back. Panic rushing into my ears and roaring there. As if I were being chased by legions of rogue secret service men and errant souls like Rijnsburger, stretching back over the decades – drawn to that place beyond the purview of elected government, where surveillance and other such features of modern warfare would always give them the upper hand.

There were more shots; I lost count.

'Van der Pol!'

I daren't turn.

'Van der Pol!' he called again.

This time I looked.

The sight that confronted me was equally confounding: he stood shin deep in water.

The tide was coming in.

The promontory, the spit, was shrinking around us. The wind wailed; fine sea spray flecked on my cheeks. The water was freezing, of course. I'd lost all sensation in my lower legs. I wouldn't have known whether I was in the water or out of it without staring.

'There have to be structures,' Rijnsburger called, as though we were out for a Sunday stroll together. 'There has to be an *architecture*,' he cried, 'at the back of it all.'

What the fuck was he talking about?

For a second I thought he was channelling Heinrich Karremans, and a vision of the dead *Rijksbouwmeester* came to me – the diving mask magnifying his staring eyes. I saw Zsolt Tőzsér, too – below the water surface, a silver trace of bubbles rising… I was about to join him.

'Self-sufficiency, energy-wise,' Rijnsburger was explaining. 'You can't erase history, but you can *edit* it.'

Rijnsburger stumbled, regaining his balance but looking curiously at his gun. His arm swung up towards me and became very straight. The gun was pointing directly at me. The sensation was dreamlike: I couldn't move, the water surface seemed to freeze. Only Rijnsburger's trigger finger was moving, again and again.

I couldn't hear a bang. Had I already died?

I heaved the air from my lungs and bowed my head. The water was moving fast once more. Rijnsburger flung the weapon aside but begun wading towards me, the hunt still on.

It would be hand-to-hand combat, then. One of us would drown.

I started in his direction. However, I was toppling seaward. The pain in my hip had taken on a glassy intensity. Rijnsburger was unbuttoning his shirt and sliding it down his shoulders. He wore a white vest, and had a startlingly in-shape torso for a man his age.

'We need to finish this,' he said. His ribcage was bowing and flexing as he breathed deeply. One shoulder dipped and shrank down, his knees buckling.

Up he rose, back out of the water, which was up to his thighs now. How had the tide come in so fast? There must be a terrific undertow.

By the time Rijnsburger got close we were waist-deep, the current pushing forcefully against my hips – pushing him towards me.

'When my organisation started, we had the chance of another way, Henk – that's the thing. The thing that I keep returning to, in times of turmoil.'

Had he gone mad? The genesis of the secret service lay in World War Two. What the fuck was he referring to, then – the Nazis? Surely not, though the far right had never left the Dutch political stage entirely, especially not since the 'immigrant crises' of recent years. At any moment, the current would lift me off my feet.

Did Rijnsburger understand the tides?

'I observed your efforts over in Driebergen,' he said, still in his Sunday-stroll voice. He was close now. Almost within arm's reach. 'And I thought how much I liked what I saw: a man who might be useful to us, one day. I don't mind telling you this now. It's something to take with you, possibly. Something to reflect upon...'

His large hand came for me and splayed round my neck, his thumb finding my carotid artery easily and forcing my neck back and down. The current was with him, and soon my head was coldly under – him on top of me. His other hand held the back of my skull like he was baptising a baby. My feet kept digging for the seabed, but I couldn't feel a thing.

I had no breath.

Rijnsburger held me there, and finally I gulped down water. Trying to cough it out caused me to drink more, its saltiness stinging my throat. My brain still worked, but weakly. In these temperatures, I had less than a minute to hold whatever breath.

I grasped and pushed and frantically tried to turn his wrist, but I couldn't feel a thing. It was as if I'd turned into a ghost. Like Joost, and the others. Pray to God the rest of my family would be taken care of.

All feeling had left my physical extremities, and a calmness began to take hold in my centre. A carousel of mental images flickered by: my father nursing a dry gin in dusty Africa; his old-fashioned moustache, much like Tommy Franks's, I now saw. Petra and Nadia, Johan… Nehalennia – a very old Zeeland goddess – Mother Sea as distinct from Father Land, with a benign-looking dog by her knee.

What struck me was the pattern of it all: the grand plan. How OK it is to leave the stage.

I closed my mouth and crossed my arms, ready to be carried on to the next place, when I glimpsed a rinsing of dark red. Shapes shifting over the water above me.

Faint shouting?

I was in another world.

\*

Cold, gritty sand pressed against my cheek. I'd arrived ashore.

On the other side? Where?

A man crouched on the beach, his face hovering over mine.

'Henk?'

I coughed and spluttered.

He shook me hard.

'Henk? You remember me?'

His face blurred and stretched as it came into focus.

'Cas?' I said, trying to sit up.

I fell back down, now aware of a foil survival blanket around me, crinkling in the wind.

'Medics should get here soon. So too our old buddy. We'll get you off this beach in short order. Better not to stay in any place longer than it takes for the fish to start smelling, as they say.'

I hadn't seen Cas in years – not since the KMar, the Royal Netherlands Marechaussee, became a separate service within the armed forces. Johan must have stayed in touch. We'd all trained together, in Norway.

'Good thing I live nearby,' he said, winking. 'Johan knew who to call.'

I sagged, closing my eyes.

'Stay with us…' Cas said, his words floating above me.

I nodded my agreement, forcing my mind to be busy, remembering their history: Queen Wilhelmina assigning the *marechaussees* the task of guarding royal palaces – a responsibility formerly held by gardeners; guarding a palace is called *klompendienst* (clog service); the KMar is anything but clog service… Two hundred *marechaussees* guarding the Queen and the Dutch government-in-exile during the war, and now it was the King's army.

'What about Rijnsburger?' I mumbled, my eyes opening – just – to become slits.

'He's not in a good way, either. I had to make a choice – which of you to save.' Cas was looking out to sea. 'We've all faced harder decisions than that one.' He smiled. 'The waves claimed him,' he clarified.

Did he know the rest?

# 36

## SIX-GUN SALUTE

CAS DID KNOW THE rest.

There was now a full-blown constitutional crisis caused by Wim Rijnsburger and his rogue faction within the secret service. The Royal Netherlands Marechaussee was one of the organs of state given extra national-security responsibilities as enquiries got underway; the *Rijksrecherche* was another. Once again, I was waiting to hear what my official role would be, bringing to justice the rogue actors involved.

Thick mist created a muffled intimacy at Joost's graveside. We were near Amsterdam, on the coast, at the Dutch Honorary Cemetery in Bloemendaal. It had been Joost's wish to be buried alongside war veterans.

The mist blurred the corners of the graves and crosses. It whited out the six-gun salute (one for each decade of Joost's life), the recoiling guns barely visible, their blasts rumbling hauntingly.

Once the last report had echoed into the distance, the King himself stepped forward to speak.

He wore a thick black overcoat, and a forbearance that spoke to something deep in my soul – as a Dutchman, and simply a man.

'We must learn to reconcile our material requirements with this nation's historic principles,' he was saying, 'like Joost van Erven did.'

I'd often wondered where Joost's confidence and sense of conviction came from. Now I knew: doing the right thing.

Petra squeezed my hand.

My wife had assumed a new role as a staff reporter at *De Telegraaf*, owing to the work she'd begun uncovering Joost's thwarted attempts to investigate informant rackets, the favours-for-energy scam, the disappearance of Rem Lottman, and – most recently – Rijnsburger's moves to clean up evidence of it all.

It had been a small faction within the secret service that Rijnsburger had led: a right-wing one, as suspected, that believed in Dutch independence and energy self-sufficiency at all costs. Extremism on home shores.

Its leader was now dead; there would be no state memorial service for Wim Rijnsburger.

'There's a point in every nation's life when its earlier hopes and aspirations must make peace with the realities of its circumstances,' the King went on, his measured breath condensing in the cold air. 'That is, if the nation is to become whole.'

I'd heard that saying before. Or at least, a variation of it.

This time, I felt its full import.

\*

The service ended, and a murmur of respectful conversation resumed. I caught a familiar face in the crowd: Marc Vissering's. A dark-green scarf sprouted from his lapels, appearing to prop up his head. The tall prosecutor approached me.

'Marc,' I said, shaking his hand warmly. 'How's Liesbeth?'

'Big.' His wife was heavily pregnant. 'But not complaining,' he said, smiling. He paused. 'Could I have a word?'

Petra caught the hint. 'I'll go and wait in the car,' she said.

Once we were alone, Marc asked, 'How are you recovering?'

I was limping, again. Hopefully not for too long this time.

'Ready to get back to work,' I replied in a low voice, referring to the rogue actors. 'Looks like there was a dozen of them...'

'Does that include the others they were controlling?'

I canted my head, unsure whom he was referring to.

'A file crossed my desk.' Marc double-checked that we were out of earshot. 'An Amsterdam gangster called Frank Hals.'

Time slowed as I waited on his next words.

'I reviewed how the Tőzsér brothers were turned from informants to providers of goods and services, as part of that favours-for-energy scam, and I wondered, could Frank Hals have been in the same boat?'

Did Marc harbour suspicions about Hals's death aboard that submarine, and my involvement in it?

'How d'you mean?' I asked warily.

'Frank Hals went on trial in 2008 accused of cultivating marijuana for resale. Do you remember?'

'How could I forget?'

'It was soon after the Tőzsérs arrived in Holland,' Marc continued. 'I've been looking at that case against Hals, and how easily he got off, and wondering whether Hals could have been recruited into a similar arrangement, in exchange for his innocence. Is that possible?'

'As a fixer, you mean? A provider of goods and services to important people?'

'Yes. Drugs – specifically MDMA – young children…'

Marc was speaking the truth. I knew.

'The case against him in 2008 was strong,' he said.

'He had a good lawyer,' I responded, looking away to the coast. I could hear the waves but couldn't see them through the mist.

Marc leaned in. 'We need to draw a line around the full extent of the wrongdoing here, Henk. That is, if we're all going to make it through this together.'

I was eager to steer him away, to a related but separate subject. 'What about Rem Lottman?'

'What about him?'

'He must have been running those people, by one means or

another. Hals and the Tőzsérs, I mean. No wonder he had to go.' I turned to face Marc. 'Where *did* he go?'

His stiff overcoat rose and fell as he shrugged. 'There's a question. He was never found, as I understand it.'

Not for want of trying on my part...

Marc added, 'Rijnsburger arranged the disappearance himself, perhaps, and took that secret with him to the grave. Lottman as another fall guy?'

Only now did I grasp how problematic Joost's opposition to Lottman had become, and the vehemency with which Joost had appealed to ministers in The Hague.

A face swept past: Muriel Crutzen's. She was formerly the energy minister, now security and justice. Willem van der Steen had gone in the post-Rijnsburger purge.

She eyed me from under a slanted hat. *The justice minister has fallen; long live the justice minister.*

And as Marc took his leave as well, something else came into focus – from my time spent searching for Rem Lottman in Zanzibar, East Africa...

\*

*Finally I found the bar, down a narrow lane in Stone Town, and dived inside it to escape the noon heat. A dog lay sleeping in the shade of the doorway. I sidestepped the creature and approached the counter – more slowly, my eyes adjusting to the gloom. A local stood behind it, watching me.*

*'Hello,' I began, 'I'm looking for a man named Nustafa.' He was the biddable one in the visa office, I'd been informed.*

*I counted off a hundred thousand shillings to get things going.*

*But the barman said nothing, and I knew instinctively that this was another false lead.*

*My wife had returned to Holland; the holiday was over.*

*It was time to rejoin her, time to go home. Zanzibar may have been a crossroads between Africa and the East – a 'New Silk Road', as those in the region called it – but the chances of Rem Lottman having passed through here felt slim to vanishing now.*

*I was wondering why this false trail through Zanzibar had been created, following a chance remark made by the energy minister at her office in The Hague, when a voice said, 'I am he.'*

*I pivoted to see a coffee-skinned, moustached man dressed in khaki. A newspaper was open on his table at the back of the bar.*

*He was older, maybe in his seventies.*

*'And you are?' He had a curiously old-fashioned voice.*

*I approached his table, scattering several flies. 'I'm looking for this man,' I replied.*

*I sat down, laying a photo of Rem Lottman on top of his newspaper. It was from* De Telegraaf, *purportedly showing him kidnapped.*

*There was no perturbation in Nustafa's face. I peeled off several hundred thousand more shillings to liven him up, in the process losing all track of the exchange rate.*

*This was crazy.*

*After a moment spent adjusting the photo so that it caught the light, he simply shook his head.*

*'You don't recognise him at all?' I let the money sit there.*

*'No.'*

*It was a tidy sum he'd received, for less than ten words.*

*I nodded resignedly.*

*My mind went to the airport, duty-free, the flight home…*

*'But* you *remind me of someone,' he said.*

*I was halfway up from my chair.*

*I sat down again.*

*'From years ago,' he continued, narrowing his eyes as though I'd teased him with a memory challenge.*

*'Pieter van der Pol,' he said, snapping his fingers. He smiled triumphantly, his memory intact. 'You could be his double.'*

*I exited the bar, stumbling out into the ferocious light, supporting myself against the ageing doorframe. Then I turned back.*

*'When?' I called out to Nustafa.*

*'Decades ago,' he replied. 'Forty years ago, maybe. I'd have to think about it...' He was still collecting together my money.*

*My father had been on the move at that time... the time that I received his last cryptic postcard. He would have been the age I was now.*

*Only it seemed too easy.*

*I went back inside and confronted him. 'Why do you remember this now, after all these years?'*

*'His circumstances were irregular.'*

*'How so?'*

*'He had a police record in South Africa, I seem to recall. He'd killed someone, if I remember correctly.'*

*'How did he get papers from you, then?'*

*'He persuaded me of his innocence.'*

*'And how did he do that?'*

*It was a redundant question. Nustafa folded the last Tanzanian bank note into his top pocket.*

*'Said it was an accident.' He shrugged.*

Good enough for me, *his gesture said.*

*'An accident?' I prompted.*

*'A man on his ship was giving him trouble.' He paused. 'Yes, that's right — he was in the merchant navy.'*

*Pieter van der Pol is not an unusual name, but it was definitely my father he was speaking of. I knew it in my blood.*

*'Said he needed to take care of things, for the sake of his family.'*

*I stared down at my hunched hands. My knuckles were white. Slowly my gaze lifted, and my eyes met Nustafa's.*

*'How did the other man die?'*

*'Drowned, he said.'*

\*

I had the sense of looking down not only on the end to Joost's memorial service, but also my father's, which I'd never had the chance to attend.

I was making my way past the orderly rows of white gravestones, when out of the clearing mist walked a man with a hat and an old-fashioned moustache.

'I thought I might find you here,' he said. 'You're limping.'

I stopped, trying not to show my surprise.

'Yes,' I said. 'Old age is a wonderful thing, isn't it?'

There were no other preliminaries.

'I still don't know who killed Heinrich Karremans,' Tommy said.

'I thought it might have been you.'

He laughed, perhaps unsure of whether I was serious.

'I got hold of the post-mortem report,' he said. 'Poisoning, then strangulation.'

I remembered the marks on the carotid artery, then I recalled Rijnsburger going for mine in the sea; could it have been him, in London?

'Did you look at that escort?'

Tommy Franks shook his head. 'Your dick was ruling your head there, Henk. But I'm not doubting that the killing of Karremans was organised. I just can't find out how, exactly.'

I began limping towards the car, and Petra.

Franks remained stationary, saying to my back, 'Come back over to London, Henk.'

'I can't do that.'

The real mystery, inside me, had been grasped. There would need to be new rules.

For the first time in my adult life, I felt a sense of calm within.

'I'm all for uncovering the full extent of the wrongdoing, but only in my jurisdiction, Tommy. In Holland. We can only control what we can control.'

Petra had started the engine.

'Right you are then, Henk.' There was more than a hint of irony in his words. 'So long.'

# Night Market

I opened the door of the car. Exhaust smoke drifted past me.
'Maybe I'll see you around.'
'Possibly,' I said.
'Possibly, or probably?'
'Possibly.'

# About Us

In addition to No Exit Press, Oldcastle Books has a number of other imprints, including Kamera Books, Creative Essentials, Pulp! The Classics, Pocket Essentials and High Stakes Publishing > oldcastlebooks.co.uk

For more information about Crime Books go to > crimetime.co.uk

Check out the kamera film salon for independent, arthouse and world cinema > kamera.co.uk

For more information, media enquiries and review copies please contact marketing > marketing@oldcastlebooks.co.uk